PRAISE FOR LILJA SIGURÐARDÓTTIR

SHORTLISTED for the Glass Key Award for Best Nordic Crime Novel

'A dark, twisty and pitch-perfect thriller. I will read anything Lilja writes ... I loved it' Michael Wood

'Icelandic crime writing at its finest ... immersive and unnerving' Shari Lapena

'Intricate, enthralling and very moving – a wonderful crime novel' William Ryan

'Tough, uncompromising and unsettling' Val McDermid

'Lilja is a standout voice in Icelandic Noir' James Oswald

'Action-packed and pacey ... The writing is crisp and clear, plotting ingenious and characterisation so vivid that I would like to be Áróra's best friend' Liz Nugent

'An emotional suspense rollercoaster on a par with *The Firm*, as desperate, resourceful, profoundly lovable characters scheme against impossible odds' Alexandra Sokoloff

'Lilja Sigurðardóttir just gets better and better ... Áróra is a wonderful character: unique, passionate, unpredictable and very real' Michael Ridpath

'Chilly and chilling ... Lilja Sigurðardóttir's terrific investigator Áróra is back for another tense and thrilling read. Highly recommended!' Tariq Ashkanani

'One of my new favourite series ... Áróra's brains and brawn, combined with the super-cool Icelandic setting, is a winning combination' Michael J. Malone

'Lilja Sigurðardóttir is good at describing the dark and cold of her native Iceland — and making you laugh ... telling a terrific tale with twist after twist' *The Times*

'Tense and pacey' *Guardian*

'Deftly plotted' *Financial Times*

'Tense, edgy and delivering more than a few unexpected twists and turns' *Sunday Times*

'The Icelandic scenery and weather are beautifully evoked – you can almost feel the autumn fog seeping up from the pages – but it is the corkscrew twists that make it both chilling and mesmerising' *Daily Mail*

'Another bleak, unpredictable classic' *Metro*

'Atmospheric' *Crime Monthly*

'Smart writing with a strongly beating heart' *Big Issue*

'Sure to please Scandi-noir fans' *Publishers Weekly*

'The intricate plot is breathtakingly original, with many twists and turns you never see coming. Thriller of the year' *New York Journal of Books*

'Taut, gritty and thoroughly absorbing' *Booklist*

'A stunning addition to the icy-cold crime genre' *Foreword Reviews*

'Three things we love about *Cold as Hell*: Iceland's unrelenting midnight sun; the gritty Nordic murder mystery; the peculiar and bewitching characters' Apple Books

'A good, engaging read, and the quick chapters make it perfect as a pick-up and put-down story for the beach' The Book Bag

'Once again expertly translated by Quentin Bates, *White as Snow* was an absolute pleasure to read. I flew through it entirely effortlessly. It's a thrilling ride, super-addictive, fast-paced and atmospheric with a great sense of setting. And the finale is breathtaking! Highly recommended' From Belgium with Booklove

'There is a real mixture of tension and emotion in this book that kept me captivated from start to finish ... all of which combines to get the tension heaving and the intrigue off the scale and had me tearing through the book at a great rate of knots' Jen Med's Book Reviews

Also by Lilja Sigurðardóttir and available from Orenda Books

ABOUT THE AUTHOR

Icelandic crime-writer Lilja Sigurðardóttir was born in the town of Akranes in 1972 and raised in Mexico, Sweden, Spain and Iceland. An award-winning playwright, Lilja has written eleven crime novels, including *Snare*, *Trap* and *Cage*, making up the Reykjavík Noir trilogy, and her standalone thriller *Betrayal*, all of which have hit bestseller lists worldwide. *Snare* was longlisted for the CWA International Dagger, *Cage* won Best Icelandic Crime Novel of the Year and was a *Guardian* Book of the Year, and *Betrayal* was shortlisted for the prestigious Glass Key Award and won Icelandic Crime Novel of the Year. The film rights for the Reykjavík Noir trilogy have been bought by Palomar Pictures in California. *Cold as Hell*, the first book in the An Áróra Investigation series, was published in the UK in 2021 and was followed by *Red as Blood* and *White as Snow*.

Lilja lives in Reykjavík with her partner. You'll find Lilja on Twitter/X @LiljaWriter, Instagram @sigurdardottirlilja, on Facebook.com/liljawriter and on her website, liljawriter.com.

ABOUT THE TRANSLATOR

Lorenza Garcia spent her early adulthood living and working in Iceland, Spain and France. She has been a full-time literary translator since 2008 and has translated and co-translated over forty novels and works of non-fiction from French, Spanish and Icelandic. She currently lives in South London with her Tibetan Terrier.

DARK AS NIGHT

Lilja Sigurðardóttir

Translated by Lorenza Garcia

**ORENDA
BOOKS**

Orenda Books
16 Carson Road
West Dulwich
London SE21 8HU
www.orendabooks.co.uk

First published in Icelandic as *Drepsvart hraun* by Forlagið, 2022
First published in English by Orenda Books in 2024
Copyright © Lilja Sigurðardóttir, 2022
English translation copyright © Quentin Bates, 2024

A catalogue record for this book is available from the British Library.

B-format paperback ISBN 978-1-916788-36-7
eISBN 978-1-916788-37-4

The publication of this translation has been made possible
through the financial support of

 ICELANDIC LITERATURE CENTER

Typeset in Garamond by typesetter.org.uk

Printed and bound by Clays Ltd, Elcograf S.p.A

DARK AS NIGHT

DARK AS NIGHT

PRONUNCIATION GUIDE

Icelandic has a couple of letters that don't exist in other European languages and which are not always easy to replicate. The letter ð is generally replaced with a d in English, but we have decided to use the Icelandic letter to remain closer to the original names. Its sound is closest to the hard th in English, as found in *thus* and *bathe*.

The letter r is generally rolled hard with the tongue against the roof of the mouth. In pronouncing Icelandic personal and place names, the emphasis is placed on the first syllable.

Aktu-Taktu – Aktou-Taktou
Áróra – Ow-row-ra
Auðbrekka – Oyth-brekka
Baldvin – Bal-dvin
Björn – Bjoern
Elín – El-yn
Elliðavatn – Etli-tha-vatn
Garðabær – Gar-that-byre
Gylfi – Gil-fee
Gufunes – Gou-fou-ness
Gúgúlú – Gue-gue-lue
Gurrí – Gou-ree
Hafnarfjörður – Hap-nar-fjeor-thur
Hellisheiði – Hedlis-haythee
Hringbraut – Hring-broyt
Hólmsheiði – Holms-haythi
Ísafold – Eesa-fold
Jahérnahér – Ya-her-tna-hyer
Jóna – Yoe-wna

Keflavík – Kep-la-viek
Kópavogur – Koe-pa-voe-goor
Kristján – Krist-tyown
Lárentínus – Low-ren-tien-us
Lárus – Low-rus
Lækjargata – Like-ya-gata
Leirvogstunga – Leyr-vogs-tou-nga
Litla-Hraun – Litla-hroyn
Miklabraut – Mikla-broyt
Mosfellsbær – Mos-fels-byre
Oddsteinn – Odd-stay-tn
Rauðhólar – Royth-hoe-lar
Sæbraut –Sey-broyt
Skeifan – Skay-fan
Smiðja – Smith-ya
Tjarnar-byggð – Tjarnar-bygth
Valur – Va-lour

SUNDAY

1

Everything went black for a moment as Áróra performed her last squat. The seventy kilos were killing her. Her back couldn't take any more and she felt as if her arms were going to drop off. This was her third rep and she only just cleared it. Not bad, though. For a woman her height to lift this weight three times in a row was not bad at all. But she seemed trapped in some kind of negative image of herself. She felt she never did well enough. She constantly missed her dad, the only trainer she'd ever had and her staunchest supporter at her weight-lifting contests – as he had been in life too. He'd always been there to cheer her on and never referred to her being too tall to do well in competition. On the contrary, he always seemed overjoyed when she came third or fourth in a tournament. And he was always so proud of her. Long after he died she felt he was there with her when she trained. It was one of the reasons why she pushed herself so hard.

'Have something to eat, girl,' Stulli said, nudging the box on the table in front of him that contained two leftover slices of greasy pepperoni pizza. Somehow Stulli had snuck into The Gym, installed himself in his favourite corner and guzzled almost an entire pizza without her even noticing.

'Good, nourishing food,' remarked Áróra, grabbing a slice with one hand and pulling down her training pants with the other. She turned her backside towards Stulli, who gave her buttock a sharp slap to numb it before he stuck in the needle and injected the steroid.

She was fully aware she shouldn't be doing this. Eating pizza and taking anabolic steroids. Her dad would have turned in his grave if he could see her now. Although lately his presence had become more remote, his influence replaced by a nagging sense of guilt over the death of her sister, Ísafold. Not that Áróra was to blame for her disappearance, but even so she couldn't help endlessly asking herself how things might have gone if she'd responded, if she'd rushed to her sister's aid the last time she cried for help.

No one knew for sure that Ísafold was dead, as her body had never been found; although the police had said there was 'compelling evidence' that she died in the apartment she shared with her boyfriend, Björn. Their theory was that Björn had murdered Ísafold in the apartment, dumped her body somewhere and then fled. He was last sighted leaving the main airport in Toronto, Canada.

Áróra clapped Stulli on the shoulder and walked out through the open garage doors. The Gym, as it was known, was situated in a large double garage that a strongman had converted into a training club for a select group of friends. Her father's reputation had earned Áróra her membership, and she was the only woman who trained there. The yard outside was secluded, shared only with the car mechanic next door and overlooked by the backs of some surrounding houses. On sunny days the previous summer they'd carried the benches into the yard to exercise outside. It felt safer during Covid to train in the fresh air with plenty of space between them, and besides, physical exertion in the open air was invigorating. Weightlifting clubs could be very sweaty places, and The Gym was no exception. Hopefully the weather would be as good this summer.

Áróra heard her phone ring inside her car and sprinted the last stretch, but the ringing had stopped by the time she got there. She didn't recognise the number and was in two minds about whether to call back. She decided to wait, at least until she was home and showered. She waved to Stulli and drove out of the courtyard, but before she'd turned onto Miklabraut the phone rang again.

'Hello?' she said, once the Tesla had paired her device with its audio system.

'Áróra Jónsdóttir?' a young woman's voice said tentatively.

'Yes, speaking.'

'My name is ... Elísabet. I'm calling about ... Well, it's all rather strange, you see...'

'Fire away,' said Áróra amicably, but the woman became still more hesitant.

'I've tried so hard to find a way of saying this that doesn't sound half crazy, but there really isn't one.' The woman gave an apologetic giggle.

'Does this have to do with the Directorate of Tax Investigations?' asked Áróra. If this was work-related she would ask the woman to call back later. When she wasn't bathed in sweat, her pulse racing from the steroids.

'Huh?' Apparently not, as the woman paused briefly before giggling apologetically once more. 'Yes, I mean no. No. This is unrelated to your work.' Áróra was surprised that this stranger should know she worked for the DTI.

'Who did you say you were?' she asked, maybe a little too sharply.

'My name is Elísabet. I'm calling because ... Well, I'm the mother of a three-year-old girl. She's called Ester Lóa, but – and this is the strange thing – she simply refuses to let us call her by her real name.' The woman gave another giggle, only this time her voice hit a shrill note as if she were over-excited. No doubt she was nervous. 'You see, our little girl insists her name is Ísafold. And that she's your sister.'

Áróra drove the Tesla up onto the pavement and slammed on the brakes. Her heart had skipped a beat when the woman pronounced her sister's name.

'Yes, my sister's name is Ísafold ... or was,' replied Áróra. Maybe this was a new witness. Someone who knew something. 'Do you have any information about my sister?' she asked.

'No, not exactly,' said Elísabet. 'But then again, yes. You see my little three-year-old daughter claims she's your sister ... I'm not sure how to put this ... reincarnated.'

2

'I realise this sounds crazy,' the woman calling herself Elísabet said for what was probably the tenth time. 'And to be honest I – or rather my husband and I – don't know what to think. We've taken her to a paediatrician and a child psychologist, but the only explanation they can offer is that it's most likely a phase. Some kind of role play. But then you'd think she'd choose a Disney princess not a dead woman.'

'We don't know for sure my sister's dead,' said Áróra, the sharpness in her voice real enough now. She didn't necessarily believe Ísafold was alive, but she still found it uncomfortable when other people spoke about her as if she were dead.

'Yes, no. Of course not ... I'm sorry,' said Elísabet. 'I've only thought of her that way since Ester Lóa started saying that in a past life she was Ísafold.'

'Hardly the language of a three-year-old is it, to talk about past lives?'

'No, not really.' Once again the apologetic giggle.

'And why do you assume your daughter is talking about my sister and not somebody else?'

'We put two and two together. Everyone knew about your sister's disappearance, and the name Ísafold is unusual so ... yes. She is only three, but she's very talkative and articulate for her age. She says to me: "I'm not a little girl, Mummy. I'm a woman," and that she wants to meet you. Her sister, Áróra. She says you always help her.'

This was the last straw. Áróra took a deep breath.

'Thank you for your call,' she said, and went to hang up, but there was a slight delay as she fumbled with the touch screen in the Tesla, and Elísabet was able to reply.

'Shouldn't we maybe meet for coffee and talk about this?'

'No, thank you,' said Áróra.

Her head was in a spin, but she had no intention of meeting up with some woman who was no doubt after money; either that or some intimate details so she could boast to her colleagues at work that she knew something about the case. There were so many crazy people around. Áróra had already encountered two – one claiming to be a medium, who said Ísafold had sent a message from beyond the grave telling Áróra to put up a photograph of her and her sister in her living room. The other a self-styled sleuth who said he'd traced Ísafold to South Africa. Daníel had investigated the South Africa claim with the police over there and concluded it was a hoax, while Áróra had dealt with the medium herself. If Ísafold was dead and sending messages from beyond the grave, no way would Áróra's interior decor be uppermost in her mind.

'But don't you want to meet Ester Lóa, er ... Ísafold?' asked Elísabet.

'Since your daughter definitely isn't my sister reincarnated, I don't see what I can do for you. But by all means let me have your email and home addresses so I can contact you if I change my mind.'

The woman duly relayed her details, and Áróra jotted them down on an old shopping list she pulled from the glove compartment, her pen hand quivering with rage. Now she had the woman's address, she could send Daníel over there, in his role as a cop, to lecture her about not harassing grieving relatives.

'I understand how crazy this must sound to you,' said Elísabet. 'We felt the same, but it's so strange the child should fixate on something like this, something that corresponds so closely to a real-life case.'

'What exactly is it that corresponds?' said Áróra, barely concealing her irritation. 'Forgive me for saying so, but you haven't told me a single thing about the case that hasn't appeared in the newspapers or the media. Nothing that makes me think your daughter knows something she couldn't have heard somewhere or that somebody told her.'

'No, you're probably right,' said Elísabet. 'And of course she has said all sorts of things that are clearly nonsense. She once said that an ice-bear killed her!'

Áróra felt the hairs on the back of her neck stand up. 'What did you say?'

'She has said all kinds of things that are clearly the product of her vivid imagination.'

'No, I mean what you said last. Could you repeat it?'

'She said an ice-bear killed her.'

The woman now gave a genuine laugh. Áróra said, falteringly, that she'd call her later and hung up. The traffic whizzing past on Miklabraut suddenly became enveloped in mist and the noise of the cars grew muffled and distant. She had trouble drawing in her breath – as if a huge paw had clasped her body and was squeezing it tight.

3

Daníel had difficulty understanding what had happened. After an uneventful weekend shift at the police station, his brain felt numb, but he could tell Áróra was in a spin. He'd managed to coax out of her that she was in her car on Miklabraut and didn't feel capable of driving home. He grabbed his jacket and ran downstairs to the traffic department to cadge a lift. The guys asked where he was going, and he told them he had to help out his girlfriend. *Girlfriend*. He still pronounced the word timidly, as if the reality it represented might somehow evaporate if he said it too loudly or too boldly.

He thanked the guys and leapt out when he caught sight of the Tesla where Áróra had parked it clumsily on the grass verge, and once again he was amazed at how badly she treated her expensive, beautiful possessions. He would never have driven the Tesla up onto the kerb like that. He'd be too terrified to scratch or dent the wing. Yet somehow Áróra seemed to use everything she owned with too much power, as if she felt anything that couldn't withstand the force of her existence would simply have to break. That was how he felt, too, sometimes. It had been his dream to have a relationship with her. To be able to call himself her boyfriend. But the role wasn't an easy one, although he wouldn't have traded it for anything in the world. His attitude was that everything worthwhile in life required a certain amount of effort, and Áróra was a perfect example of this.

He got into the car, put his arm over Áróra's shoulder and drew her to him. Often when she felt bad, she would push him away, harden herself, give a little growl and shake herself the way a dog would, but this time she leaned into his embrace, limp and exhausted. He stroked her hair and held her for a while before asking what the matter was.

'This is what's the matter,' she said, handing him the crumpled piece of paper bearing her illegible scrawl.

'Is this the woman who you said called you?' asked Daníel.

Áróra nodded, drying her face with her T-shirt. She was still wearing her sports gear so she must have come straight from the gym. She was often a bit on edge after training because she pushed herself hard and seemed not to eat enough afterwards.

'What did she want?'

'She says her three-year-old girl is Ísafold reincarnated.'

Daníel was dumbstruck.

'Well, well,' he breathed. 'It seems there's no end to the number of crazy people out there.'

'Indeed.' Áróra gave a faint smile then grew serious again. 'And yet something the woman said struck me. She told me her daughter said ... or rather her daughter as Ísafold said...' She paused for a second. 'She said an ice-bear killed her.'

'Huh?'

'Yes. And what struck me about it is that Ísafold always used to call Björn her *ísbjörn* – "my Ice-Bear".'

4

Lady Gúgúlú, real name Róbert, was pretty sure the time had come the instant his phone rang. Something about the ringtone was different from usual, as if it contained a premonition that his life, as he'd been living it for the last four years, was over.

'Hello?'

'Hi, darling.' It was Stebbi, the bartender and manager at the nightclub. 'A man came here asking about you.'

Fuck. Róbert felt his blood run cold. Even so he managed to hold his nerve and control his voice.

'Was he cute?' he asked, and the question made Stebbi laugh.

'Not exactly your type,' he replied. 'A bit rough around the edges, to be honest. And he was wearing a polo shirt. I can't see you dating a man who wears a polo shirt.'

'Absolutely not!' declared Róbert theatrically. 'What did he want, anyway?'

'He showed me a video of you doing your *Gúgúlú and the Great Escape* show. And I told him what you asked me to say: that your name is Haraldur, Harry for short, and I have no idea where you live.'

'Good,' said Róbert. 'Thank you for that.'

'But there was something weird about him, so when he left I took a peek outside and saw him get in a car with two other people in it. I didn't catch a good glimpse of them but they looked like men in suits to me. Then it occurred to me this could be the stalker you told me about, so I thought I should warn you.'

Róbert was inwardly relieved that he'd prepared for this moment. Stebbi had done exactly the right thing.

'Thanks. I owe you,' said Róbert. 'Take me off the programme will you, darling, I need to keep a low profile for a while.'

He said goodbye to Stebbi then heaved a sigh. His good friend deserved a proper farewell, but Róbert was better off playing this down. Making out he was taking a temporary break, to escape his stalker. It would create unnecessary drama if he announced that he was leaving for good. He glanced about and felt a pang of regret when his eyes alighted on the costume that lay almost finished next to the sewing machine. The butterfly gown he'd planned to wear that weekend. In a spectacular drag show to be called *Gúgúlú Crawls out of the Chrysalis.* But it was no use having regrets. This was a question of do or die. He clambered onto a chair and reached on top of the wardrobe for the rucksack he had packed and ready, with everything in it except the box.

He pulled on a pair of hiking pants, a thin wool jumper and then his parka, put on his hiking boots and laced them tight. Afterwards he turned out the lights and stepped outside. Pausing an instant, he glanced across the lawn at Daníel's apartment and felt another pang of regret. Damn. These had been fun times. He sniffed hard, picked up the rucksack and closed the door behind him.

Inside the shed he grabbed the little fence post he'd whittled flat at one end so he could use it as a shovel, and took it with him into garden. Kneeling down next to the rocks at the far end, he pushed the post into the ground. He had to dig through the top layer of soil then he could scoop out the sand around the box with his hands. The excavated earth formed a mound on the grass; he wished he'd put a plastic bag next to the hole – the signs of his digging would be visible. And there was no way he could do this neatly with this crude, improvised tool. Glancing about, his eye alighted on the large pot containing the cherry tree he'd bought the year before. Its grey, leafless branches were probably dead. But it would have to do.

5

Áróra could smell her own sweat as they walked into the café in Borgartún, and regretted not having gone home first to change. But she felt they needed to meet this woman Elísabet straightaway. They'd called her back and she had agreed. In fact she seemed happy to leave the house at a moment's notice; perhaps she feared Áróra might change her mind. For her part, Áróra wanted this strange affair to be over and done with.

They glanced about the café, unsure who they were looking for, but a woman seemed to recognise Áróra and stood up and waved to them, smiling amicably. She seemed over-excited, like a child at Christmas. It was as if she were struggling to suppress a wave of joy that might burst forth at any moment from her big, childlike face. Áróra thought she saw her hop up and down as she stood next to the table and waved.

'I'll get us some coffees,' Daníel said, heading straight for the counter while Áróra walked up to the woman and greeted her.

'Sorry about the get-up,' she said. 'I've just come from the gym.'

'Oh yes, of course, you do weightlifting,' said Elísabet, and again Áróra experienced a feeling of unease. It wasn't enough that this woman knew where she worked; she knew she lifted weights as well.

'That's right.' Áróra sat down, and suddenly all the questions she'd lined up to ask the woman seemed to evaporate. Her pulse was racing and she found she couldn't speak. Not that this mattered, because Elísabet was evidently the talkative type. She launched into an apology, as she had on the phone, her words punctuated by artificial laughter. Only, behind the artificial laughs Áróra now detected a bell-like tinkle that threatened at any moment to erupt into a genuine belly laugh. It was as if by letting out the occasional stilted *ha ha ha*, the woman was holding back a fit of the giggles.

'Of course this is terribly strange, and I know better than anyone how it sounds. As I told you on the phone, we, that's to say my husband and I, are at our wits' end. We've taken the child to every kind of specialist, *ha ha ha*.'

Daníel approached the table with their coffees and before he had a chance to introduce himself Áróra cut in ahead of him.

'This is my boyfriend, Daníel,' she said.

Daníel shot her a glance then smiled at Elísabet. Áróra could tell he understood her thinking. It was better Elísabet didn't learn straight off that Daníel was a cop. That way she'd be more likely to lower her guard. Be more open about what she wanted from Áróra.

'Have you believed in reincarnation long?' said Daníel, removing his jacket and draping it over the back of his chair. He spoke in a friendly manner, smiling mildly.

'*Ha ha ha*, no. Actually, I haven't. Which is why I'm finding it very difficult to believe my own daughter,' replied Elísabet, no hint of a defensive tone.

Daníel broadened his smile and sat down. 'So you and your husband don't belong to a sect that believes in reincarnation, or anything like that?'

'Huh? No, no. Only the Church of Iceland. So to speak. We had our daughter baptised the day we married, but we don't attend mass or anything. We're no different from most other Icelanders.'

Daníel nodded, continued to smile amicably and took his time sipping his coffee. This had the effect of keeping Elísabet talking.

'We're very ordinary people, you know, like all our friends. We're not yoga or reincarnation fanatics, or anything like that.

It came as a complete shock to us when Ester Lóa began insisting she wasn't a child, but a woman called Ísafold.'

'When did it start?' asked Daníel.

Áróra's pulse was still racing. It was a relief that Daníel was taking it upon himself to ask the questions she felt too upset to articulate. She wouldn't have had the presence of mind to put them in the correct order. And she wanted to know everything about this child, everything she'd said. Right now.

'Six months ago,' replied Elísabet. 'She'd already started to talk a lot from the age of around two, and then about six or seven months ago she started to tell people who asked her name that she was called Ísafold. I thought this was just some nonsense. Something she'd got from a cartoon. That there was a character somewhere called Ísafold. But when we asked her why she kept saying her name was Ísafold, she said: "Because I'm not a child, Mummy. I'm not Ester Lóa. I'm a woman. And I'm dead."'

6

Outside the café Áróra stood watching the woman as she'd climbed into her car and waved goodbye to them. Daníel studied Áróra's face, trying to read her expression: it betrayed some sort of longing or regret. As if Áróra wished with all her heart that she could follow the woman home and meet the mysterious child who spoke about a past life. Daníel didn't believe this rubbish for a moment, and hoped Áróra would view it all with a big dose of scepticism. But he wasn't just suspicious of the woman. He was anxious as well. He had to be careful now not to fuel Áróra's anxiety; instead he had to coax information out of her in a calm way.

'What do you make of all this?' he asked tentatively. Áróra turned to him and he saw tears glisten on her eyelashes. 'Hey, hey,' he said softly and pulled her to him. 'Shall we go to my place. I'll make us something nice for dinner?'

She nodded, cleared her throat huskily, wriggled free and strode purposefully towards the Tesla. She installed herself in the passenger seat, indicating that she wanted him to drive. He did so with pleasure. The Tesla was out of this world. It drove like no other car, and he never missed the opportunity to sit behind the wheel. He would even sometimes refrain from having a glass of wine or beer with a meal when they went out so he could be their self-designated driver.

He turned on the Tesla's engine, and the central display screen lit up, casting a harsh blue light on Áróra's face. Even though she'd shaken him off just now and retreated into her shell, he could see clearly she was in a bad way. Her face was puffy, the rims of her eyes red.

'Áróra, do you remember, at the height of the investigation

into your sister's disappearance, when the forensic team was combing her and Björn's apartment?' he ventured. 'I told you and your mother where most of the bloodstains were found. Do you remember that?'

'Of course I remember,' Áróra said, a hint of irritation in her voice as she looked at him quizzically.

'Did you tell anyone else about those findings?'

'No.' Her response was short and to the point.

'Think carefully,' he insisted. 'Go over in your head who you've spoken to about this in the last three years.'

Áróra hummed, stared straight ahead for a moment then shook her head. 'No,' she said. 'I haven't told anyone about what was found in the apartment.'

'Do you think your mother might have?'

'There's a chance she may have said something about the case to her sister and to a friend of hers in Newcastle. They go round to her house every day for tea. But I doubt it. Firstly because Mum refuses to believe Ísafold is dead. She clings to the hope that she's in Canada with Björn. And secondly because she's English. She avoids discussing awkward subjects. It's her way of protecting herself from too much suffering.'

'So it's unlikely she mentioned it to anyone here in Iceland?'

'Very unlikely,' said Áróra. 'Now stop playing the cop with me, Daníel. Why are you asking me about this?'

He shifted in his seat and turned towards her. 'Because this young woman, Elísabet, said something I'm almost certain was never made public. Namely where the majority of bloodstains were found in the apartment. As far as I know that information never got out. Apart from the police, I think you and your mother are the only two people who know that most of the bloodstains were found in the kitchen and on the inside of the bathroom door.'

7

Róbert set his rucksack down on the scrubby patch of land between the bridleway and the stables, then scrambled up to the end stable. He was grateful for the network of bridleways that ran around the city's periphery. Generally speaking there was no street lighting, signposts or CCTV on bridleways. Even so he'd played safe, keeping the hood of his parka up at all times as he used them as a detour to get here.

He was out of breath after the hike yet didn't exactly relish the thought of mounting the horse. He was no horseman, although he'd more or less mastered the art of staying on the animal's back and getting it to move forward. And they had a long journey ahead of them. Longer than he cared to inflict on himself or the horse, but he had no choice in the matter. He had initiated plan B. Now everything had to go smoothly.

The horse seemed surprised to see him and became skittish when it saw Róbert gather up the tack. He'd done a few practice runs to accustom both himself and the horse to the alternative bit he'd made from bone and woven leather strips, but that was a while ago and the horse was bound to find it uncomfortable. The bone that went into the animal's mouth was a good deal wider than a normal bit and Róbert prayed the horse wouldn't chew straight through it because he only had one replacement. He slipped the saddle blanket over the horse's back and placed the saddle on top of it. He had a cobbler adapt the girth so that instead of a buckle it had a clasp made of wood and leather. With any luck it would hold out until he reached Suðurland, on the far side of Hellisheiði.

He led the horse outside and gave it a clap on its hindquarters. It was a ten-year-old bay with a darker tail, mane and fetlocks, but what most appealed to Róbert about the horse, and indeed what had made him choose it, was that it changed colour with the seasons. A bit like Róbert himself. When its winter coat came through, white hairs would mingle with dark ones, turning the horse gradually grey, as if it wanted to camouflage itself, blend in with the snow. In spring, however, the horse's coat grew darker and it became a splendid bay again. Right now it was in that awkward in-between stage, shedding its winter coat even as the dark hairs came through, making it look rather scruffy.

'Both of us are transitioning now, darling,' he said to the horse as he led it away. He came to a halt where he'd deposited his rucksack, lifted it onto his shoulders and found a hummock to stand on to enable him to mount. One of the stirrups he'd made from a large animal bone threaded with leather gave a snap or crack as he placed his foot in it, and he prayed it hadn't broken. With any luck they would hold out until they reached their destination.

He also prayed that the foreign-made plastic horse shoes with which he'd fitted the animal would survive the rough Icelandic terrain on their way across Hellisheiði.

8

It was calming to feel the hot water from the shower pummel the nape of her neck. Áróra closed her eyes and tried to make sense of the thoughts swirling in her head. Daníel had told her to jump straight in the shower and relax while he started cooking. She had stripped off her training gear on the way to the bathroom, kicking off her knickers just before she stepped into the shower. Water always had a soothing effect on her, and after three years living in Iceland she now allowed herself to enjoy hot water Icelandic style. She would soak in the tub for hours, topping up the hot water as and when needed, or stand under the shower for a good twenty minutes with the jets on full, breathing in the steam and feeling her muscles go soft.

Her pulse was still racing, which was normal after a steroid injection, but now it was keeping pace with the thoughts that whirled around and around in her head: the words Elísabet claimed her daughter had spoken. She told them her daughter had said the ice-bear struck her in the kitchen. Then he stabbed her with a knife so she bled and bled. Afterwards she ran to the bathroom and tried to shut the ice-bear out, but he pushed against the door while she pushed on the other side. She'd pressed against the door with her back and hands, her feet braced against the floor, but the ice-bear was too strong and he burst in and grabbed her round the throat so she couldn't breathe.

Images of the child's description flashed through Áróra's mind like a film reel, and she only had to replace 'ice-bear' with 'Björn' for it to seem plausible. Björn had regularly been violent towards Ísafold, and his abuse got worse each time she went back to him, after Áróra had found her safe places to stay at the Women's Refuge, or at a hotel. Her injuries became more and more serious, Ísafold in worse and worse shape, and Áróra evermore exasperated each time her sister went back home to Björn.

This description of the events that took place in the apartment tallied with the forensic department's findings, namely that most of the blood was found on the kitchen furniture, the kitchen floor and the inside of the bathroom door. Áróra had seen that Daníel was dubious about Elísabet's story and suspicious of how she knew where the blood was found. No doubt he suspected Áróra or her mother had blabbed, and the story had reached Elísabet's ears. Or else he suspected a leak at the station. The one thing he didn't suspect was that the story might be true. That Ester Lóa really was Ísafold reincarnated and could remember the moment of her death.

Áróra gave a few gasps and felt herself burst into tears. She tilted her face towards the shower head and let her grief flow forth. Was the child really describing Ísafold's last moments? Was her end so tragic? Full of pain and fear of the man she loved. And loneliness, as she fought for her life, only months after she – Áróra, her sister, who should have protected her – had given up and turned her back on her.

9

Daníel heard Áróra turn on the shower as he switched the light on in the kitchen and caught sight of the piece of paper lying on the table. A note from Lady Gúgúlú.

But instead of the usual elaborate diagram telling him she'd borrowed his toaster, or some physics equation that Daníel was supposed to understand but never did, it contained a brief, hand-written message:

> *Darling. Just to let you know I've moved out. I've had to go abroad unexpectedly, a family matter, and I won't be back anytime soon. Forgive the short notice. I've paid three months' rent into your account. Love u. Miss u. Bye.*
> *P.S. You can throw out all the junk in the garage, I've taken everything I want to keep.*

Daníel was more or less accustomed to being gobsmacked at his eccentric neighbour and tenant, but this took the biscuit. He reread the message several times but could make neither head nor tail of it. It was stranger than any physics equation. He went into the living room and opened the French windows. The garage lights were out, but Daníel crossed the lawn anyway, and as he approached he glimpsed the key in the latch. Opening the door, he fumbled for the switch and was even more astonished when the light came on. Nothing in Lady Gúgúlú's converted garage apartment had changed. Everything was as usual – messy and complicated. The bed at the far end was unmade, two crumpled beer cans stood on the bedside table, and there was an iPad on top of the duvet. Draped next to the sewing machine was what looked like a finished costume adorned with brightly coloured butterflies, each of them hand-stitched. The hours of work that must have gone into making that dress. Daníel vaguely recalled something about a magnificent butterfly drag show, but truth be told he didn't always pay full attention to Lady's detailed descriptions of her performances and outfits. Opening the fridge he discovered food and an unopened six pack; there was rubbish in the rubbish bin and in the tiny bathroom a mug containing Lady's toothbrush and toothpaste, as well as what appeared to be most of her toiletries on the shelf. Wasn't it strange to travel abroad without at least taking your toothbrush and razor?

He went back into the main room and glanced about. This was altogether more than a little strange. And strangest of all was that her mobile phone in its pink glitter case lay on the table. Who went abroad without taking their phone? Daníel felt a wave of unease go through him. It wasn't the dread of death he often experienced when he entered a space where someone had passed. Not exactly. This was more like a mixture of shock and sadness. Lady Gúgúlú, or Haraldur, as she was officially named, was the closest thing Daníel had to a friend outside work. As unalike as they were, somehow, by accident, they had become each other's support network. Daníel had resolved various issues for Haraldur, and Haraldur, it turned out, was brilliant with Daníel's kids, who regarded him as their weird and wonderful auntie who lived in the garage.

Daníel locked the door behind him and started back across the lawn, but then came to an abrupt halt and stood open-mouthed in the middle of the garden. At the centre of the wild patch next to the rocks stood a tree. Roughly as tall as a man, still without leaves in the early spring and, judging from the mounds of soil around it, recently planted. Evidently the lady in the garage had received some kind of dispensation from the elves to mess with their enchanted patch. Daníel himself had never managed to cut the grass there, because, curiously enough, the lawnmower always broke down or the shears fell apart. Clearly Lady had taken the trouble to do a spot of gardening before she left, but not to say goodbye to him.

10

Róbert hadn't planned to break his journey because he wasn't confident he'd be able to remount, still less that the wretched horse would get going again if given a few minutes' rest. But after they'd come down off Þrengslin moor south of Reykjavík and were heading along Hlíðarendarvegur, the zip on his parka broke and it was too gusty to have it flapping about him like that. He steered the horse into a small hollow at the side of the road, halted and dismounted. His whole body was groaning and the horse looked like it felt the same way. The animal spluttered and champed at the bit, shifting on its feet, then stood with its head drooping despondently, like a condemned man.

'We have a way to go yet,' he told the horse. 'But the ground will be softer.' The horse didn't look up, apparently unconvinced by his reassurances. Maybe it realised that, as of today, life would never be the same. It would never go back home to its stable, because somewhere south of Selfoss a different life awaited. And it was gradually dawning on Róbert that his own life there would be a lot more monotonous and lonely than it had been these past four years. In fact he'd been incredibly lucky that they hadn't caught up with him sooner. The drag shows had probably been a mistake. Although it wasn't allowed, the audience took photos and videos, and posted them online. Clearly wigs and thick make-up didn't fool the face-recognition software they used. Or maybe it was pure coincidence. Maybe someone had simply recognised him.

The zip on his parka had softened and felt like putty between his fingers. The teeth wouldn't close. He opened his rucksack and pulled out the remedy of all remedies: duct tape. He bit into it, tore off a few strips and taped the flaps of his parka together. He thought he heard the horse groan when he remounted. He'd stiffened up himself during their brief halt, so he assumed the animal had too. All the more reason not to linger but continue their journey. Keep his eyes and ears open, veer off the road if he heard a car coming, but otherwise allow the horse to walk at a leisurely pace until they reached the mouth of the river Ölfusá. Then he had to watch and wait until he was sure no car was near and gallop across the bridge as fast as the horse would take him. From there it was only a short trek across heathland to the bridleway that would lead them all the way home.

Home. What a fluid concept that was. In the same way his own character was fluid. Now he was saying farewell to Lady Gúgúlú and everything associated with her. That chapter in his life was over. Prior to that he'd said farewell to his life as Róbert Þór Gíslason, maybe without knowing what he was getting himself into when he'd asked people to call him the anglicised Thor Gislason. He had subsequently cast off that name for another, which he'd then dropped before assuming yet another. He'd gone by various names since his troubles began. And now he was moving into a new phase. With any luck it would be the last, because he'd run out of back-up plans. He had neither the money nor the energy for another emergency escape.

From now on he'd be plain Robbi. Back to the beginning. To when he was a nonentity. When people called him Robbi.

'If you want to change your persona or your self-image, now's the time to do it,' he said to the horse, and as if by magic the animal slipped into the ambling *tölt* gait unique to the Icelandic breed, and Robbi felt himself glide across the sands. Perhaps the horse was simply celebrating being on soft ground. The accursed rocky terrain had taken its toll on them both. Robbi had bought the horse relatively cheaply on the understanding that it had a fine *tölt* but had never got the hang of the flying pace or 'fifth gear' that, apparently, both of its progenitors had mastered. But Robbi couldn't have cared less. The horse had gone a long way towards fulfilling its obligation. To carry him safely from one place to the next.

11

Áróra wrapped her hair in a towel and slipped into Daníel's bathrobe, which he kept on a hook on the back of the bathroom door but never used. She had wept in the shower, the hot water washing away her tears as they flowed, and her heart now felt lighter. Meanwhile, out in the kitchen, Daníel seemed heavy-hearted. He sat hunched over the table with a magnifying glass, examining some bits of papers. When he glanced up, his face had a worried look.

'My tenant has vanished,' he said.

'Lady Gúgúlú?' Áróra knew Lady well. She'd been a fixture at Daníel's place since they first met. A kind of honorary member of the family, who nevertheless did her own thing and didn't always follow convention.

'Yes, Haraldur,' said Daníel, returning to the papers. Then he sighed and set aside the magnifying glass. 'This note is all he left, but I can hardly believe he went without saying goodbye to me. Just to leave a note is so...' He paused. 'Hurtful.'

Áróra could see from Daníel's eyes that he was wounded. She knew him well enough by now to be able to read his feelings. Although he usually had a calm exterior his eyes always betrayed his emotions.

'Did you try calling him?'

'That's what's bothering me,' said Daníel. 'There's no point, because he left his phone behind. And his iPad and his TV, and a whole lot of other valuables, which he says in this note to throw away. He doesn't seem to have taken his toiletries or other personal things either. He's left a new costume he was finishing for his next drag show. A magnificent dress it must have taken him hours to make. I just don't get it.'

Áróra sat down next to Daníel, stroked his back and read the note. The message was brief, although it did contain those terms of endearment Lady sprinkled about her as if she were sowing seeds, and which always seemed to issue from her lips in English: *Love u. Miss u.*

'What's with the magnifying glass?' Áróra asked, adding in a playful voice: 'I wasn't aware detectives still employed Sherlock's methods.'

Daníel gave a faint smile at her attempt to be funny. 'I've been comparing this note to some of the other notes he's left, and it's definitely his handwriting. But something doesn't add up.'

Áróra nodded. A lot of things that day didn't add up. 'It's been a strange day,' she said, and Daníel placed his arms about her and drew her close.

'I forgot I was going to cook for us,' he said. 'Why don't we order pizza and open a bottle of wine, snuggle up on the sofa and console each other?' Áróra nodded, and Daníel let go of her and rose from his chair. 'Can you order a pizza while I call Helena at the station to ask her to put out an appeal on Gúgúlú?' Áróra stared at him in surprise. He seemed to catch her expression: 'When people disappear without taking essential items with them,' he explained, 'it suggests they're thinking of killing themselves.'

The thought hadn't crossed her mind. And now she realised it wasn't exactly hurt she'd see on Daníel's face. His eyes were clouded with fear. She stood up and went to fetch her phone from the bathroom. Now they really could do with pizza and a bottle of wine.

12

Here it was. His back-up plan. His fallback position. In his head, Róbert had called his next step plan B, but he'd moved so far down the alphabet now, this was more like a plan L or M. Still, he had learned from his experiences over what was now almost a decade. Learned and understood from each of his failures that it wasn't enough to change countries and keep a low profile. Or to change his name and sail under a false flag. He needed to renounce his ties with the world altogether. And the time to do so had come.

The solitary house stood to the far southwest of Tjarnarbyggð, and Róbert had bought the plots on either side so he wouldn't have neighbours. All around was an endless plain over which the sky had seemingly capsized like a vast, translucent white dome. The lowland stretched south as far as the eye could see down to the sea at Eyrarbakki, where, on a clear day, you could make out the tower of Litla-Hraun prison. To the north, in the distance, a chain of blue-white mountains rose, spreading as far east as the Eyjafjallajökull glacier. This clear view, extending for several kilometres in all directions, made it impossible for anyone to approach without being seen.

The only route to the house was via a complicated series of roundabouts and turnings, and beside the last roundabout, leading to the turn-off to his house and the two vacant plots, stood a post box. Not that there would be any post, except possibly junk mail, because no one officially lived at the address. It was registered as a summer house in the name of an acquaintance of Róbert's. An acquaintance who couldn't be traced back to him. An acquaintance who himself was only vaguely aware he possessed the property, and who in his alcohol haze had most likely forgotten he once signed a document to the effect that he was the legal owner of a summer house and that Róbert's mother was his sole heir. A convenient arrangement that benefited both parties, since Róbert had arranged for regular payments to be made to the owner of the summer house. Hiding from the world was hard work.

And Róbert's back-up plan had been nothing if not hard work. In fact for years it had been a kind of hobby. He had drawn all the plans himself, designing the house from the ground up, and once the footings were laid and the windows and outside insulation installed, he had done more or less everything else himself.

He felt a release of tension as the horse lumbered into the final stretch, and pitied the poor creature when he had to force it back onto hummocky ground to take a detour to avoid being seen by a car before joining the road again. He brought the horse to a halt and dismounted about a hundred metres inside the gate that was clearly marked: *Private Road – No Access*. He was stiff all over and had pins and needles in his feet, so he leaned against the horse until he felt the blood begin to circulate in his legs again. The hole was where he'd left it, likewise the gravel he'd placed at the bottom to prevent frost heave. He took off his rucksack and extracted the box, held it out before him for an instant and closed his eyes. How curious it felt to be holding this little box containing the curse. For years he had kept it so close, yet hidden it from sight. He had considered hiring a digger to bury it somewhere so damned deep its power would be vanishingly small, but that wouldn't lift the curse. It might turn out that he could regard the curse as a blessing. His life insurance at the eleventh hour. In the worst-case scenario there was a chance they would be happy to take the box and let him go. Unlikely, but it gave him a glimmer of hope.

He placed the box inside the hole and used his hands to cover it with soil. He sensed the horse gazing at him with curiosity and maybe even a touch of disdain, which was hardly surprising. How could the animal possibly comprehend what the man who'd dragged it on this arduous journey was doing, kneeling by the roadside, grubbing around in the dirt? He clambered to his feet then stooped once more to smooth over the traces of fresh soil so they'd disappear more quickly. When he'd finished, he felt a sudden urge to do a little Gúgúlú number. He blessed it by crossing himself. 'Rest in peace, darling,' he pronounced over the tiny grave then winked at the horse. It gave a tired snort.

He had purposefully refrained from burying the box as deep as he had in the garden at home in Hafnarfjörður. *Home*, he thought and shook his head. Home was no longer there. From now on he lived here. Home was here. He felt a pang in his heart when he thought of Daníel, and could only pray he didn't come looking for him. Perhaps that was the one loose thread he ought to have tied up better. Maybe he'd been in some kind of denial. Refusing to face the fact that the day might arrive when Daníel would no longer be in his life. Or his crazy kids. Róbert swallowed hard. He was better off not thinking about the kids right now. Not when he was so exhausted and scared. It was just too much. He couldn't permit himself to break down until later.

It was good to have the box closer to the surface here, because its sphere of influence covered a longish section of road and served as an extra security barrier. Anyone attempting to ram the gate or drive straight through it would find their engine stall when they came near the box. So no vehicle could get right up to the house.

Róbert tugged gently on the reins to urge the horse on. But the bay seemed suddenly rooted to the spot, as if it was in two minds about moving into the outhouse.

'Easy, easy,' Róbert said to the horse. 'Come on. I've made a nice stall for you. And there's food and water waiting. Giddy-up.' The animal reluctantly obeyed Róbert's command, and he led it through the outhouse doors and into the stall. The animal clearly felt the same as he did after the journey. Stiff and sore all over. He removed the saddle and bridle, and the horse seemed relieved to be rid of the rough bone in its mouth. Róbert grabbed a cloth that hung on a hook and gave the animal's back and haunches a brisk rub down.

The outhouse was stocked with everything he needed to keep a horse for a fairly long time. He didn't know much about horses, so back when he was installing the stable he'd searched online for information from the Agricultural College as well as a few experienced horse breeders. He was relieved now that he'd done his homework. He had the whole plan worked out – knew exactly in what order to do things. He cut open one of the bales, grabbed a few handfuls of hay and also gave the horse a generous scoop of pellets. Then he filled the water trough and set the timer on the light switch.

'Bed at ten, old boy,' he told the horse as he left. 'But you can watch me through the porthole if you want.' He indicated the window he'd placed directly opposite the stall, pointing towards the main house. He had no idea whether horses suffered from boredom, but it had occurred to him at some point that the window would at least be a sort of eye onto the world. Like TV for horses.

He closed the outhouse door and walked over to the main house. The lights came on automatically, although there was no real need for them, now that spring was here and the days were lengthening. But it was good to know that at least one of the electrical circuits he'd installed worked properly. He glanced back at the outhouse and saw the horse clearly through the lighted window. It had its head in the manger, and Róbert felt a warm sensation course through him. Maybe he and the horse had formed a bond of some sort during these past few arduous hours. Maybe he should christen the horse. Choose a name that suited its character. Then again, it was probably foolish. Better he didn't. Safer not to develop any emotional ties to the horse. It would only make it harder for him to kill the animal if the need arose.

Daníel had woken before six with an uneasy feeling in the pit of his stomach. He'd made himself a coffee and sat down to go over the case file on Ísafold's disappearance yet again, only this time in light of what this woman Elísabet had told them the previous day.

Closing the file, his mind drifted to other matters. He'd called the station towards the end of the night shift to check if there was any news on Lady Gúgúlú, but there'd been no reports of a body found in the sea or at the foot of a tall building, or hanging from a tree somewhere. Obviously this came as a relief. Nor had his colleague Helena had any joy calling round hospitals, psychiatric wards and other places where the police typically looked. He'd done all he usefully could for the time being, and now he settled down to grapple with himself over the fundamental question of when and under what circumstances people had the right to disappear. Needless to say, this was a difficult thing to do in a country like Iceland where the national civil registration system meant the authorities could keep close tabs on its citizens and their activities within society. A few individuals had succeeded in falling off the radar, but only abroad. It was easier to make yourself disappear in bigger countries where they had no system of national identification, and where many people, like the British, seemed to consider disappearing and starting a new life an inalienable right. In fact Lady Gúgúlú – Haraldur – had lived in the UK once. Maybe he'd gone back there? In his note he said he'd had to go abroad unexpectedly because of a family matter. Now Daníel regretted not having asked him more about his past. He knew nothing about his family except that his mother lived in the Canary Islands. Actually, he knew remarkably little about this eccentric fellow, who, during his years in the garage, had come to play such a big part in his and his children's lives. The few times Daníel had tried to delve into Lady's past, he had the clear feeling it wasn't a welcome topic of conversation. Truth be told, in his opinion people had a right to leave their past behind. It was just painful all of a sudden to become part of that past himself.

'Good morning,' Áróra said as she came into the living room, back in her gym gear, hair brushed and ready to go. He received a volley of kisses from her, and would have been more than willing to take her back to bed. But she seemed in a hurry to leave.

'Don't you want coffee?' he asked, but she shook her head.

'No. I'm going to jog home on an empty stomach. Burn off some fat.'

He looked at her and smiled. 'You don't need to,' he said. 'You're thin enough as it is.'

She adopted an air of mock-offence. 'Hold on a minute, are you complaining?'

He laughed. 'Not at all,' he said. 'You're the most beautiful, desirable woman I know.'

'Just as well,' she retorted, kissing him once more.

He smiled and refrained from saying what was really on his mind: that he was concerned she might be training too hard. She never felt she was strong enough and was too critical of her own body.

'Have you looked at Ísafold's case file again?' she asked, crouching in the hallway to tie her laces.

'Yes,' he replied. 'And I think what I said yesterday was right. Apart from the police, only you and your mother knew about the location of the bloodstains in the apartment. We took the decision not to make that information public.'

'And I haven't discussed it with anyone, and I very much doubt my mother has either. At least not with anyone here in Iceland,' said Áróra.

Daníel nodded. Became pensive. The description of the attack inside the apartment that Elísabet claimed came from her daughter tallied perfectly with the evidence.

'We need to meet Elísabet again,' he said. 'Maybe I should go and see her on my own, wave my badge at her. It might pressure her into coming clean.' Áróra winced visibly. And then that look appeared on her face that he knew only too well. Her defensive expression. The signal that she was about to withdraw into herself. Back away from him. Grow distant. So he quickly added: 'But you're in charge of this, of course. Just let me know how you want to deal with it.'

She seemed reassured. 'Let's talk later today,' she said, blowing him a kiss before disappearing through the door.

He felt the familiar panic settle in his chest. The fear that she might leave him. They didn't even have to quarrel; it was enough for her to adopt that distant look and his heart would start to hammer in his chest. He longed to call her straightaway, insist he wouldn't do anything regarding her sister's case, or this mysterious woman, without discussing it with her, and then try to read what Áróra was thinking. In her tone of voice. Her choice of words.

He felt relieved, then, when the bell rang. She must have come back to talk it over some more, or she'd forgotten her key. He bounded over to the door to let her back in. Only it wasn't Áróra who stood outside, but three strange men. The one nearest to Daníel placed a hand on his chest and pushed him back inside the apartment. The other two followed behind.

'We need to talk to you about Róbert Þór Gíslason,' said the man who entered last, closing the door behind him.

15

The last time Daníel experienced anything like this was when he did his police interrogation training, except it was clear from the atmosphere now that this was no training exercise. The men had pushed him onto a kitchen chair and taken away his phone. He couldn't really say they'd been violent, because he hadn't resisted, but they'd certainly intimidated him. Three against one was always intimidating, and the threat didn't need to be verbal to be understood. It was obvious he wouldn't get away from them, even if he tried.

'When did you last see Róbert Þór Gíslason?' the one who spoke Icelandic repeated.

Daníel shook his head, trying to maintain a calm exterior despite the swirl of thoughts in his head. 'I refuse to answer your questions until you tell me who you are,' he said for the third time.

They hadn't introduced themselves, and he couldn't make out what organisation they might be working for. He knew two of them were foreigners, because the Icelandic speaker whispered to them in English and they whispered back, and although Daníel couldn't make out exactly what they were saying he managed to overhear the odd word. These men were no ordinary criminals. If they were, they would have beaten a response out of him by now. They were all in their twenties, similarly dressed in black suits and black T-shirts, and had a formal air about them that made him think they'd probably been through police training. Yet their refusal to tell him who they were and in what capacity they were interrogating him didn't add up.

'Are you with the Police Commissioner's Office?' he asked, addressing the Icelander.

The man's face remained impassive, and he continued to pace up and down as if he had trouble staying still. Meanwhile the two foreigners were virtually immobile. One of them sat on a chair, rested his elbows on the kitchen table and stared straight at Daníel. The other stood stock-still, arms folded, also staring. It was as if they were expecting him to break down at any moment and tell them everything they wanted to know.

'How long did Róbert Þór live here?'

'I don't know who you're talking about,' replied Daníel. 'I don't know any Róbert Þór.'

'Your tenant,' said the Icelander. 'Or maybe he's your lover?' A kind of twisted grin now appeared on the man's face.

'Implying that I'm queer doesn't offend me, if that's what you think, but I don't have a male lover,' said Daníel. 'And my tenant's name is Haraldur, but he also goes by his stage name, Lady Gúgúlú. He's been renting my garage apartment for just over four years. And now I insist you tell me who you are or I'll report you to the Police Commissioner's Office for breach of protocol, and then all hell will break loose.'

One of the foreigners slammed his fist down on the table, making Daníel jump. The Icelander leaned forward and hissed in his face, his acrid toothpaste breath stinging Daníel's eyes.

'You'll do no such thing!' he yelled, and the man who had struck the table added in English:

'Forget this visit and don't mention it to anyone. And you can forget about your tenant, too.'

16

Áróra stood in front of the mirror, debating whether to put on full make-up or just a dab, as was her custom of late. On a normal day she would have used a light face cream, a bit of mascara and a pale lipstick. But these were unusual circumstances and she felt strange, so the idea of painting her face as if she were going out on the town didn't seem too crazy. Wearing a kind of mask that veiled how she felt gave her a degree of protection. Hid her flushed cheeks, the sweat on her upper lip, created a thin shield against the situation.

She shook her head at her own foolishness. If the child really was her sister, Ísafold, it didn't matter how she looked. She shook her head again, surprised at herself. Of course the child wasn't Ísafold. In the cold light of day her misgivings felt deeper and stronger, and what the little girl's mother, Elísabet, had told them yesterday seemed even more far-fetched. And implausible. Yet Áróra had arranged to meet her again, and this time she was going alone. She wanted to see the little girl for herself, allow her intuition to guide her, without Daníel stepping in and challenging everything head on. Maybe she simply wanted to believe.

As she ran a comb through her hair she felt a few spots on her scalp. Fucking steroids. The spots meant she needed to make a decision about when to stop taking them. Today was a rest day and tomorrow she'd do weight training and have an injection. It would be fine if she stopped in a couple of weeks. She wouldn't let her voice deepen. She just wanted to increase her strength, build a bit more muscle on her arms and thighs. Her thighs were going well and most of her jeans were on the tight side now, but her arms were taking longer. Her back was always the limiting factor. She couldn't put more strain on her arms than her back and shoulders were able to take. The steroids helped and she was pleased to find she was growing stronger by the week. She felt more confident, too. And Daníel hadn't complained about her increased libido, although he never ceased to be surprised by Áróra's daily demands for sex. Sometimes twice a day. Áróra smiled to herself and at the same time felt a surge of remorse. Daníel wouldn't be at all happy to know she was taking banned substances. Even if it was only temporary.

She pulled a thin jumper on over her shirt and grabbed her bag and coat on the way out. She burned up the Tesla all the way to Bakkahverfi and turned the radio on full blast. She didn't recognise the music, but the thumping bass kept pace with her pounding heart, and she had the impression that if only she drove fast enough her anxiety about this meeting wouldn't get its claws into her. She parked the Tesla in the big car park in front of the building and searched for the house number. The block had two floors and was U-shaped, with a garden and play area and a few sturdy-looking trees in the middle. It was clearly built back in the seventies but had been well maintained. She found the correct entrance, leading off the garden, and she pressed the bell. Elísabet's voice answered, and soon after the entry system buzzed her in. Áróra pushed open the door, walked inside and ran up the stairs. Just then she felt an overwhelming desire to pull out. Turn on her heel, run back to her car and forget about the whole thing. But it was too late, and she forced a smile when Elísabet opened the door and ushered her inside.

When the little blonde girl with a shock of curls came bounding over and literally flung herself at Áróra, her anxiety transformed into something else, some powerful, inexplicable emotion that burrowed its way into her heart – it was as if her heart were melting, the blood flowing out of it, making her belly feel warm and fuzzy.

'Áróra,' cried the little girl, and Áróra sank to her knees, returning the child's embrace hesitantly, even though the little girl clutched her so tight she could scarcely believe such a shrimp had this much strength.

'Troll sister,' she whispered in her ear, and Áróra burst into tears.

'Elf sister,' she whispered back, misty-eyed. 'My darling little elf sister.'

17

Robbi awoke to the sound of birdsong and instantly felt raven-
ous. He had wolfed down a Pot Noodle and a chocolate bar the
night before while setting up the CCTV and alarm systems.
After that he'd loaded both shotguns, stood one of them in the
alcove by the front door and stashed the other beneath his bed,
placing a box of cartridges within easy reach of both. Then he'd
lain down on the bed and fallen asleep almost immediately,
much to his surprise, as the last thing he remembered was his
heart pounding and a nagging sense of fear.

Now, with the sun coming in through the windows and the
sound of birds twittering, somehow his fear seemed irrational.
As if yesterday's nightmare had softened into a sweet dream that
filled his head with thoughts of beauty and freedom. He knew
this was a fantasy, of course. He would probably never be free,
but there was no harm in dreaming. He boiled the kettle, prepared coffee in the cafetière and opened the pantry door. The
floor-to-ceiling shelves were crammed with tins and jars, and
bags of dried food he had vacuum-packed to extend their use-
by dates. He brought out some oatmeal, long-life milk and a bag
of raisins, cut through the plastic packaging and made porridge,
thinking to himself he'd only be happy once he learned to use
the bread-making machine. He preferred having toast and jam
with his morning coffee. Porridge was more of a midday meal
for him, but today it would have to do.

In order to look up any information, however, whether it be
recipes or tips about the self-sufficient life-style he had embarked
upon, not to mention keeping abreast of world events, he would
need to get online and create new usernames for everything. At
least he could have fun inventing a new online persona. She

should have a common name like Guðrun or Anna, and be middle-aged or late middle-aged. He'd need to be careful not to use her name to look up anything relating to his previous life.

He sat down at the table with his porridge and coffee, and contemplated the CCTV screens. The main camera was focused on the gate and showed the nearby stretch of road. In fact he could see the gate through his kitchen window, but the camera gave him a close-up view, so that if a car approached he'd be able to see the driver. Beside it was a motion sensor, which would set off an alarm inside the house if anything bigger than a sparrow went near it. The other cameras were fixed to the house and pointed in every direction, giving him a rapid overview of the entire area. All of them had zoom, so he could survey the land around in detail. He'd installed a camera in the stable, as well, just for fun. And it appeared the horse was awake and hungry. His first task that morning would be to feed the animal and let it out into the paddock to stretch its legs. Judging from his own aching muscles the horse must be hurting too.

Robbi finished his porridge and coffee then rose from the table and stretched his sore limbs. He had a busy day ahead of him. He needed to settle in, take an inventory and go out for supplies. His last trip for a while.

18

This was exactly the way interrogations worked. Daníel was exhausted. He was hungry, tired and angry, and despite his attempts to remain calm he had lost his cool and raised his voice a few times. And he'd blabbed. He'd let himself be drawn into an argument with the men, which resulted in him giving them information but failing to extract anything from them in return. He was no closer to knowing who they worked for, but he did have an idea they were in law enforcement, because they used the same techniques he did when confronted with people who were tough to interrogate. Patience and tenacity. But despite knowing their game he found it hard to defend himself against it. And so they went on, taking turns to ask him questions. One minute they were friendly and tried to get through to him; the next they made oblique threats.

'I've told you everything I know,' said Daníel. 'I've always been under the impression that Lady Gúgúlú's name was Haraldur and the rent was paid by Gúgúlú Ltd. I can't tell you any more than that.'

The three men continued to stare at him piercingly, as if they were trying to read his thoughts, to see whether he was hiding anything from them. He often used the same technique. Said nothing and gazed, waiting for his interlocutor to fill the silence.

A phone vibrated in the Icelander's pocket. He took it out and put it to his ear.

'Okay,' he said into the phone. 'I'll be right out.' He turned on his heel, and as he left the kitchen murmured something in English to the other two about the removal van having arrived.

'What are you doing?' shouted Daníel. 'I demand to see a warrant. You're not taking a single thing out of that garage unless I see a warrant.'

One of the foreigners picked up Lady Gúgúlú's note and waved it in the air. The Icelander had translated it for them.

'Why should you care about this junk. Róbert doesn't,' he said. 'In his note he says you can throw it all away, so you can be thankful we're saving you the trouble. The garage will be all clear and ready for the next tenant.'

'Who the hell are you, anyway?'

'The important question, and the one to which we want an answer is: who is Robert Thor?'

'You seem to know that better than I do,' scoffed Daníel, choosing not to correct the man's pronunciation of the name Róbert Þór.

The other foreigner drew up a chair, and sat so close to Daníel their knees were touching. 'Have you ever noticed anything strange about Robert Thor?' he said, leaning in confidentially.

'Yes,' replied Daníel. 'If Lady Gúgúlú or Haraldur, as I know him, is indeed the Róbert Þór you're looking for, then yes. He's the strangest person I've ever met.'

The man hummed. 'What I mean is, have you ever noticed ... how can I put this ... any mysterious phenomena occurring around him? Anything that's ... er ... difficult to explain?'

'What sort of phenomena, exactly?' Daníel asked, unable to conceal his astonishment.

'For example, did your car break down more often than usual? Or did your domestic appliances stop working? Any TV or radio interference, or clocks that go backward?' The man's serious face was so at odds with his curious line of questioning that Daníel burst into laughter.

'Are you asking me whether Lady Gúgúlú is an extra-terrestrial?' he said laughing, but his laughter was rudely cut short by a punch in the face. He raised his hand to feel his mouth, but his lip and jaw had both gone numb. His teeth seemed to be in place but the blood on his fingers showed he had a split lip. He took a few deep breaths to quell the adrenaline that was now pumping through his veins, demanding he hit the man back.

'This is no fucking joke!' hissed the man, and Daníel had to agree. That punch in the face proved to him these guys weren't cops. But in that case who were they? And why were they taking Lady Gúgúlú's stuff out of the garage? Why all these bizarre questions?

Daníel took the kitchen roll the other man handed him and dabbed his mouth. Flickering in his mind's eye was the newly planted tree in the wild patch out in the garden.

19

Áróra sat watching the child as though in a trance, scarcely aware of Elísabet pacing back and forth in the kitchen and bringing coffee cups out to the low table. The little girl scampered about the rectangular living room. Over by the far wall was a window where a play area had been set up with a rug and some padded IKEA boxes that contained toys. The child busied herself plucking one toy after another from the boxes and running with them over to Áróra, who hardly had time to show her appreciation before the little girl ran off again.

'What's your name?' Áróra asked her for a second time.

'Ísafold,' replied the little girl.

'But isn't it also Ester Lóa?' her mother asked with a hint of reproach as she emerged from the kitchen carrying a coffee thermos and a milk jug.

'Yes,' said the child. 'But also Ísafold Jónsdóttir. Ester Lóa Ísafold Jónsdóttir.'

She was a slender child, and when she wasn't flinging herself into Áróra's arms, skipped nimbly round the room on her toes. She had pale-grey eyes and her big head was wreathed in blonde curls, which stuck to her cheeks and temples from sweating as she dashed about. When Elísabet disappeared into the kitchen again, Áróra used the opportunity to probe the child.

'Do you remember our dad?' she asked, at which the little girl promptly flexed her arms and cried:

'Strongest daddy in the world!'

Áróra swallowed the lump that kept rising in her throat. Their father had never actually won the title of world's strongest man, but he'd been both Icelandic and Scottish champion.

'Do you remember what he told us to eat?'

'Elf food and troll food!' cried the little girl.

This was what their father had always said. He encouraged Áróra to eat mostly protein, and Ísafold carbs, because Áróra practised weight lifting and Ísafold ballet and gymnastics. How in the hell could this three-year-old child whom she'd never met know that? Elf food and troll food were expressions used only by the family, and as far as she knew they hadn't shared them with anybody else.

Elísabet returned to the living room with a packet of biscuits and sat down next to Áróra on the sofa. She made a rustling noise with the packet as she opened it then offered one to Áróra.

She couldn't have swallowed a thing and shook her head. 'No, thank you.'

Elísabet took a biscuit herself and munched on it as the two women sat side by side, watching the child as she emptied the toy boxes and placed the contents in a pile around Áróra, who sat there feeling numb, her eyes brimming with tears.

'She's been diagnosed as hyperactive but without the attention deficit,' said Elísabet, plucking another biscuit from the packet. 'But the child psychiatrist wants to run a few more tests, due to this Ísafold thing. Also because it's not normal for a child so young to talk about death the way she does.'

Áróra swallowed hard and then coughed to clear the lump in her throat. 'Has she said anything about where...' She paused an instant, unsure about how she should word this. Should she say *body*? *Where her body was buried*? Ísafold's body wasn't necessarily buried anywhere. She could be at the bottom of the ocean. Áróra cleared her throat once more. 'Has she said anything about where Ísafold is resting?'

Elísabet took a bite of her biscuit then washed it down with a mouthful of coffee.

'Hm,' she said and nodded. 'Yes. Not the exact place. She doesn't know that. But she's described the surroundings quite well.'

20

They had emptied the garage apartment of everything. They'd even taken the wardrobe, the washing machine and the little stove that came with the tenancy. All that remained were the bare walls and the floor, which, oddly enough, looked as if it had been scrubbed. There wasn't a single footmark or any of the dust bunnies you find lurking under furniture when it's moved. The place was sparkling, and, indeed, ready to rent out. But that wasn't the plan. This mysterious visit by the men had convinced Daniel that Lady, Haraldur, hadn't left of his own free will, but was on the run, probably from these individuals. And although this concerned him, because they weren't exactly easy-going guys, it was a relief to know his friend hadn't voluntarily abandoned him.

And if his departure was forced then he was almost certainly in need of help. Daniel locked the garage and went back out into the garden. On his way over to the house he stopped at the wild patch, contemplated the tree and wondered whether Haraldur had hidden something there in a hurry before he left. He gave a sigh. The patch was under some sort of spell. Lady Gúgúlú claimed that hidden folk lived in the nearby rocks and didn't take kindly to human meddling. It was a source of endless vexation for Daniel, who kept the rest of the lawn immaculate all summer but never managed to mow that spot. Each time he tried the lawnmower broke down. The engine stalled. The gear slipped. The blade bent. Even the garden shears had fallen apart right there when the bolt snapped. Eventually Daniel decided to follow Lady Gúgúlú's advice and leave the patch well alone. Yet now it seemed Lady herself had disturbed it, and Daniel was determined to find out why. Could it have some connection to the mysterious men's questions? Entering the little tool shed to fetch a spade, he noticed traces of soil on the floor, and next to them a stick he hadn't seen before, like a fence post flattened at one end. Daníel never replaced any tools in the shed without first cleaning them meticulously, so clearly someone else had been in there, tossed the muddy stick on the floor and left a mess. And since his upstairs neighbours never did anything in the garden, only one other person came to mind.

Daníel drew a deep breath before he stepped on the spade and plunged it into the soil. He was half expecting it to bend out of shape, like the old one had when he'd attempted to dig up the turf beneath the wild patch. Before Lady Gúgúlú's elf story gave it protected status. But the edge cut easily through the loose earth and in no time at all Daníel had extracted the recently planted tree. Inside the hole, however, he found only sand and soil. He dug down deeper until the spade hit frozen ground. There was no way anyone had hidden anything in there. He shovelled half the soil back into the hole, replaced the tree, filled up the space with the remaining soil then tamped it down with his feet.

This left only one thing for him to check. The pink glitter phone he had decided not to mention to the men and which, since yesterday, had been languishing in the pocket of his trousers, now hanging on a hook on his bedroom door. He massaged his bruised cheek and congratulated himself on having achieved at least this small victory.

21

Robbi sauntered down to the gate, carrying the battery under his arm, making sure to give the spot where the box was buried a wide berth. He wasn't going to let a brand-new battery get ruined before he'd even used it. He opened the bonnet of the jeep, slotted the battery into place, screwed it down and connected the leads. Then he climbed inside, reached below the passenger seat and pulled out the bundle he'd stashed there. He removed the oilcloth encasing the shotgun and loaded the chamber with cartridges he took from his pocket. He'd sawn off the barrel so he could fire it out of the window while driving, but now, as he contemplated the grassy yellow plain stretching towards the white-capped mountains, the idea of taking a shotgun with him on a shopping trip to Selfoss seemed ludicrous. Yet this was his reality. He was pretty sure that if things went pear-shaped the shotgun wouldn't help him much, but it gave him a sense of security.

The engine spluttered to life, and Robbi smiled to himself. Everything was going smoothly – for now at any rate. He moved off slowly to give the jeep time to warm up, as he hadn't driven it in a long time, but it all sounded fine. Not even a squeak from the brakes. The jeep was grey, an older model that was less complicated than the newer ones, meaning he could do most of the maintenance on it himself. He had a second spare tyre in the outhouse together with the necessary tools, and in the event he did need a mechanic it shouldn't be a problem as the vehicle was registered to the owner of the summer house. Who also, unbeknownst to him, paid the insurance and the road tax. It would no doubt come as a big surprise to the man himself to know what an active, responsible member of society he was.

Before turning onto the main road, Robbi put on his cap and face mask. Although masks were no longer obligatory in shops, quite a few people still wore them, and it suited his purposes now to be able to cover his face without drawing too much attention. He needed to avoid getting caught on any CCTV or traffic cameras.

His first stop was the petrol station. He put on a pair of sunglasses, resting them on top of the mask, then got out of the jeep, making sure to lower his head when he inserted the summer house owner's credit card into the pay-at-the-pump machine. Petrol stations were crawling with CCTV. He filled up the tank and two jerry cans he kept in the back. Then he drove into Selfoss, admiring the new buildings in the revamped town centre. The town authorities had planned this new development and thumbed their noses at the capital by building replicas of houses that had been demolished in downtown Reykjavik. The multi-coloured iron- or wooden-clad facades of the timber houses had a pleasantly familiar feel, even though this exact street scene had never existed before. The double- and triple-pane windows were either painted the same colour as the roof or stark white, which Robbi always found more beautiful. He longed to take a stroll, stop at a café, have fun exploring the town, but that wasn't possible for him now. Nor would it be in the future. Reality had caught up with him, and he was down to his last back-up plan. He'd better not mess this one up.

At the supermarket, he picked a large trolley and started in the freezer aisles. He grabbed five bags of mutton chops, two whole boxes of cod heads, two bags of breaded haddock, a box of chicken breasts, a bag of salmon fillets and filled the rest of the trolley with trays of minced beef. Then he wheeled the trolley over to the checkout and asked the cashier if she would keep an eye on it while he continued his shop. He fetched another trolley, half filled it with frozen vegetables and berries, then took two whole boxes of butter, four huge slabs of cheese, a few tubs of caviar and emptied the shelf of tinned pâté. Pâté was freezable. He had plenty of jam in the pantry, as well as tins of French pâté, which he could keep until he'd finished the frozen ones. Then he took all the fresh vegetables he thought he could eat in the next ten days, along with five bags of potatoes. Finally he piled the trolley to overflowing with sliced bread and pastries, and wheeled it over to the checkout.

The girl looked at him curiously, and he murmured something about an equestrian gathering at a summer house. She nodded as if this were a plausible enough explanation. She would remember him, and he was glad of the face mask, even as he prayed nobody ever asked her about the customer who did an enormous shop.

It was a relief to be leaving the town again, the jeep stuffed to the gunnels with all the food he needed. Now all he had to do was drive down to Stokkseyri and pick up the hens.

22

Áróra hadn't yet collected herself by the time she arrived back at Daníel's house. She still felt emotional and a bit choked up, her pulse racing as if she'd been running flat out. She didn't know whether this was because of the steroids or because for the first time in over two years new information had surfaced about her sister. It was probably a combination of the two. The steroids made her much more sensitive, and trivial things that wouldn't normally affect her did so now. It was no surprise, then, that news as big as this had sent her heart rate into exercise mode.

She'd searched for so long. Every summer, and well into autumn, she had tramped the roads and trails around the capital with a camera drone high up in the sky. She would film huge swathes on either side of these roads then examine the recordings for anything unusual. During her quest she'd collected a fair amount of litter from the grasslands and lava fields on the Reykjanes peninsula, because once she was satisfied the pale or colourful blotches on the landscape weren't the wrapping encasing her sister's body, but plastic sheeting, drums, foam trays or all sorts of other things, she would put it all in the boot of her car and take it to the recycling centre. Because regardless of what she'd said to Elísabet, Áróra had never stopped trying to find her sister's body. There was no evidence to suggest Ísafold might be alive somewhere, and Áróra was sure her sister was dead. What's more she'd always felt she was lying somewhere in the lava. And today this little girl had confirmed that intuition.

When she tried to open the door to Daníel's apartment she found it locked. Yet she knew he was at home because his car was outside. Her door key was in the Tesla so she rang the bell. Maybe he'd flicked the latch because he wanted to be left alone.

Despite being a cop, Daníel usually left the door unlocked when he was at home. He'd got into the habit as his children grew older and constantly drifted in and out, invariably forgetting their keys. It amused Áróra that he'd kept up the tradition, as his children now lived with their mother in Denmark and only spent one week with him every three months.

Áróra gave a start when Daníel came to the door. His lower lip was bruised and swollen and had a big cut on it that extended down towards his chin.

'What happened to you?' she asked, reaching instinctively for his head. She cupped his face in her hands and inspected his wounds.

'I got hit,' he said. 'Punched in the face by some British guy who came here with his colleagues looking for Lady Gúgúlú.'

'An angry ex-lover, or...?'

'No,' said Daníel. 'The men were some kind of...' he hesitated. 'Cops.'

'What?' Áróra gaped at him in astonishment.

'Yes, or maybe they're with a security firm,' Daníel replied. 'I got the feeling they think Haraldur – Gúgúlú – is somehow dangerous.'

Áróra led Daníel into the kitchen and ordered him to sit down while she opened his first-aid box and made a butterfly stitch out of a piece of plaster.

'This almost needs stitches,' she said, pinching together the skin below his lip and fastening it with the plaster. 'In any case you mustn't smile for a while,' she added. The word was enough to bring an incipient one to Daníel's lips. 'No, don't!' she said, bursting into laughter, and for a moment Daníel struggled to keep a straight face. But then they became serious again.

'Are you going to report these men?' she asked. 'How does that work, anyway? Do cops call the cops?'

'I intend to call certain people, yes,' he replied firmly. 'And I'm determined to find out who these guys are and what they want from Gúgúlú.' Áróra rummaged in the freezer, found a pack of frozen peas and handed it to Daníel. He dutifully pressed it to his jaw and rose from the chair. 'Do you mind if we go into the living room?' he said. 'Those guys kept me in the kitchen for over two hours. And I found out my kitchen chairs aren't exactly comfortable if you sit on them for too long.'

In the living room, Daníel flopped onto the sofa and spread his arms. Áróra sat down beside him and he drew her close.

'I went to see the little girl,' she whispered.

Daníel looked at her and frowned. 'Áróra!' he said. 'I asked you not to go there on your own.'

'I know, I know,' she said hurriedly. 'But I had to see her. Talk to her calmly. And she is just a very lively little three-year-old, but...' She faltered.

'But what?' demanded Daníel.

Áróra wasn't quite sure how she should put her thoughts into words.

'But on some strange level she also seems to be Ísafold. She knows things which, apart from Ísafold, only me and Dad and Mum knew, expressions which...' She was relieved when Daníel didn't say anything else, although she could almost feel in his body that he was simmering with doubt. 'And Daníel,' she said, her voice breaking. 'She says my sister is lying in black lava.'

23

Helena had always felt best when she was at work, but nowadays she didn't really feel good anywhere except at work. Her personal life had become, to put it bluntly, a little sad. She found herself in the very situation she'd tried so hard to avoid: she loved only one woman – with all the suffering this entailed. Up until now, she'd refused to become attached, had pursued multiple relationships with women and had always kept her emotions well protected, buried deep in the core of her being, where nobody else could gain access, a place she daren't expose for this very reason.

Admittedly she couldn't have foreseen having a lover who was not only in prison but married to another woman. However, this was her current situation. And what hurt Helena most of all was that, as her spouse, Bisi was permitted to visit Sirra whereas she wasn't. She knew perfectly well, of course, that for both Sirra and Bisi the marriage was one of convenience, so that Bisi would be granted leave to remain in the country, and then, with any luck, would eventually gain citizenship. Bisi had been trafficked to Iceland, and when the authorities only offered her a few months' protection before deporting her back to Nigeria, Helena and Sirra decided to help her. But now that Sirra was serving a prison sentence of several months for an old extortion charge, Helena missed her dreadfully, and it cut her to the quick to know that Bisi got to go to the prison that evening and stay over. Helena would have given her right arm to be able to snuggle up next Sirra that night. Instead Bisi was going to be with her; they'd stay up late playing board games and sleep primly side by side like good little sisters. What a waste of a conjugal visit. But they needed to keep up the charade, because immigration was no doubt watching them and the marriage had to appear genuine. So as well as feeling sad and lonely, Helena found herself in a position she hadn't expected to be in again: back in the closet.

She'd volunteered for another night shift, in traffic of all places; anything rather than stay at home obsessing over Bisi's visit with Sirra. But she was told she'd done too much overtime that month and to clear off home. It came as a relief, then, when Daníel called her with an assignment. Two, in fact.

'Keep this between us for now,' he told her, and she rejoiced inwardly. This was exactly what she needed to keep her mind occupied. To stop her from thinking about Sirra and how much she yearned to be in Bisi's place, spending the night with wonderful, soft, loving, sexy Sirra.

'Fire away,' she said, pen poised above her notepad.

'It's about Gúgúlú,' he said. 'Could you stop by my place later to pick up her phone and get it examined? I need to stay with Áróra today, you see. She's not in very good shape mentally ... Which brings me to the other thing I want to ask you to do.'

'In connection with what?'

'Ísafold Jónsdóttir's disappearance.'

'I'm on my way,' Helena said, grabbing her coat from the desk chair. She clocked off, then bounded down the police station steps two at a time.

24

In all the articles Robbi had read on self-sufficient living, keeping hens consistently topped the list of things to do. He had thought long and hard about whether to have a cockerel as well and allow them to multiply, breed his own chickens, but he realised he would dread having to slaughter them for food. So he'd bought himself six hens with the idea in mind that once he'd exhausted his supply of frozen food, he could get the protein he needed from eggs, in addition to the tinned produce.

He walked up to the main house, fetched the wheelbarrow and pushed it down to the gate. The frozen food seemed all right for the moment, so he decided to start by transporting the three cardboard boxes containing the hens. He stacked them on the wheelbarrow and conveyed them to the hen coop beyond the house. He opened the door to the coop and surveyed the hens' quarters. The perches were all set up, likewise the nesting boxes he'd made, and the rubber tyre with sand in the middle. He trotted over to the outhouse, grabbed an armful of hay from the bale, returned to the coop and distributed it evenly among the nesting boxes. Then he filled the food dispensers and the water trough at the tap outside. Lastly, he opened the air vent and closed the door. According to his research, hens should be kept inside for the first three days, after that they would consider the new coop their new home and from then on would return there before it got dark.

He opened the first box and lifted out one of the hens. The other one sat as though paralysed, but the instant he set it down on the ground it joined its sister, who was strutting about, investigating the new quarters. He opened the other boxes and was alarmed when two of the hens instantly started fighting, as if both resented the proximity of the other in this new dwelling. Robbi felt a flash of panic. Aside from what he'd read and his memories of staying with his grandfather in the countryside as a boy, he knew nothing about hens. Maybe this hadn't been such a good idea after all. But what was done was done, and he reminded himself he was a nuclear physicist, so it could hardly be beyond his wit to do a bit more research and figure out how to deal with the problems that could arise in a flock of hens. People everywhere kept poultry in their back yards, so it couldn't be that complicated.

The scuffle ended with one of the hens huddling in a corner while the other, a white Sussex, strutted about as if it owned the coop. The four other hens contemplated the white Sussex and seemed united in their decision to bow before its authority. Robbi scattered a scoopful of sunflower seeds on the ground. The hens instantly pecked at the seeds, save for the harassed one in the corner. He hoped it would be okay. Now he wished he'd installed CCTV in the coop, like he had in the stable, so he could keep an eye on them. Truth be told he was surprised he hadn't thought of it. But it was easily remedied. He had a few spare cameras in the house – he could set up some of those.

He contemplated ways in which he might ameliorate the shock this move to a new place must signify for these slow-witted souls, and his inner Gúgúlú burst forth.

'*Wilkommen! Bienvenue! Welcome!*' he sang, and the hens glanced up from their sunflower seeds, staring at him in apparent alarm. 'I'm only welcoming you,' he said by way of explanation, and resumed singing his favourite song from *Cabaret*.

When he'd finished he took a bow, but the hens showed no sign of applauding or cheering. They were a poor substitute for the rowdy audiences at his old drag shows, who made one hell of a din with their yells, shouts and wolf-whistles. But the hens hadn't booed either, even though maybe this wasn't his best performance. Which was some consolation at least.

25

Áróra and Daníel were coming out of the empty garage apartment just as Helena pulled up outside the house. She embraced Áróra and asked her how she was. It had been an emotional day and Áróra could feel herself choking up again.

Helena was less sympathetic towards Daníel. 'What the hell happened to your face?' she asked, scrutinising him.

'Long story,' he said with a grin.

Áróra knew Daníel and Helena were genuine friends, and that they'd become accustomed to engaging in the badass banter that was apparently common among cops. No doubt people who were constantly exposed to trauma in their work found it hard to fuss over something as trivial as a split lip.

Daníel pulled out the phone with the pink cover and handed it to Helena. 'Could you ask Rannveig to unlock it and send me a transcript of the contents. Also ask her to keep it off the record. And tell her I said hi.'

Helena took the phone, nodding as she slipped it into her pocket.

Daníel then turned to Áróra and placed his arm around her. 'Actually we plan to spend the evening consoling one another,' he said. 'Áróra had a bit of a strange day, too.'

Áróra felt the lump in her throat grow bigger. She swallowed hard and gave a little cough as she tried to think of the right words to explain what had happened. But there really weren't any, so she just gave it to Helena straight.

'I'm a mess because this woman contacted me. She has a little girl who says ... she's my sister reincarnated.'

Helena's mouth opened then closed again, and she looked searchingly at Daníel. Áróra saw his eyebrows dart up and down to indicate he considered the story complete humbug. She felt slightly irritated by this, even though she could see why neither of them would swallow it. Daníel hadn't met the child in person – he hadn't sensed the familiarity. That intimacy you only have with someone you know well. But she had sensed the connection that had existed between her and her sister when they were little.

'I know it sounds crazy,' she said to Helena, 'but I met the child this morning and she said things nobody outside the family could know about. For instance, that Dad called me troll girl and my sister elf girl and he always gave us different food to eat.'

'Sometimes in these situations we hear what we want to hear,' said Helena.

Áróra felt a strong urge to scream at her, but her tone was so good-natured and benevolent, and her own common sense told her that of course she was right. This was what spiritual con artists preyed on. The credulousness of grieving people who want to be in contact with their deceased loved ones.

'What bothers me about this,' Daníel put in, 'is the mother's account of her daughter's description of the attack she says ended in Ísafold's death. It coincides exactly with the bloodstain patterns we found in the apartment.'

'Ah,' said Helena, and Áróra could see she was taken aback.

'Yes,' Daníel said simply. It was as if he and Helena were communicating through gestures. There was some meaning behind Helena's frowns and the way Daníel nodded his head.

'Could you send me these people's details?' asked Helena.

Daníel nodded and now Áróra felt as if she were no longer there. As if there weren't three of them standing between the garage and the driveway but that she was looking on while the two of them communicated in their secret language, as if they'd appropriated her experience, this thread she had finally been handed. This clue, the first in a long time, to the puzzle of her sister's disappearance.

She felt a tide of anger rise inside her. Not the usual kind of irritation but full-blown steroid rage. She stormed off across the garden into the apartment, to avoid shouting something she might later regret.

26

Daníel said goodbye to Helena and then took his time following Áróra across the garden onto the porch and through the French windows into the apartment. He didn't hurry because he'd learned from experience that Áróra could be quick to flare up when she lost her temper, but she was equally quick to calm down again. She wasn't in the living room, so he looked in the kitchen, but she wasn't there either. Nor in the bedroom. He paused to listen through the closed bathroom door, and when he heard the sound of running water he went to the kitchen, opened the cupboard doors and considered the dinner possibilities.

'Can't we just order a takeaway?' Áróra said behind him, as if she were reading his mind.

'Again?'

'Sure. I'm up for another pizza.'

Daníel looked at her and frowned. It wasn't like Áróra to be this casual about food. If anything she was too strict about eating protein and two kinds of vegetable with every meal, along with all the body-building supplements she took. Recently, though, her habits had changed. There was no denying it. Compulsive exercise and disordered eating. Not for the first time it occurred to him she might be struggling with some sort of eating disorder. Whatever the case, now wasn't a good time to bring it up.

'I could go out to fetch a roast chicken,' said Daníel, and Áróra nodded distractedly. Walking up to her, he made to take her in his arms but she placed her hand on his chest and pushed back against him.

'I need you to have faith in me,' she said. 'To have faith in my intuition about this little girl and what she's saying. She knows things only Ísafold and I knew about. Trivial things that were between us and our dad. And...' Áróra pursed her lips. 'And I need you. I need your support.'

Daníel clasped her hand and kept hold of it as he dragged up a chair for each of them and they both sat down.

'You have my support, Áróra, all the way,' he said his eyes seeking out hers. 'I do have faith in your intuition, and in the little girl. But I'm a cop, and in my experience there are an awful lot of people out there willing to exploit other people's grief.' He felt Áróra stiffen and he tightened his grip to stop her from pulling away.

'But I don't see what she has to gain from it. The mother, I mean. She hasn't asked me about anything or demanded anything from me.' Áróra was talking nineteen to the dozen, so Daníel just gave the occasional nod to show his agreement. 'This problem with their daughter is costing them a lot of money and stress, dragging her back and forth between psychiatrists and psychologists, looking for answers. They're as confused as I am about this.'

'Everything you say may be true, Áróra, darling, but you know I led the investigation into your sister's disappearance and therefore I need to view this new evidence with a critical eye. This woman Elísabet claims her daughter has information that hitherto only the police knew about, aside from you and your mother. I need to look into it. You do understand that.' Now it was Áróra's turn to nod while Daníel gave an inward sigh of relief. He'd been right to take this approach. To place the emphasis on the investigation rather than his real motive, which was of course to protect her. He didn't doubt for a moment that these people wanted something from Áróra – money or information – and he was going to make sure they didn't get away with it. 'Tomorrow Helena and I will go and have a chat with Elísabet and her husband to see what we make of them. But I promise to keep you in the loop and tell you everything straightaway. Okay?'

Áróra nodded, breathed deeply and glanced out of the window just as a gaggle of geese took off from the Hamarskotslækur river amid a great clamour.

Daníel kissed the top of her head as he rose to his feet. 'I'm going to pop out and get a chicken for dinner,' he said.

She nodded distractedly, still gazing out of the window. But when he was out in the hallway she called after him. 'Daníel!'

He retraced his steps and stood in the kitchen doorway. 'What?'

'The little girl, Ester Lóa, said that Ísafold, or should I say Ísafold's body, is lying in black lava.' Áróra's eyes weren't brimming with tears now, they oozed sorrow. 'Didn't I always say I had the feeling Ísafold was somewhere in the lava?'

27

By focusing her attention on Áróra's strange story, Helena managed to avoid thinking about what Sirra and Bisi were doing right then, and to stop herself getting angry and upset again about missing out on her conjugal visiting rights. She'd never come across a scam involving reincarnation before, and she'd encountered enough of them in her time. Car dealer scams offering people cut-price import luxury vehicles, romance scams promising marriage to lonely hearts up there in the far north if they parted with the price of a plane ticket, fortune-telling scams that predicted calamities that could be averted for a price. And then of course there were the endless emails from Africa that flowed into Westerners' accounts, most often excruciatingly written using Google Translate, informing people of an inheritance or a lottery win they could claim for a mere hundred dollars. Helena often felt like tearing her hair out in despair over the numbers of people who let themselves be duped by this nonsense, swindled out of more money than they could afford, and who only went to the police when it was too late. She thought they were idiots, whereas Daníel always calmly maintained that people were simply credulous. Maybe it wasn't just his generous attitude towards everything and everyone that made him say that; perhaps he was simply right. Most people had trouble believing other people wanted to do them harm. And ninety-eight percent of human beings were decent and honest. The problem lay in detecting the other two percent.

The fuel light on the dashboard came on as she turned into Vesturlandsvegur, so Helena stayed in the right-hand lane and headed for the petrol station on Ártúnsbrekka. She would take Lady Gúgúlú's phone in to Rannveig then go home and do some online research into this couple who were possibly trying to scam Áróra. Helena empathised with Áróra. She was in a tough situation. Probably one of the toughest situations a cop like her ever came across in their work. The thing about missing-persons cases was that as long as there was no proof the person was dead, their loved ones held on to a glimmer of hope that they might be alive. It was human nature, plain and simple. Because no matter how illogical or unlikely it was that Áróra's sister Ísafold was alive, in theory it was still possible. And it was this theoretical possibility, however small, that kept the missing person's loved ones in a state of perpetual mourning. Delaying their acceptance of death, the final stage of grief. It was better to be able to bury a body. Say goodbye and gradually move from grieving the missing person to accepting that they've gone forever.

Outside the garage apartment earlier, Daníel had whispered to Helena that Áróra was going through a tough time mentally. That she'd been up at the eruption site on Reykjanes every day last spring and summer, traipsing back and forth along the edge of the red-hot lava flow, terrified it might cover her sister's hidden grave.

Helena was so immersed in these reflections about Áróra and Ísafold's disappearance that she failed to notice the two men who came racing towards her the instant she stopped her car at the pump and got out. One of them grabbed her upper arms while the other searched her pockets and inside the waistband of her trousers.

'I'm holding my card in my hand,' she said, in the hope the man would stop groping her.

But he just snorted. They weren't after her credit card. Glancing about, Helena considered whether or not she should scream, but the traffic noise on Vesturlandsvegur would most likely drown out her cries, and she was facing into the wind so her voice wouldn't carry to the convenience store, where there were people milling about. No one else was at the pumps and no cars were entering the filling station. But she didn't need to think for long, because the other man who had leaned inside her car now straightened up with a triumphant cry.

'Got it,' he said, brandishing Lady Gúgúlú's phone with a smug look on his face.

His colleague released Helena, and just as the two men marched off, a car pulled up and they climbed inside. Helena grabbed her own phone and took a shot of the vehicle as it drove away then hurriedly zoomed in on the image. As luck would have it she'd managed to snap a photo of the registration plate.

28

Daníel had told Helena not to worry, to let things lie, write out her report and save it on her home computer but not file it in the system just yet. Before they lodged a complaint, he would speak to someone in the International Department of the Police Commissioner's Office to verify whether these men were working in an official capacity, and if any local police interference might jeopardise an ongoing investigation. That said, he had every intention of protesting strongly over the way the men had behaved, and of demanding to see the warrants that permitted them to interrogate him, seize Lady Gúgúlú's property and frisk Helena. He told Helena to chill out at home that evening, and if she found herself at a loose end maybe she could do some research into the Áróra case.

For his part, Daníel couldn't resist running a search on the vehicle registration number Helena had sent him. The result came as a surprise. No such registration number existed. Under normal circumstances, he might conclude that the number had been written down wrongly or misremembered by the witness, but Helena had sent him a photograph of the plate, so it was on his phone in black and white, no mistake. The number had never been registered to any vehicle in Iceland, yet the plates were Icelandic. He shook his head. He found it hard to believe that operatives from a foreign law-enforcement agency were driving around in a vehicle with false plates. This made it more likely the men were criminals. Which didn't allay his concerns for the safety of Haraldur – Lady Gúgúlú.

He was drifting off to sleep on Áróra's shoulder as they lay entwined on the sofa, watching a movie, when Helena called back. He extricated himself and went into the kitchen, his phone glued to his ear.

'You've been a busy bee,' he said, and Helena laughed.

'I was bored,' she said. 'And I couldn't fall sleep. But I think I've now dug up all the online information there is on Elísabet and Lárus, the parents of the reincarnated child.'

'You don't say,' replied Daníel, amused at how commonplace Helena made it sound to talk about a reincarnated child. 'I'm all ears.' He pushed the kitchen door to, as he didn't want Áróra to pick up any fag ends.

'As far as I can see you were right,' said Helena. 'I don't think these people have been entirely honest with Áróra.'

'Really?' It came as no surprise to him that something fishy was going on but he was on tenterhooks, nevertheless.

'They host an Icelandic true-crime website and a podcast in English. The website address is Crime.is; the podcast the same.'

So that was it. They were angling for information, or an interview. Daníel felt his gorge rise. They'd chosen a very roundabout way of approaching her. He remembered going to fetch a distraught Áróra stranded in her car on Miklabraut. Why hadn't these people simply asked her for an interview?

'As for the "troll girl", "elf girl" thing,' Helena went on. 'I had no difficulty finding the reference in an interview with their dad when he was crowned Iceland's strongest man. There's a cute photo of him holding his two little girls, one in each arm. He was a giant of a man.'

'Okay,' said Daníel. 'Will you come with me tomorrow to talk to these people?'

'Yes, sir,' said Helena. 'What time do you want me there?'

'Come round to mine at about nine.'

'Okay. Shall I file this? Are we reopening the case, or following a new lead, seeing as how the investigation is still open—'

'No,' Daníel cut in. 'We're just saving Áróra from these crackpots.'

Stulli jabbed her buttock and pumped in the steroid. Then he offered her an extra-large sub sandwich. Áróra took a seat next to him in the corner. It was early and The Gym was deserted. Most of the guys came there at midday and some in the late afternoon, only the pros and a few others trained in the mornings.

'You need to eat,' he said. 'You won't build muscle just with testosterone; you need calories as well.'

'Maybe I'm not so interested in bulking up,' said Áróra, accepting the sandwich. Stulli was right, she should eat more. Everyone was telling her how skinny she'd got.

'Really, so why are you doing it?' asked Stulli.

'I want to be stronger,' replied Áróra.

'The two go together,' said Stulli. 'To increase your strength you need bulk.'

'Maybe I mean mental strength,' Áróra said, peeling the cling film off her sandwich. And as she reflected on it now, maybe that was the heart of the matter. Because although she had a shorter fuse on steroids and was often on the verge of losing control, they also gave her a pleasantly detached feeling. As if the small stuff no longer mattered and anxiety was a mere illusion. Recently she'd found herself wondering whether men actually felt like that all the time, given their main sex hormone was responsible for this effect. What the steroids didn't do was to take away her feeling of guilt. And loss. Or silence that nagging question that had haunted her for over three years. The question of what happened to her sister Ísafold.

'You need to take care of yourself, girl,' said Stulli. 'Steroids are addictive. I can give you a shot of butyric acid to calm you down if you want.'

Áróra shook her head, took a bite of sandwich and chewed. She would have chosen a different one but it was edible. Some sort of processed meat with egg and a vegetable of dubious origin. Stulli was right about the steroids too. She'd been having the injections for four weeks now and should probably stop before she got hooked. She'd heard of people who had difficulty stopping, even though steroids didn't give you a high. The kick came from seeing your body change so fast. It was a small victory in the battle against weakness.

'Do you take them much?' she asked, and Stulli shook his head.

'I can't anymore,' he said. 'My heart has grown too big.'

Áróra grinned. 'Are you sure you didn't always have a big heart?'

Stulli smiled back. He'd been something of a disciple of her father's when he was a young man and she was still a child, and she recalled how touched her mother was when he offered to help with the funeral arrangements.

'Are you calling it a day, then?' he asked.

This was her chance to quit. But Áróra shook her head. She had felt her strength grow day after day, and at each training session she was able to lift more weight. Just now she'd done three seventy-five kilo squats, and only the day before yesterday she'd struggled with seventy. She was advancing ridiculously fast.

'Two more weeks. I want to make eighty on the squats.'

30

Helena watched Daníel talk to the couple sitting side by side on the sofa opposite them. Having worked with him for all these years, she could clearly see how his mild manner and friendly questions were aimed at getting one of them to give something away. He was on a fishing expedition. The couple seemed tense and at the same time excited, as if Helena and Daníel had come to tell them they'd won the lottery. The husband, Lárus, kneaded his hands constantly, while his wife, Elísabet, scurried back and forth to the kitchen of the tiny apartment, fetching more things to place on the table before them. There was already a coffee thermos, cups, a jug of milk, a bowl of sugar, some teaspoons and two packets of biscuits. Helena poured coffee for herself and Daníel from the thermos and added a drop of milk to her cup.

'When Áróra introduced you as her boyfriend I didn't realise you were a policeman,' said Elísabet.

'So you didn't know I worked for the police?' Daníel eyed her over the rim of his cup as he sipped his coffee.

'No,' said Elísabet and giggled nervously. 'I had no idea. How could I have known?'

'You seem to know a good deal about Áróra – you've been researching her,' Daníel replied, raising his eyebrows, but still with a faint smile on his lips so she wouldn't take what he'd said as direct accusation.

'Well, not much, to be honest,' she replied. 'Of course, I looked her up on Facebook and whatnot when Ester Lóa started this Ísafold thing.'

'So it wasn't the other way round?' asked Daníel. 'You didn't familiarise yourselves with Áróra first and after that Ester Lóa started to say she was Ísafold?'

'What are you implying?' Lárus now asked, looking at Daníel peevishly.

'What I'm implying is that when parents discuss things in front of their children, the children sometimes absorb and understand what's being said without their parents realising.'

Helena admired Daníel's diplomacy – how he managed to say what he meant, but obliquely. What he was really asking the couple was whether they had trained their daughter to say these things. Coached her.

'No, that's not how it happened,' said Elísabet, who didn't seem to be taking any of this personally. 'Though of course I remember when the case was in the news a few years ago.'

'Three years ago. Around the time Ester Lóa was born, isn't that right?' Daníel put in.

'Yes, and that's what makes it so strange.'

'I agree with you there,' said Daníel. 'It's altogether very strange.'

Helena decided it was time for her to intervene. She set her cup on the table and looked straight at Lárus.

'You host a podcast and a website called Crime.is, where you discuss Icelandic true crimes,' she said, and for an instant Lárus's eyes darted between her and Daníel, as if he were searching their faces for some clue as to why Helena had asked this question.

'Yes?' he replied, in a questioning tone.

'It's a strange coincidence that a couple who host a crime podcast have a daughter who claims she was the victim of an unsolved crime in a past life,' said Daníel, and once again Helena was thankful for how synchronised they were. It came naturally now, almost as if each knew what the other was thinking. 'I can see how that might grab your listeners' interest.'

'We haven't discussed the Ísafold case on our podcast, nor do we intend to,' Lárus said resolutely.

'Of course we want to attract listeners, but we made a decision not to put our daughter on show for all the world to see,' put in Elísabet.

'So what exactly is it you want from Áróra?' asked Helena, taking care to soften her tone.

'I don't really know,' said Elísabet, and Lárus shrugged in agreement. 'Maybe, like you, we're just looking for some explanation for our daughter's strange behaviour.'

A silence descended upon the room. Helena found it awkward, even though she was familiar with this tactic of Daníel's – keeping quiet for a while and simply staring at his interlocutors, because people had a tendency to want to fill silences, and when they spoke without thinking they often gave things away. But on this occasion it misfired. The couple simply sat and stared back at Daníel. Lárus with the air of a condemned man, and Elísabet smiling and at last giggling nervously.

'We also find this very strange,' she said.

Daníel sighed. He clearly felt they weren't getting anywhere with this conversation. 'What I find strangest of all,' he said then, 'is your daughter's account of the attack. I assume, since you host a crime podcast, that you have a source within the police and that's how you got your information about where in the apartment blood was found?'

'Huh?' Lárus seemed genuinely taken aback.

'No, we have no source in the police,' said Elísabet.

'In other words, you're confirming that Ester Lóa's account is accurate?' Lárus seemed to cheer up all of a sudden. 'That the ice-bear attack coincides with the traces found at the scene?' Lárus's casual use of police parlance grated on Helena's nerves, and she could tell from the way Daníel grimaced that he felt the same way. Clearly they were lying about not having an inside source of information.

'I'm confirming no such thing,' said Daníel rising to his feet.

Elísabet followed suit and accompanied him out into the

hallway. 'Might you want to talk to Ester Lóa in person? To have a better idea of what's going on. It's amazing to hear her speak about her past life. She's at nursery now, but I can fetch her...'

'That won't be necessary,' Helena said behind her.

Elísabet moved aside to let Helena enter the cramped hallway. As she began to put on her shoes Helena told herself for the umpteenth time that she needed to wear shoes like Daníel's, something she could slip on and be ready to leave. It was embarrassing to have to crouch and ask for a shoe horn when you've practically insulted people.

'I want to make it clear that regardless of the fact Áróra is my girlfriend and it makes me angry when people hurt her, we take a dim view in the police of people who harass relatives and friends of crime victims, especially when a case is ongoing. An open case means open wounds. Kindly bear this in mind and stay away from Áróra.'

The couple stood awkwardly in the hallway while Daníel gave his speech. Helena could see Lárus redden with rage. She gave an apologetic smile as she closed the door behind them and hurried down the stairs to catch up with Daníel who was already halfway to the bottom.

'Wasn't that a bit harsh?' she asked.

Daníel stopped at the foot of the stairs. He heaved a sigh and leaned against the wall next to the main entrance. 'Maybe,' he said. 'But this has been incredibly hard on Áróra. She's less preoccupied with her sister these days, but instead she trains and trains, and runs and runs. She's obsessed with body-building and protein powders, and now I suspect she may be taking steroids.'

Helena gave a start. She hadn't seen Daníel this distraught in a long while. He seemed to have shrunk into himself. She contemplated his face.

'Hang on ... Is there something you need to tell me about that split lip?'

31

Áróra arrived a little late to the meeting and gave a contrite smile as she slipped into a seat at the table alongside the investigation team. She wasn't on the permanent staff as she'd never wanted to be permanent anywhere. She was her own woman. Her job title was 'expert consultant' and she knew for a fact Agla had hired her to dig around in areas where the permanent staff weren't permitted to look. Agla herself was an ex-con. Sentenced for financial crimes in the wake of the Icelandic banking collapse, when she was CEO of one of the country's largest banks. And now she had a job at the Directorate of Tax Investigations. After her conviction she was banned from using the title of director, but everyone knew she headed all the investigation teams. It was a stroke of genius, because who better to find money than those who knew how to hide it. The rumour was that during the crash Agla had hidden away billions of krónur in tax havens.

She was already presenting her team with their latest assignment:

'For over a decade now the biggest cryptocurrency producers – or miners, as these companies like to call themselves – have been operating here in Iceland. The reason for this is because we have cheap energy and a cold climate, and their hardware generates a lot of heat and their cooling systems require a constant supply of air and water. I estimate that some of the biggest producers buy electricity from us to the tune of two billion krónur. However, our cheap energy and cold climate aren't the only reasons why these companies like Iceland. It's also because our government is dragging its feet over how they define cryptocurrency and therefore how it is taxed.'

'Not to mention how damaging it is for the environment,' put in one of the rookie investigators. He was yet to learn that Agla generally ignored any comments unrelated to the topic under discussion. But on this occasion she made an exception:

'This is true,' she said. 'Many people believe it's wasteful to use all this energy on creating cryptocurrency, which is simply a series of complex calculations, when central banks can print ordinary money at very little cost.'

'The energy would be better employed in greenhouse farming.'

Agla now looked at the young man with a mysterious expression that almost resembled a smile. 'You may be right,' she said. 'However, we're not looking for eco-fraud. We're looking for tax fraud. Keep your eyes on the money.' The young man nodded and sat up straight in his chair. 'We'll proceed in the usual way,' Agla went on. 'Since tracing the profits of cryptocurrency itself is a complex inter-state affair – although cryptoassets are now taxable – we'll start with the expenses and then look at the transactions. Is it the overseas parent companies who invoice for expenses such as computer hardware? Or do they buy from unaffiliated companies here in Iceland? And so on. Divvy up the companies among yourselves and do what you do. Áróra, come to my office and I'll give you your assignment.'

Agla stood up and left the room, and Áróra followed suit. Agla was already seated when Áróra entered her office, and she passed her a file across the desk.

'Here's the information on the first group of companies we're looking into,' she said.

'Okay,' said Áróra, sitting down opposite her. 'How are things with you otherwise?'

Agla frowned. 'Yeah...' she said, drawing out the word. 'Everything's fine.' She didn't return the question. Agla wasn't very good at small talk and always grew slightly uneasy when people tried to engage her in chit-chat. It seemed her comfort zone was limited to work, and she had little interest in straying outside that.

'Glad to hear it,' said Áróra, smiling amicably. Agla returned the smile but hers was wooden. This woman's social skills, or lack of them, would make a great research topic. 'I'll go about it in the usual way, shall I?' resumed Áróra, and Agla's face and body showed palpable relief, Áróra almost heard her breathe a sigh.

'Yes. Look at the owners, who's behind them and how they make their profits. It should be pretty straightforward for you.'

Áróra rose and Agla was obviously delighted that she didn't intend to sit there making endless small talk.

'I'll get cracking on it straightaway,' she said, thinking to herself she'd need every ounce of concentration to start on such a big, tedious project when all she wanted was to sit and watch the little three-year-old girl who said she was her sister.

32

Róbert turned on the fuses in the box he'd fitted in the greenhouse and plugged in the electric heater. He hadn't had the foresight to run a pipe into the greenhouse when he installed the heating in the main house, but now he'd moved in maybe he could remedy that. He would enjoy designing some sort of energy-efficient heating system for the house. And of course it would be good for him to have a project to work on as time wore on. When he started to get bored. Because that was bound to happen sooner or later. Going out on dates and hunting for guys wasn't on the menu. Gay clubs and dating apps were the first places they'd look, so he was better off steering clear of all that. The best way to combat loneliness was to keep himself busy.

The temperature outside was more or less average for April, around five degrees centigrade, and with the help of the electric heater he could easily get it up to fifteen or sixteen in the greenhouse. He plugged in the heating pads and arranged them on the bench. Then he put coir grow cubes into the trays, placed them on the heating pads and filled them with water. The cubes swelled up and the trays quickly warmed. He went back into the house to check on the freezer. The light on the side indicated it was in fast-freeze mode, so the food he'd bought yesterday should be fine. He went into the kitchen, put two slices of bread into the toaster and fetched butter and cheese from the fridge. He would miss the cheese when it ran out, but then he'd have all the frozen pâté. He needn't venture out to buy food for a long time. According to his calculations he had enough provisions to last him a year – even if in the last few months he might be living off dried and tinned goods from the pantry. And eggs of course, as well as vegetables from his greenhouse. With any luck his hens would lay and his greenhouse would be plentiful.

He felt a knot tighten in the pit of his stomach, and he drew a deep breath to try to relax. He was a physicist. His PhD thesis had attracted international interest. There was nothing he couldn't learn. He could memorise everything he read, and was told his deductive reasoning powers were excellent. Growing food, a fundamental skill that most of mankind had mastered, should therefore not be beyond him. It all came down to self-confidence. Whenever they'd caught up with him his self-confidence had taken a battering. He needed to keep reminding himself that each time this happened he had managed to elude them. And this time his plan was so bulletproof he must be safe. Providing he didn't show his face in any towns and was careful not to leave any tracks for them to follow when he went online.

The toast on his plate was finished but he'd forgotten to enjoy it. He was so immersed in his thoughts and anxieties he'd eaten it without realising. He may as well have gobbled down a bowl of flavourless cereal. Not to savour good cheese was truly wasteful. He must rein himself in. Use some self-discipline. Reflect. Calm down. The last four years had been fun, but he'd gone a bit wild. A lot of drinking, a lot of partying, and loads of guys. And at the same time he'd used his brain very little, and hadn't had a new idea for ages. Yes, he'd elaborated his back-up plan. Driven south over Hellisheiði practically every week to work on the house, read everything he could find on self-sufficient living and apocalypse preparation, but he'd made no new discoveries himself. And that wasn't good for his brain. The brain was like a muscle – it grew stronger with use.

He got to his feet, left the plate in the sink and drained his glass of water. Then he went into the pantry, fetched the plastic seed trays and grabbed three bags of potatoes on his way out.

33

Elísabet hadn't even wanted to open the door properly, but had kept it half closed and peered through the crack. Inside the apartment beyond, Áróra could hear Ester Lóa playing, and she longed to push her way in, sit on the floor with the little girl and play with her. Talk to her. Embrace her. But the expression on Elísabet's face had been almost beseeching and she spoke in hushed tones.

'Actually, your boyfriend told us to stay away from you,' she said. 'And we don't want to be upsetting you like this. It's a very emotional subject, naturally, and even though we believe Ester Lóa, we can't prove any of it's true. That she really is your sister.'

Áróra was fuming with rage now as she drove, a little too fast, in the direction of the police station. Daníel had told her he would talk to them, not ruin everything. She texted him while she was waiting for the lights to turn green on Sæbraut and asked him to come downstairs. She needed to speak to him. Daníel would know what this meant, as whenever she picked him up from work Áróra always parked on Rauðarástígur, the street that ran alongside the police station. And that's where he was when she drew up. Standing on the pavement waiting next to an empty parking space.

She had planned to begin by asking him exactly what he'd said to Elísabet, but before she knew it she had leapt screaming from the car, her mind a blind fog, with an overwhelming urge to break something.

'Why the hell did you have to ruin everything?' she shouted at him, slamming the car door hard. Seeing Daníel flinch did nothing to calm her. He took a few steps back and raised his palm in a defensive gesture while she kept yelling. 'She wouldn't even let me in to talk to the child. This is the first contact I've had with my sister in three years!' Daníel murmured something which she couldn't hear above her own yells. 'I ask for your help, your support, and then you go meddling and ruin everything! How is that supposed to help me? Eh?'

She calmed down when she heard Helena's voice ring out sharply next to her. Áróra hadn't noticed her arrive, but it was obvious she'd come running, as she was out of breath.

'The couple hosts a true-crime podcast!' snapped Helena. 'Weekly episodes, plus a whole website in English exclusively devoted to Icelandic crimes. What the hell did you think they wanted from you?'

It was like an ice-cold jet of water in her face. Both the information and how it was delivered. Helena seemed furious.

'Huh?' Áróra gazed in bewilderment at Daníel, who had backed up as far as the grey wall of the police station, and then again at Helena, who stood on the pavement, a look of determination on her face, arms folded across her chest.

'Maybe you should take a few breaths and ask before losing your rag,' Helena said, her eyes drilling into Áróra.

'They've clearly coached the child in order to extract information from family members,' said Daníel gently, his voice was filled with compassion.

'But the little girl knows things only Dad and I and Ísafold—'

Áróra broke off when Helena lifted up her phone to show her an article with a photograph of Áróra's father holding her and her sister. Áróra took the phone from her and zoomed into the image. It was an old interview with her father taken when he won the Strongest Man in Iceland title.

'He talks about his two daughters being complete opposites, both in physique and personality. You're a troll like him and Ísafold is a skinny little elf girl.'

Áróra felt her knees suddenly buckle, and she collapsed onto the bonnet of the car. Could this be true? Was it that simple: Elísabet and Lárus dug up an old interview and some articles about her family and Ísafold's disappearance, taught their daughter a few key phrases which, in her desperation to learn something about her sister's fate, she had fallen for hook line and sinker?

'Maybe mind the buttons on the back pockets of your jeans? I mean so as not to scratch the paintwork on the Tesla.' Daníel said this in a soft hesitant voice, but it irritated Áróra all the same.

'Ugh, Daníel, is this my fucking car or yours?' she snapped without thinking, and instantly regretted it.

'Maybe we should all go back to our jobs?' Helena said, addressing herself to Daníel. She plucked her phone from Áróra's hand and started back towards the police station.

Daníel hesitated for a moment, as if he expected Áróra to say something, then he nodded and followed Helena. Áróra was left behind with a hollow feeling inside. This glimmer of hope, the bittersweet pang of joy that Elísabet's phone call had sparked in her had now died out. So the whole thing was a hoax. Or was it? Elísabet's parting words whispered hastily through the half-closed door just now flashed into her mind. She called after Daníel and Helena.

'But how did the child know that Ísafold was put in a suitcase?' The two stopped dead in their tracks on the corner, as if they were playing grandmother's footsteps. Then they wheeled round as one.

'Huh?' Daníel came walking back towards Áróra, a look of bewilderment on his face, Helena following fast on his heels.

'Elísabet whispered through the crack in the door that the child said the ice-bear put her in a suitcase and carried her out to the car.'

34

It felt cosy inside the greenhouse even though the thermometer only showed ten degrees. The house sheltered it from the cold spring breeze and the lights added a bright, summery feel. It was as if the grow lamps tricked the brain into thinking they were radiating sunlight. He would install a chair in the middle of the greenhouse and sit there to read. It would be a good way to ward off depression. But right now he had work to do. The water in the drip trays was sufficiently warm and the swollen grow cubes moist enough for Robbi to begin sowing his seeds.

First he planted a row of regular tomato seeds. Then one of cherry tomatoes. A total of fourteen tomato plants of which, according to his research, he might expect half to come up. Afterwards he planted two rows of cucumber seeds, two of courgette, three of spinach and finally half a row of parsley and half of basil. He would plant the herb and spinach seeds at ten-day intervals to ensure he always had a supply.

Later that spring he might sneak up to Hveragerði in a face mask and buy some nice fruit trees, such as a grapevine or fig. Perhaps a cherry tree if they had one. He could drive the long way round and he knew of an old ramshackle nursery where they certainly didn't have CCTV.

He planted the sweet-pepper seeds in a big flower pot. Eight in total. With any luck four of them would come up. He gave the soil a good soaking and congratulated himself on all his research into growing vegetables. That was two years ago now, yet he remembered everything he'd read. Everything he needed to remember. He could retain information in his head endlessly and retrieve it whenever necessary. It was only his emotions that were always in some kind of turmoil. They were what made him doubt himself.

He placed the covers on the seedling trays and stretched some plastic over the pot with the sweet-pepper seeds, then went out of the greenhouse, carrying the bags of potatoes. He took them into the outhouse and emptied them onto the floor. The horse was out in the paddock but now it ambled over, as if to see what Robbi was up to. Robbi had fenced off the horse's side of the outhouse by erecting a simple barrier made out of some old pallets so it couldn't get at the potatoes, even at full stretch.

'They should sprout in here, old boy,' he said to the horse, which stood with its hindquarters outside, as though ready to bolt if Robbi tried to catch it. Clearly the animal was in no mood to take another trip anytime soon. 'I know how you feel,' said Robbi. 'I'm as bow-legged as a cowboy today. And I imagine you're exhausted too, darling. That's what comes of too much *riding*.' The horse didn't respond to his feeble joke and headed back out to the paddock as soon as Robbi left the outhouse. Tomorrow he'd fence off a bigger area for the horse. And begin digging his potato patch.

35

'She doesn't look right to me,' said Helena on their way up the stairs to their office. 'She's not her usual self. It's strange seeing her so angry.'

'She's always had a quick temper,' said Daníel, aware of how he sounded – excusing bad behaviour.

'But that wasn't normal rage just now,' said Helena. 'I think maybe you're right about the steroids.' She took hold of Daníel's arm, and he pulled up short. 'Did she hit you?' she asked, pointing at his face. 'Did she do this?' Helena looked so concerned he couldn't help giving a chuckle.

'No, Helena,' he said. 'It was the guys who took the phone off you at the filling station. The ones looking for Gúgúlú. Which is why I don't think they're cops.'

'Okay,' Helena said raising her finger, as if she were a school ma'am. 'But this is no laughing matter. Men are victims of domestic violence, too, and it's something we need to take seriously.'

'Absolutely,' Daníel said, looking straight at her and nodding his head. 'You're a good friend,' he said smiling. 'Looking out for me like this.' Now it was Helena's turn to feel self-conscious and she bounded up the last few stairs.

'Lay off,' she said bashfully and knocked on the commissioner's door, which swung open almost the same instant.

'I have three minutes,' said the commissioner. 'Spill it.' She strode back to her desk, which seemed incongruously small in the airy room, and stood rifling through some papers.

Daníel did the talking. 'I'll send you a more detailed email, but in a nutshell a couple has come forward claiming their child is some sort of medium between the living and the dead. Under any other circumstances we'd dismiss this as nonsense, naturally. However, their account of the events surrounding the disappearance and possible death of Ísafold Jónsdóttir is significant.'

The police chief immediately glanced up from her papers, her eyes lingering on Daníel's lip for a second. 'Significant in what way?'

'Because their description of the attack on Ísafold coincides with the bloodstain patterns we found in the apartment, and now they're saying she was put in a suitcase and driven away in a car. Forensics identified a large urine stain in the boot of Björn's car that contained traces of blood, but no hair, skin or clothing fibres. On the other hand there were scratch marks around the rim of the boot, suggesting a heavy object had been dragged out of it. The car had been thoroughly cleaned, so it was difficult to tell how recent the damage was, but it could have been made by a suitcase.'

'This nonsense spouted by these mediums, or whatever they are, sounds like a leak coming from our department,' said the commissioner. 'And we need to plug it.'

Daníel and Helena nodded as one. The odd pretext they'd given her didn't matter, all they needed was the commissioner's permission to follow this lead. 'By all means utilise the station's resources to look into this, but if we officially relaunch the investigation we'll need to put someone else in charge because of your personal connection with the case, Daníel.'

'Absolutely,' he replied, and Helena nodded beside him.

36

Ari Benz Liu, chief superintendent in the International Department at the Police Commissioner's Office, was sitting at his computer with his headphones on and didn't hear Daníel knocking at his half-open door then walking in. Ari was immersed in something and listening to music at the same time, it seemed, from the way his head bobbed rhythmically up and down. Daníel tapped his desk, and finally Ari looked up and removed his headphones. His face broke into a broad smile.

'Daníel, old man!' he exclaimed. 'How are things?'

'Fine,' said Daníel, sitting down on the chair opposite Ari. 'I wanted to ask you something I think you might know about.'

'Go ahead.' Ari rested his elbows on the desk and leaned forward.

'I wanted to know whether any foreign law-enforcement agencies are operating in Iceland right now. Or any undercover intelligence agents or anything like that?'

'Ah.' Ari sat up in his chair. 'Actually there aren't, and even if there were you know I'm not really at liberty to tell you. This kind of stuff is on a strictly need-to-know basis. Why do you ask?'

'Because I think I may have had a run-in with some of them.' Daníel pointed to his lip. 'It's a bit of a long story, but my tenant, Haraldur, has disappeared—'

'The drag queen?' Ari cut in, astonished.

'Yes, Lady Gúgúlú. You remember her from that barbecue one time.'

'How could I forget?' said Ari. 'Are you telling me your drag queen has disappeared?' Daníel doubted the appropriateness of Haraldur being referred to as 'his' drag queen, but he let it go.

'Yes, and then three men came looking for him and I had the impression they were agents of some sort.'

'Did they behave like agents?' Ari rose abruptly to his feet. His manner was now different and his voice sounded slightly forced, as if he were trying to seem jovial despite the furrow that had appeared on his brow. 'There's nothing like that going on here at the moment,' he said. 'I can assure you of that Daníel, old man.' Ari gestured for Daníel to stand up then strode over to the door, continuing in the same forced tone, his voice overly loud: 'Come out to the parking lot with me. I want to show you my new car.'

Daníel stood up and followed him into the hallway and down the stairs.

'Two of them were British, I think, and there was—' began Daníel, but Ari cut him off.

'As I said, there's no undercover stuff going on. We'd know about it if there was. Foreign agents can't operate here in Iceland without our knowledge. Now, what make do you think my new car is?'

'I'm guessing it's a Benz?' Daníel said, increasingly puzzled by Ari's behaviour. Not that there was anything unusual about Ari wanting to show Daníel his new wheels. He had a thing about driving shiny new cars. But even so he was acting very strangely.

'Naturally,' Ari said. 'Naturally it's a Benz!' He marched ahead of Daníel into the parking lot and towards his new steel-grey AMG coupé.

'How do you afford it?' asked Daníel contemplating the car.

Ari laughed. 'You didn't know I was heir to a fortune?'

'Huh? No, I had no idea.'

'Yes, yes. I descend from a line of Asian nobles.'

'Really? Is that true?' Daníel said, bewildered.

'No, it's a joke!' said Ari. 'My father owned a small hotel and when he died it was sold and I inherited the money. I have no mortgage and my mother doesn't need my support, so I have my whole salary to play with.'

'Hm. Nice,' Daníel murmured as they reached the car.

Ari opened the driver's door, and for a moment Daníel

thought he was going to offer to take him for a ride, but instead Ari tossed his phone onto the front seat and gestured to Daníel to do likewise.

And then at last it dawned on Daníel. Ari thought their phones were tapped.

Daníel also placed his phone on the seat, after which Ari shut the door and walked a few steps away from the car. Daníel followed suit and they came to a halt side by side, contemplating the car as if they were admiring its qualities. Only it wasn't horse power and acceleration that was on Ari's mind.

'We may have some possible intelligence about certain agents operating here at the moment. Something hush-hush that the authorities are nevertheless aware of,' said Ari in a half-whisper. 'This didn't go via the usual channels but through some sort of diplomatic route. Maybe the Foreign Office. I don't think I'm even supposed to know about it.'

'Do you mean to say a foreign intelligence service is operating here in Iceland?'

'Possibly,' said Ari. 'But you didn't hear it from me, and if you run into those guys again my advice is to give them a wide berth.'

'One of them is Icelandic...' said Daníel.

'That's all I know, I don't know what else to tell you. Only that we aren't allowed to arrest these men or even make a report if they get into trouble, which it's clearly assumed they will. Those are our instructions. I'm not happy about this presumption that they will act unlawfully. If I were you I wouldn't go poking around trying to find out who they are.'

'And you think they're tapping people's phones...? Mine? Yours?'

'I assume they are,' said Ari. 'I think it's that sort of, er, organisation.' Ari strode back to the Benz, but before he opened the car door he turned to Daníel and whispered: 'I just don't see how your drag queen is connected to this.'

37

Robbi scrubbed the dirt off his hands in the kitchen sink then dried them on a dish cloth, thinking to himself that now that he'd become something of a farmer he needed to improve his hand-washing hygiene. From now on he would wash them in the bathroom. He also needed to write out a daily schedule for himself. When you had living creatures that depended on you it didn't do to sleep late and laze about. While he was making coffee he outlined a schedule in his head. Coffee – see to animals – exercise – bake bread – see to plants – have lunch – relaxation and reading – walking, running or exercise bike – coffee – inventions and improvements – cooking – dinner – see to animals – rest and TV or reading. He would seriously limit the time he spent surfing the net, even if he did so as a bustling, late-middle-aged, organically minded housewife called Guðrun. Guðrun was the name he was considering using for his online identity. Somehow it had a more earthy ring to it than Anna. As if it were more natural for someone called Guðrun to look up information on how to grow potatoes and make compost.

Running through the schedule reminded him he hadn't checked on the hens. He abandoned his cup of hot coffee, went out into the hallway and pulled on some shoes. This proved the need for a schedule. He'd led a disorderly life for too long, sleeping half the day, working nights – if you could call drag shows and partying after every performance work. But back then he had decided to live his life to the full for as long as he could – before it was too late. Before he had to resort to plan B and become a self-sufficient farmer with the discipline that entailed. Or be killed. Because that would definitely be his fate if they caught up with him.

He carefully opened the door to the coop and peered inside. The hens eyed him suspiciously, fleeing from under his feet as he went to look at the feed tray and the water trough. Both were fine, they'd barely made inroads into the feed. He might get away with refilling it once a week. Nor had they drunk much of the water. Maybe one litre out of twelve. He grabbed a handful of seeds and sprinkled them on the ground. The hens perked up and appeared to overcome their fear of him, save for the little harassed hen, which had ventured out of its corner but remained apart from the flock. He tossed a handful of seeds the hen's way and it managed to peck at a few before the big, feisty Sussex went scurrying over to gobble them up. It was a bit like human life. Some people simply didn't stand a chance against the bullies.

Then he went to check on the nesting boxes, more for form's sake than with any real expectations, but when he lifted the lid his heart leapt. In the middle box sat a brown egg. He picked it up; the egg was still warm to the touch. Cupping it in his hands a feeling of pure joy invaded him. This was easier than he'd thought. Only twenty-four hours after he got his hens he had his first egg.

'Oh my God, thank you, hens!' he said, wondering which one of them had laid the egg. But none of them showed any particular interest; they just continued pecking at the sunflower seeds. As a sign of his gratitude, he tossed them an extra handful of seeds from the bucket on the shelf.

Back in the kitchen he considered whether to celebrate the occasion by boiling the egg and eating it straightaway, but he didn't have the heart, so he placed it in a bowl on the kitchen counter, where he could take delight in gazing at it. This was a mark of achievement, if not on the level to which he was accustomed. He hadn't actually produced the egg himself, so the pride he felt was of a different nature. The egg was a gift. A true miracle. If he'd kept a cockerel the egg would have been a blueprint for life itself. All that was necessary to bring forth a living creature from the cosmos. Then again, this egg was so insignificant. It was infertile and would therefore never be anything other than an egg. Barely half a breakfast for a grown man.

The egg was a little bit like him. Full of the promise of great things that might have been, but in reality as insignificant as this egg. He didn't doubt they would kill him if they got hold of him. The thought wasn't a pleasant one. His biggest fear, however, was that they might try to torture him first. To get the information out of him. The formula. Because that's what they were really after.

38

Daníel had sent Áróra several texts but had received no reply. He'd also tried calling her and she didn't pick up. Evidently she was still mad at him. And here he stood banging on her front door and ringing the bell, but she didn't come to the door. Her Tesla was sitting on charge, so he was pretty sure she was at home, and sticking to her decision not to speak to him. He tried peering in through the frosted glass panel on the door, but he couldn't see anything. He resisted the temptation to walk round and tap on her windows. Of course, she had every right to ignore him.

He was the one really struggling here. She seemed perfectly happy to freeze him out for days at a time when they quarrelled. In fact this had only happened twice before – he couldn't even remember why – but both times he'd felt awful. With an uncomfortable tension in his body, his heart rate elevated and the constant feeling that he needed to make things right between them. And that's how he felt now. Although Áróra had yelled at him, he was pretty sure he was at fault. He should have talked it over with her more. He could have done things in a much calmer way. He'd allowed his hero complex to take over, determined to fix the problem for her instead of putting all their cards on the table and discussing with her what she wanted to do.

Daníel drove home slowly, checking his phone at each set of traffic lights in the hope there'd be a message from Áróra, but the screen remained empty apart from a reminder from his smart watch that it needed charging. Áróra had given him the watch. She liked to monitor his heart rate, daily step count etc., then compare their stats. Needless to say, she always came out on top. The woman exercised like a machine and ran whenever possible, while Daníel dutifully trained with his colleagues to stay in good enough shape to pass the low-level endurance police fitness tests, which was more than a lot of middle-aged police officers could boast about. He had lucky genes. His mother was strong and sinewy like her parents. But he knew nothing about his father, and his attempts to find out had failed. Or rather he'd given up trying to extract information from his mother and grandparents, who all seemed to stiffen up whenever he asked them about that half of his biological roots.

Daníel parked outside his house and his heart sank when he remembered the abandoned garage apartment. Somehow it felt so desolate to think there was no one in there. Not that he and Haraldur had lived in each other's pockets, but it had felt comforting to know he was out there and that Daníel could show up with a six-pack and knock on his door for a chat after a tough shift or when he was lonely. And it seemed to work both ways. From time to time Haraldur would stop by for a chat, although his musings on life and existence often seemed to hover somewhere on the boundaries of physics and philosophy, and were very different from the rational way of thinking favoured by someone like himself, who was trained to look for cause and effect. But the fact that they seldom understood each other hadn't mattered. Their friendship wasn't based on that.

When Daníel put his key in the door and turned it, he didn't hear the customary click. Had he forgotten to lock it? As he gently pushed open the door, a hand shot out and grabbed his coat sleeve, yanking him so hard he lost his balance and stumbled headlong into the hallway, where the three men from the day before were waiting. Together they threw him to the floor.

39

Áróra wasn't used to her mother having a soothing effect on her – it was normally the other way round – but now Violet's composure seemed to calm the thoughts boiling and bubbling inside Áróra's head. She had just told her mother about Elísabet and her little girl who said she was Ísafold reincarnated, and she could picture Violet sitting with her cup of tea in the chair next to the living-room window in her little house in Newcastle, looking out at the garden as she spoke on the phone with her daughter.

'You're not the type to get taken in by this sort of nonsense, Áróra darling,' she said, and Áróra felt a sudden longing to be home. Home at her mother's table in the little living room, where mementoes of her father, and her and Ísafold's childhood, adorned the walls in the form of photographs and trophies; to see the trees she and her sister planted in the garden when they were little, now grown tall and leafy.

'No. And of course Daníel's right,' Áróra said. 'I just can't stand it when people meddle in my affairs.' Now that her mother had pacified her Áróra felt ashamed about not opening the door to Daníel earlier. She'd been seething with righteous indignation and wanted him to suffer, which he always did when she gave him the cold shoulder. Only now it felt childish. Idiotic.

'These people clearly want something from you,' said her mother. 'And it was dishonest of them not to have said so from the start. If only they'd asked you whether you wanted to be interviewed for this ... cast thingy...'

'Podcast,' Áróra cut in.

'Yes, podcast. They should have been upfront and approached you on that basis. As for this carry-on with the little girl, I don't like the sound of that all.' Áróra agreed wholeheartedly with everything her mother said, knowing at the same time she would instantly have said no if Elísabet had called and asked for an interview. It was precisely this thing with the child that had reeled her in.

'I know all that, Mum,' she said. 'I was just so sad when Daníel told me these people were most likely fakes. That they'd probably duped me. It felt like some precious thread that might have led me to Ísafold had slipped through my fingers.'

Áróra heard her mother sigh, and her eyes pricked with tears when, instead of saying she should have known better, Violet whispered:

'I know, my love. I know.'

Áróra was about to tell her mother she was going to buy a plane ticket straightaway and come home for a few days, but before she could think it through properly her mobile pinged once more telling her she had a new message. She removed the phone from her ear, expecting to see yet another entreaty from Daníel, begging her to reply, suggesting they meet up, talk things over, but instead of a text an image of his swollen, bloody face appeared before her.

Áróra placed the phone to her ear again. 'Mum,' she said. 'I need to go now. We'll speak again soon.'

She hung up before she could hear her mother's parting words, and tapped in Daníel's number as she rushed into the hallway and grabbed her coat off the hook.

40

Bearing in mind what Ari Benz had said about there being ears everywhere, Daníel refrained from explaining anything to Áróra while they were in the car and simply told her he'd encountered some thugs who'd beaten him up. Probably because he was a cop. Maybe in connection to some case he was working on. Then he asked her to drive him to a nearby pharmacy. Áróra protested and wanted to take him to A&E, but Daníel knew there was no serious damage. The men could easily have broken some of his bones if they'd wanted but they didn't. Even his nose had escaped relatively intact, despite bleeding like a fountain. He was just a bit battered and bruised, and had a few scratches; all he needed was a cold pack, painkillers and some plasters. If he went to A&E and it emerged he was a cop, he'd have to report the assault, which might result in an even worse one. He didn't want to go there. He'd deal with this a different way.

When the car came to a halt outside the pharmacy Daníel pulled out his phone and made a big show of placing it in the Tesla's glove compartment. He motioned to Áróra to do the same, pressing a finger to his lips to tell her not to say a word. Áróra hesitated for a moment but did as he asked, then followed him across the parking lot towards the pharmacy.

'What on earth is going on?' she asked when they were halfway there.

Daníel stopped in his tracks. 'I'm not quite sure to be honest, but it's very strange. As you know Gúgúlú – I mean, Haraldur – has disappeared, and I suspect the guys who are after him might work for some intelligence agency or similar organisation, as they seem to have permission to operate here and tap people's phones independently of the Icelandic police authorities.'

'And you think they're tapping my phone?' Áróra asked in astonishment.

'I think it pays to assume they are,' said Daníel. 'They seem to feel at liberty to spy on me as well as to beat me up.'

Áróra's eyes filled with tenderness and she gently placed a hand on his cheek. 'I'm sorry about today,' she whispered, and he put his arms around her and drew her close.

'So am I,' he said. 'I acted too hastily. I should have talked it over with you more.'

'You needn't apologise, it was the cop in you taking over.'

'I should've been more of a boyfriend and less of a cop,' Daníel said, and tried to smile, but it was too painful. In addition to yesterday's split lip he had a cut at the corner of his mouth where one of the guy's fists had hit him repeatedly.

They had wanted to know what Ari Benz told him in the parking lot outside the Police Commissioner's Office. This made it clear they were tapping either his or Ari's phone, since their questions only referred to their conversation after they'd shut their phones in the car. The guys already seemed to know what had gone on between them prior to that. And they'd let Daníel feel it. They punched him a few times as a punishment for talking to Ari Benz. Then kicked him a few times as a reprimand for continuing to look into 'his boyfriend', as the Icelander put it. He received an extra kick for laughing at their attempts to use homophobia to punish him or force him to talk. In the big scheme of things Daníel couldn't care less if people thought he was queer. And then he sustained a volley of kicks and punches for having tried to hide Gúgúlú's phone from them. And after they punched him for every question he answered in a way they didn't like. But Daníel had stood up under pressure, maintaining that he and Ari had talked about his new car, as they often did. Ari was always boasting about his cars, Daníel said. This was true, and it paid to stick to his story. He'd interrogated enough people to know that telling half-truths was better than trying to lie under pressure. Not that his interrogations bore the slightest resemblance to this mockery. Daníel was burning to know what organisation gave their operatives licence to behave this way on foreign soil. He was determined to get to the bottom of it. And Áróra was going to help him.

In the parking lot outside the pharmacy they swapped assignments. Áróra would search for Lady Gúgúlú or Haraldur or Róbert Þór Gíslason, as the thugs insisted he was called, and Daníel would finish looking into Elísabet and Lárus and their mysterious child.

41

It was strange keeping up the pretence that she and Daníel were still quarrelling now that they'd kissed and made up. But Daníel insisted it was necessary, and that for her safety they should have as little contact as possible over the next few days. She'd scarcely heard anything so crazy, but this case had definitely roused her curiosity. She dropped Daníel off outside his house, and when he asked her to come in behaved as if she were still angry with him and said she wanted time to think. She was still upset and thought they should take a break from the relationship. It was weird hearing herself say this even as the two of them smiled and gazed into each other's eyes while Daníel caressed the back of her hand gently with his thumb.

Then she watched him hobble inside and close the door behind him. She waited until the light had come on in the kitchen and he'd waved to her through the window to let her know everything was okay, then she turned the car round and drove off. It pained her to see him in such a state, and she wished she could have followed him into the house, helped dress his wounds and tucked him up in bed. But he was quite capable of putting on a few sticky plasters, applying a cold pack and swallowing some painkillers. She would be of more help to him by trying to find Lady Gúgúlú. This was his greatest anxiety, and if what he'd told her was true then he couldn't possibly do so himself without drawing the attention of these mysterious men who'd attacked him.

Áróra headed straight for work, because there she could go online on the office computer, which was – supposedly – well protected against spyware. She parked the Tesla, glanced about then released the central locking system and climbed out. Áróra had no desire to run into the three mysterious men, after what Daníel had told her about the way they'd treated him and Helena. Although she'd have liked nothing more than to pay them back for what they did to Daníel, she knew she couldn't take on three men at once. Especially if Daníel was right and they were highly trained – some sort of intelligence agents.

She installed herself in front of her computer in the main office, but then changed her mind and decided it would be safer to switch to her colleague's computer and log in using her password. This was easy enough, because, despite the security officer's and Agla's lectures, this good colleague's password was her pet dog's name. Seppi was the subject of much discussion during coffee breaks; as well as being a show dog Seppi was apparently a canine genius.

She had some information about Lady Gúgúlú that Daníel had given her, and he'd asked her to start by running a name search on Róbert Þór Gíslason, which she did. There was no one of that name on the national register, although a Róbert Þór Gíslason born in 1986 was registered deceased four years ago. This was both strange and frustrating. The mysterious thugs appeared to be looking for a dead man. The name itself was a dead end.

Áróra felt her stomach rumble and while she considered her next move she went out to the staff kitchen to find something to eat. The cupboard was almost bare and the only communal food was the rock-hard digestive biscuits some colleagues dunked in their coffee, like poor imitations of biscotti. She opened the big cupboard with the labelled shelves. Since hers was empty, she rifled through those of her colleagues and at last found a packet of flatbread from which she extracted two half-moon shaped slices. This thin rye pancake, which the average Icelander, including her late father, seemed to think was the best bread on the planet, was in fact a second-rate bakery product invented during a flour shortage in a bygone era; it had nevertheless carved a niche for itself as some kind of cultural legacy. The bread was just about edible if you slathered it in butter, preferably adding another layer of fat such as cheese or salami. She found a tub of spreadable butter on the top shelf of the fridge along with a packet of sliced cheese, also the property of a colleague. She didn't suppose he'd miss a couple of slices, so she peeled off two and placed them on top of the thickly buttered flatbread then stuck the two half-moons together. She took a bite and headed back to the office, munching and reflecting on which avenues she could go down in her search. She should probably start by following the money. Which was her forté.

She sat down once more at her colleague's computer and used as her starting point the information Daníel had given her. Gúgúlú Ltd, owner Haraldur Gunnarsson, paid Daníel a monthly rent directly into his account via standing order, it seemed. Áróra located the company's yearly financial statement and sifted through the expenses column. The payments to Daníel were listed there as rent for the artist's workplace. This was more or less valid since Lady Gúgúlú's costume-making took up quite a lot of space in the garage, although she clearly lived there too. However, Áróra wasn't on the trail of a tax fraudster right now, and anyway she wouldn't have given such minor breaches a second glance. Her job consisted of exposing much bigger cases of tax evasion. Other expenses listed on the statement included fabric for costumes, travel and heating costs, meetings, which Áróra assumed were restaurant bills, as was frequently the case, and finally the internet connection in Daníel's garage. The company didn't pay out any salaries, but profits were taken out every two months to the tune of two hundred thousand Icelandic krónur – about eleven hundred pounds sterling – and transferred to Haraldur Gunnarsson's bank account. This wasn't a very large disposable income, which meant Lady must have some alternative source of funds. Áróra looked up Haraldur's national identification number in the tax system and was surprised to discover that he was on disability benefits. This wasn't so extraordinary in itself – after all, he rented a garage apartment and besides the drag shows didn't appear to have a steady job. What did come as a surprise was that according to official records Lady, or Haraldur, owned some plots of land for summer houses on the other side of Hellisheiði, as well as a half-finished summer house, registered as a stage three dwelling, which meant the basic structure had been built but the property wasn't weather-proofed.

It also came as a surprise to Áróra to discover that Haraldur received housing benefit, not for Daníel's garage apartment but for an apartment in downtown Reykjavík on Öldugata. This was exactly the kind of clue Áróra had been hoping for. She logged out of her colleague's computer and grabbed her jacket from the chair.

42

'I'll be out on parole soon, my love,' whispered Sirra down the phone as Helena dried her eyes with the back of her hand. She'd become as weepy as a middle-aged woman, Helena told herself. She'd noticed other changes in herself too – changes that showed she was trapped in exactly the relationship cage she used to pity her friends for being caught in. Not that she missed her old life-style; she didn't. She no longer wanted to drink and go partying; she didn't want that carefree feeling that came with only having to think about your own needs. And she had no desire for any other woman but Sirra.

'I'm counting the days,' she said, and laughed.

'You mustn't be jealous of Bisi,' said Sirra. 'This was a joint decision, remember?'

'I know,' said Helena. 'I'm not jealous. I envy the time she gets to spend with you though. And I just miss you dreadfully.' And it was true. Sometimes she felt sick with longing. As if her heart were swollen and had somehow spread through her entire body so she couldn't eat and felt a constant lump in her throat.

'You'll be able to visit in a few days,' Sirra said reassuringly.

'There's something so sad about talking to each other through glass,' said Helena, aware of how her voice sounded, like a whiny kid.

'Soon we'll be able to meet properly,' said Sirra. 'It's only behind glass for the first three visits.'

This cheered Helena up. She'd be able to touch Sirra. Embrace her. Breathe in her scent. Stroke her hair.

'Sirra,' she whispered into the phone. 'I'm ready now.'

'Ready for what?' Sirra whispered back.

'I'm ready for us to be together all the time. I don't think I need to have my own space anymore. I've always felt I wanted it, but now when you're not around I suffer. I just want to be with you all the time. Sleep together, wake up together, eat together, watch TV together. I want to be with you every free moment of my day.'

Sirra didn't reply and then Helena heard her clear her throat.

'Maybe we've got ourselves into a bit of a fix over this, I mean because of the whole situation with Bisi,' she said and laughed, but Helena heard a catch in her voice.

'Can't we just find a solution?' said Helena, and Sirra laughed again, this time joyously.

'Yes, of course we can,' she said, and now Helena could hear the old confidence in her voice. The confidence that had attracted her so strongly to Sirra from the beginning. 'Of course we'll find a way out of it.'

'I love you,' whispered Helena, and she heard Sirra blow kisses to her at the other end of the line.

'We'll be together soon,' said Sirra. 'Just be sure to keep busy until then. It'll take your mind off things.'

Helena nodded. Work had always been her greatest comfort and refuge. 'That won't be difficult,' she said. 'We have fresh evidence about the disappearance of Áróra's sister, Ísafold. As of tomorrow morning Daníel and I will be working a new lead.'

43

A man of about forty came to the door of the big house on Öldugata and peered quizzically at Áróra. It was one of those tall concrete structures right next to the pavement but with what looked like a big south-facing garden at the back. Judging from the doorbells there were two apartments in the building, and Áróra had begun by pressing the top one because she saw a light in the first-floor windows.

'I'm looking for Haraldur Gunnarsson, otherwise known as Lady Gúgúlú,' she said.

The man seemed about to say something but shook his head and frowned, perplexed. 'Haraldur?' he then said tentatively.

'Yes,' said Áróra.

'Haraldur is certainly a bit gaga but he's far from being a lady. That's why I had to let him go.'

'So he is, or was, your tenant?'

'Yes,' replied the man. 'The poor fellow always paid his rent on time, first of every month, by standing order. Someone must have set it up for him, as there was no way he could have kept track of when it was due.'

'So he doesn't live here anymore?' asked Áróra.

'No. He rented the basement flat, but things got so bad I couldn't subject my family to that. Endless parties and a bunch of people like him tramping in and out day and night. The garden littered with beer cans and empty bottles.'

This didn't sound quite right, and Áróra wondered whether the man's description didn't conceal some prejudice. Daníel had mentioned Lady bringing men home and said he played his music a bit loud late at night, but that he only had to knock on the door and everything went quiet.

'What do you mean by "people like him"?' she asked.

The man was covered in confusion. 'You know, what do we say nowadays, er ... street people. What we used to call winos.' The man appeared to interpret Áróra's puzzled expression as some sort of accusation so he leapt to his own defence. 'I have small children. I can't tolerate this kind of behaviour in my home. I was forever expecting him to set fire to the house. I disconnected the cooker, but he had a microwave and an electric kettle, and he smoked like a chimney. I had to redecorate the apartment to get rid of the stench after he left. But just so you know I tried to keep him here for as long as I could, because he's a perfectly nice man and I felt sorry for him. He just drinks like it was going out of fashion. And his memory is shot to pieces. After every spell on the psychiatric ward he just gets worse. He's shown up here on several occasions, trying to get into the basement because he's forgotten he doesn't live here anymore.'

Áróra raised her hand and nodded vigorously to calm the man down. 'I'm not accusing you of anything,' she said. 'I understand that you can't have people like him living here.'

The man sighed. 'Yes. But I still feel bad about kicking the poor fellow out. When he's come here and I've had to explain to him why he no longer lives here, he bursts into tears. It breaks my heart. But I just can't be responsible for him anymore. You need to take over and do your job.'

'We?' Áróra asked, astonished. 'Who do you mean by we?'

'Social services. You are from social services, aren't you?'

44

Based on the man's description, Áróra scarcely felt any need to check whether the Haraldur who'd rented the basement apartment on Öldugata was Lady Gúgúlú. All the same, she drove down to the homeless shelter and asked the supervisor if there was someone there by the name of Haraldur Gunnarsson.

He pointed to a man wandering in the corridor, toothbrush in hand, a look of confusion on his face.

'In here, Haraldur,' said the supervisor, steering him into one of the rooms. 'Your bed is at the back.' He looked at Áróra searchingly. 'Is this the guy you're looking for?'

She shook her head. She'd never seen this man before and what most baffled her was that he didn't look at all like he was born in 1986, as it said in the national register. His skin was rough and pitted, his cheeks red, and he had the shambling gait of an old man.

'Good night, mate.' The supervisor closed the door behind Haraldur and accompanied Áróra back to the foyer.

'He should be in some kind of residential care. They're trying to get him a place in a nursing home, but he doesn't really belong in one – he's too young. He's not badly off financially, either. He receives benefits and a small monthly sum from a relative or someone. His social worker gives him a weekly allowance so he doesn't drink away a whole month's money in one go – or lose it. Haraldur's fallen through the cracks in the system, and nobody quite knows how to help him. We have several cases like that here.'

'And was he really born in 1986? Thirty-six years old?'

The supervisor gave a rueful smile. 'Yes. This is what happens when people with brain damage abuse alcohol. Allegedly, a few years back, Haraldur was given electro-shock therapy for his depression. Only it made him lose his memory and he never recovered it.' They'd reached the entrance to the shelter and the supervisor held open the door for Áróra. 'So he's not the man you're looking for?'

'No,' said Áróra. 'Haraldur Gunnarsson is a common enough name, I suppose. But he's the wrong one.'

'What's strange,' said the supervisor, 'is that you're the second person to ask about Haraldur today.'

Áróra gave a start. 'Really?'

'Yes,' said the supervisor. 'He seems popular at the moment. I think it was the cops who came looking for him earlier. Or rather a different Haraldur. Like you.'

'I see,' said Áróra, a feeling of unease creeping up her throat.

Áróra stepped out into the night, the chill piercing her coat as she reflected on the supervisor's words. The men Daníel had described as possibly belonging to some shadowy intelligence service – must have traced the same steps she had taken in her search for Haraldur. The realisation sent a jolt of urgency through her. The thought that they were already ahead of her in the search was unsettling. She would have to move faster, think smarter, stay one step ahead. For if indeed they did belong to some intelligence service, they would have access to resources she didn't. She climbed into the Tesla and sat for a while, deep in thought, contemplating the men standing with their backs against the wall of the shelter, smoking. In fact, she'd told the supervisor a lie, because although the man with no memory in the shelter wasn't Lady Gúgúlú, he wasn't the wrong Haraldur. What she needed to do now was find out why Lady had been using this man's name and national identity number all these years. Finding Haraldur had been too easy – child's play. And the mysterious men must have thought so too. People who adopted someone else's identity could carry on a fairly normal life so long as nobody doubted their name. Especially if the real owner of the name was a social drop-out who was unlikely to file a complaint about identity theft. But now it seemed everyone who was looking for Lady knew that Haraldur was just a front.

Áróra was hungry again so she stopped at a drive-in and ordered a hot dog with everything, and a chocolate milk shake, both of which she devoured in the car. Crumbs and bits of fried onion fell off the hotdog while she was driving. She imagined the look of horror on Daníel's face if he could see her now. He was forever offering to clean the car for her, even though she'd explained to him that she hired a valeting company to do it for her once a month. Then he'd get that funny look on his face, the one he always adopted when she paid other people to do things she could do herself. Since she started earning good money she'd grown accustomed to this level of luxury. She certainly hadn't been a spoilt kid growing up – she and Ísafold had had to earn their pocket money and save up if they wanted to buy expensive stuff. And they were also made to do housework, which included cleaning the family car, something Ísafold enjoyed but Áróra found onerous.

Back in the office Áróra sat down again and logged onto her colleague's computer. She must go to work now, carry out an in-depth search. She cast her mind back, this time to when she first met Daníel. Lady Gúgúlú was in the garage by then, and probably had been for a while. It was annoying that she couldn't simply text Daníel and ask him how long Lady had rented his apartment for. However, if the three mysterious men really were tapping Daníel's phone and found out she was looking into Lady's disappearance then both she and Daníel would be in danger. She decided to start her search ten years back. Surely then she could trace the start of it all. When Lady Gúgúlú first began using the name Haraldur Gunnarsson.

WEDNESDAY

45

'I'm not having any more injections,' Áróra said to Stulli when they met at the entrance to The Gym, she on her way out after weight training, he on his way in. 'I nearly beat up my boyfriend yesterday,' she went on. 'So I'm quitting.'

Stulli nodded his head. 'You already lift a good weight for a woman your height. That long back of yours is strong as an ox. You should be happy with how much you can lift.'

'I know,' she said.

'But I understand you want to improve. You're not your father's daughter for nothing. We all know about the competitive spirit.'

He gave her a friendly clap on the shoulder with his great paw, and for a moment Áróra had the impression it was her father laying a comforting hand on her.

'Yes. We want to be competition fit all the time,' she agreed. 'But since I'm not competing it makes no sense. To tell the truth, I don't know why I keep plugging away like this.'

'Old habits,' said Stulli. 'And of course you grew up in a weight-lifting gym. I remember you training with your dad when you were still a shrimp. So part of it is probably to remember him.' Áróra gazed intently at Stulli. His words showed insight.

'What do you think about reincarnation, Stulli?' she asked. 'Do you believe we can be reborn into a new body after we die?'

Stulli shrugged. 'Is it any more incredible than sprouting wings after we die?' he asked.

Áróra grinned. 'Probably not,' she said, and gave Stulli a quick hug before setting off at a sprint towards her car.

It was close on seven am and she had a lot to do that day. Her flight to Gran Canaria left at midday and she still had to fling a few things in a bag. She'd spent yesterday evening digging deep into a decade of Haraldur Gunnarsson's finances, which were a complete mess until four years ago, when he changed overnight into a model citizen. Not only did he settle his tax debt, he also began to pay his bills on time and received a monthly sum of two hundred thousand krónur from Gúgúlú Ltd. Soon after that, Haraldur bought some summer-house land in Tjarnar-byggð, between Selfoss and Eyrarbakki and subsequently imported a prefabricated house, registered as partially built because it wasn't weather-proofed. A woman named Fríða Ró-bertsdóttir stood to inherit both the house and the land. According to her national identity number, Fríða Róbertsdóttir was born in 1954, and Áróra found other information that gave her address as Gran Canaria. Lady Gúgúlú did all her adminis-trative business as Haraldur Gunnarsson, hence the absence of any paper trail in her real name, whatever that was. And given what Áróra knew about the men who were pursuing her, or him, she, or he, had every reason to go underground.

However, Áróra found no connection between this woman Fríða in the Canary Islands and Haraldur, besides the fact she was his sole heir. Then again, Daníel did say he thought Lady Gúgúlú's mother lived in the Canary Islands, and Áróra had a sneaking suspicion she must be Fríða. And where did people go when they were in a fix and there was no way out...?

46

Helena sat in her car in the parking lot outside the block in Bakkahverfi, awaiting Daníel's text. Her thoughts strayed to her conversation with Sirra the evening before, and she wished she hadn't been so sad and depressed. People in prison really shouldn't need to comfort those sitting at home, who were free to do as they pleased. But all Helena wanted was to be with Sirra. Still, Sirra's prison term at Hólmsheiði was drawing to an end, and after a short stay at a halfway house she would serve out the rest of her sentence doing community service. Helena couldn't wait. Of course it would be complicated to arrange things so she and Sirra could live together, without immigration services suspecting Bisi's and Sirra's marriage was a sham. Maybe Helena could 'rent' the front room in Sirra's apartment in Laugardalur, which was actually where Bisi stayed.

Helena's phone pinged, rousing her from her daydream. Daníel had sent her a thumbs-up emoji. She knew what it meant so she got out of her car and hurried towards the block. She was supposed to take Elísabet down to the station for an 'informal chat' while Daníel fetched her husband, Lárus, from his workplace. They'd decided to synchronise in this way to prevent the couple from talking to each other and getting their stories straight for the police. Assuming they hadn't done so already.

Elísabet seemed surprised to see her but was all smiles when Helena asked if she'd accompany her to the station. If anything, she seemed enthusiastic. Helena even thought she looked thrilled by her request.

'I'm so glad you're looking into this, because everywhere we go we hit a brick wall,' she said to Helena as they descended the stairs in the block. 'It's as if no one quite knows what to tell us. In the meantime, we're becoming more and more alarmed at the things

Ester Lóa is saying, and to tell you the truth I'm a little afraid. I hardly dare ask her about her past life, because all she talks about is how she died. The ice-bear and all that.' Helena hummed every now and then to show she was listening, but otherwise didn't respond to what Elísabet was saying. She'd have plenty of time to get the details out of her down at the station. She and Daníel had booked two interview rooms equipped with audio devices, as well as two officers who were at that very moment reading up on the Ísafold case so they could help her and Daníel assess whether the information the couple gave them was relevant to the case in any way at all.

'I thought you'd be in a patrol car,' Elísabet said as they walked out into parking lot, her voice oozing disappointment.

'Mine will have to do,' said Helena, unlocking it remotely with the key fob. 'I might be able to bring you home in one, though.'

'That would be fun,' said Elísabet. 'I've never been inside a patrol car before. Not even on the back seat because I was caught speeding or something.' Helena darted a glance at the woman. She seemed so earnest, so ingenuous, she reminded her of a ten-year-old kid. She didn't exactly fit the profile of someone who would make up stories about her daughter or be involved in a missing-person case and keep quiet about it for three years. She didn't seem the type to keep quiet about anything.

'Patrols cars are terrible old rust buckets,' Helena said as she got into her car. 'I'm afraid you'll be disappointed.'

'Oh, not at all!' Elísabet said, installing herself in the passenger seat. 'This is the kind of detail that makes our true-crime podcast interesting. I doubt many people know that patrol cars are rust buckets.'

As she drove out of the Bakkan parking lot and headed downtown, Helena wondered whether someone hadn't provided the couple with such 'details', as Elisabet put it, about Ísafold's disappearance for their podcast. Someone, therefore, who had links to the case. Or some cop who'd leaked information. Either way she and Daníel would get to the bottom of it today.

47

Áróra hadn't dried her hair after taking a shower and the back of her shirt collar felt damp as she stood on Agla's doorstep. Agla came to the door, dressed and ready for work, and clearly surprised to see her.

'I just need five minutes,' said Áróra.

Agla opened the door wide and stepped aside. 'Come in,' she said. 'I've just made coffee.'

A boy aged about seven sat in the kitchen in his pyjamas, munching Cheerios out of a bowl and watching *Sponge Bob* on his tablet. He barely glanced up when Áróra walked in. But Elísa, Agla's wife, welcomed Áróra with a warm embrace, as she would a special guest. Áróra had always considered Elísa and Agla a particularly ill-matched couple. Not because of their age difference but because they were such opposite characters. Agla was so stiff and formal and elegant, whereas Elísa wore jeans and had sleeve tattoos on both arms. She was open and outgoing and laughed all the time.

'What's it like working for the tax inspectorate?' she asked Áróra.

'I love it,' said Áróra. 'Although actually I've come here to ask Agla if I can take a mini-break.'

'Sit down, darling, sit down, I'll bring you a coffee,' Elísa said, and poured her a cup while Áróra took a seat between the little boy and Agla.

'Is something the matter?' asked Agla cautiously, and Áróra felt a little pang in her stomach because she was about to tell a lie. Or, more accurately, a half-truth.

'Yes and no,' she replied. 'This sounds really weird, but some people have come forward. They say their daughter claims ...

she's my sister reincarnated. They've been harassing me a bit, and Daníel and his colleagues are following it up because it seems they have information that was never made public – about blood in the apartment where Ísafold was attacked.

Agla and Elísa stared at her open-mouthed.

'Wow,' Elísa said, while Agla placed a hand on Áróra's arm and gave her a quick squeeze.

'Whatever you need,' she said. 'Take as much time off as necessary to deal with this.'

'I realise it's a bit presumptuous to ask for time off at such short notice and then go sunbathing, but I'm thinking of spending a week in the Canary Islands to recharge my batteries. Get right away from everything.'

'That's a great idea,' said Elísa. 'You need to heal.'

'It's not presumptuous at all,' added Agla. She seemed so much more relaxed and natural at home than at work. 'Don't worry about the assignment. I can look into the cryptocurrency creators myself. I doubt we'll find much of interest, in any case.'

'Really?' Áróra was surprised. 'So why investigate them, then?'

'Good question,' said Agla, shrugging and taking a sip of coffee. 'I get the feeling right now that a lot of countries are collaborating to try to tax cryptocurrency creators every way they can in order to make life difficult for them while they wait for their own central banks to create cryptocurrencies.'

'And you think that's in the pipeline?'

'I suspect it is,' said Agla. 'It'll be cheaper and more eco-friendly, because central banks could control production without the need for all those calculations and computations. They would oversee the process themselves and wouldn't have to set up huge mining farms with their energy-guzzling super-computers.'

'But it totally goes against the idea of free-floating currencies remaining independent of the big global currencies,' said Áróra.

'It also makes life more difficult for criminals,' said Agla. 'Freedom is good, but other things spring up in its shadow.'

Áróra couldn't help smiling. It was somehow surreal, sitting having this conversation with a former bank fraudster. The irony evidently wasn't lost on Agla, as she smiled too.

48

Áróra pressed her forehead against the aircraft's porthole and looked down at the Reykjanes peninsula. As the plane tilted and turned east she found herself directly above the eruption site in the Geldingadalir dales. Reykjanes had always appeared black but the new lava field gave the word a fresh meaning. It was black as pitch. In contrast with the older lava that blanketed the cape, grey from the weather and sea salt, speckled green with moss and clumps of wispy grass. Now, as she gazed down at this vast expanse of new lava, she was gripped once more by the panic she'd felt nearly the entire time the eruption lasted. What if her sister's body lay under this new lava? Stuck beneath a layer of molten rock several metres deep. What if they never found her grave? What if they never got any closure? Then Áróra would be doomed to wait forever in this agonising limbo she'd been trapped in these past few years.

She always had this strange feeling when she was on Reykjanes. A powerful sensation that hit her like a wave, the sensation that Ísafold was somewhere nearby. That she was on the verge of discovering her sister's final resting place. Then again, she'd felt the same way at Þingvellir, on Hellisheiði and around Þrengslin, in fact in all the places where she'd searched with the drone, down dust tracks and along pathways, anywhere a body might conceivably be hidden. But now Reykjanes had this added dimension – what the little girl had said about black lava. That Ísafold was lying in black lava.

The plane rose through the cloud cover, obscuring Áróra's view of the ground below, and she settled back in her seat. Her mother and Daníel and Helena were right, of course. It was utter nonsense. It was only her grief and guilt that made her susceptible to such foolishness. She had to trust in Daníel to find out whether or not Elísabet, Lárus and their little girl really did have any information to give them regarding Ísafold's disappearance.

She pulled out her phone, plugged in her earbuds and put them in her ears. She would listen to some music, have the flight attendant bring her a beer and relax for a few hours. She would be ready then to carry out the task she'd taken on. That of finding Lady Gúgúlú. For some reason she was convinced Lady was in the Canary Islands, being looked after by her mum. Which was why Áróra had decided not to announce her arrival and simply show up at the house. Because her intention wasn't only to find Daníel's tenant and friend Lady Gúgúlú, or whatever his real name was, but to discover why he'd been going by the name Haraldur Gunnarsson, and, last but not least, who or what Lady was running from.

49

'Why don't you pick up Ester Lóa from the nursery and bring her down here to the station? Then you can hear it straight from her?' Lárus seemed more frustrated than angry.

These informal chats had dragged on. In fact Daníel was amazed that neither Lárus nor Elísabet appeared to want to call it a day, just get up and leave, as he'd explained to them repeatedly they were at liberty to do. On the contrary, he had the impression they wanted to stay longer. As if they felt this conversation were necessary. And it only occurred to Daníel fairly late in the morning that this was because they themselves were looking for explanations for the things their daughter was saying. Of course, the case took on a whole new aspect if this were true.

'Who is Ester Lóa in regular contact with, apart from the people she meets at the nursery?'

The question seemed to throw Lárus. 'Just us and our friends and relatives,' he said.

Daníel texted Helena to tell her to ask Elísabet the same question in the other room.

'Presumably her grandparents?' said Daníel. 'Aunts and uncles, cousins? Anyone you leave her with regularly?'

Lárus shook his head slowly. 'We don't use a child minder, as such. She goes on visits but always with her mother and me. If we go to my sister's, for example, Ester Lóa will play with her kids while we grown-ups chat over coffee.'

'And how old are your sister's children?' asked Daníel.

'Two and five,' said Lárus.

'And they haven't exhibited similar behaviour? They haven't talked about these things?'

'No,' Lárus said, folding his arms across his chest and leaning back in his chair. He looked sullen, as if his patience was wearing thin.

'Okay,' Daníel said, smiling amicably. 'You understand we're obliged to look into this, to make sure there's no leak here at the station.'

Lárus nodded. 'Yes, yes, of course.'

Daníel pushed a notepad and pen across the table to him. 'I'm going to ask you to write down the names of everyone Ester Lóa has been in contact with during the last few months, or since she started saying she's Ísafold.'

Lárus sat up straight, seized the pen and leaned over the pad. 'I may not remember every last person we've met,' he said.

'That doesn't matter. Focus on the people she's been in frequent contact with, anyone she's been alone with, people you've left her with, people she's visited, etc. It would be good if you could also give us the names of the nursery teachers she spends most time with. We'll print out a staff list ourselves, so just write down the names you can remember.' Lárus sighed and muttered something under his breath but then began writing out a list on the pad.

Daníel had started for the door when Lárus called him back.

'Daníel.' He wheeled round to find Lárus gazing at him in despair. 'I understand that you have your procedures, but you're wasting unnecessary time and energy looking for someone who might have told Ester Lóa what to say. You should try talking to her yourselves, then maybe you'll understand what we're talking about. It's, you know. Spooky.'

50

The hens seemed to feel at home in the coop now, and Robbi looked forward to letting them out the following morning. He had the impression they felt safe in there, even though they still regarded him with suspicion, as if they hardly dared believe he was really going to feed them. He scattered a handful of maize kernels on the ground, and their mistrust gave way to greed as they pounced on the kernels and began to peck at them. The big white hen was the pushiest, and most of the others gave it a wide berth. Any that ventured too close to the maize it had its eye on received a sharp peck on the head and scurried off to concentrate on the kernels further away. Only the little harassed hen didn't seem to get much of a look-in, but when Robbie tried again to toss it something, two other hens attacked it, scaring it away from the food altogether.

He longed to step in, scold the bullies, tell them the hen they were taunting and humiliating was probably far cleverer than they. Just as his mother had after the boys at school beat him up and pissed on his school bag, and he had sat on the steps, battered and bruised, crying over his urine-soaked *X-Files* backpack, and she had arrived to fetch him. He couldn't quite remember if that was at his second or his third school. At times it was the kids who scared him away; at other times his teachers. His teachers would scold him for solving all the maths problems in his exercise book on the first day, or get angry when he corrected them, the kids called him a poof or a freak. In many ways the teachers were worse. After all, the kids were just aggressive kids, but the teachers should have known better than to humiliate him in front of his classmates, who generally interpreted a scolding from the teacher as a signal for open season.

But it was probably understandable. According, anyway, to the pedagogues in the States, where he went to take a course. They maintained that for the average teacher educating children like him was problematic. Children who were highly talented. Gifted children. So they devised a programme for him and his mother that involved him taking courses all over the world, and they also found him a mentor back home in Iceland, a man named Jónas, a professor of physics at the University of Iceland, who invited him to sit in on his lectures. Jónas also met with his primary-school teachers to discuss appropriate reading and study material for Róbert. He had them move him up two grades and went over Róbert's homework himself outside school. Robbi always felt a pang in his stomach whenever he thought about Jónas. When he earned his PhD at Oxford, Jónas had called to congratulate him, but lost his temper when Robbi told him he was going to work for BH Dynamic Systems. Jónas had muttered something about Robbi wasting his talent, told him he didn't know what he was doing, but Robbi laughed and asked Jónas scornfully whether he seriously imagined he'd apply for a job at the University of Iceland! Jónas had hung up on him and they hadn't spoken after that. Yet Robbi had wept three years ago when he saw Jónas's obituary in the papers. And he'd always regretted not listening to him.

Looking back now he felt sickened by his own arrogance. It was laughable to think he'd seriously believed he could change things. That he could change the world and mankind for the better. He, who didn't even know how to deal with bullying in a flock of hens. He was just a nobody. Worthless. All they wanted was the box and the formula. And, failing that, to make sure no one else got their hands on it. Which was why his life was in danger.

He became aware his life was in danger three years after he went on the run. He had buried the box in a plastic container filled with sand in the middle of a field he rented from a horse breeder near Coventry. After paying the man extra for his discretion, he had taken off. He took care never to stay in the same place for too long, and he travelled by road or rail wherever possible, so he needn't give his name. He realised they must be looking for him through Interpol, because when he did disclose his name, entering a country, booking a flight or reserving a hotel, they caught up with him soon after. As a result he stayed mostly at B&Bs, brothels and other places where they didn't ask for any ID, and often with men he picked here and there. That was how he met Ole, who was Danish. They fell into conversation at a gay bar in Thailand, where they both looked visibly Scandinavian, and being far from home the old tensions between Icelanders and Danes fell away and they became almost as brothers. For his part, Robbi avoided the subject of Danish colonial rule in Iceland , and Ole didn't comment on the underhand way in which Iceland had declared independence when Nazi Germany occupied Denmark at the start of WW2, so neither felt the need to apologise.

After spending several nights together at Ole's rented apartment, it seemed only natural that Robbi would stay on. They had a lot of fun together, a vigorous sex life, and within a few weeks Ole had developed a bit of a crush on Robbi. They scooted round Pattaya on Ole's pale-pink Vespa and went for foot massages every evening before storming the dance clubs. However, Robbi never got the chance to decide whether he felt the same way about Ole. Before that happened Ole was dead.

They'd gone on a sightseeing trip to Bangkok, and since they only planned to stay one night, Robbi stupidly used his card to pay for the hotel. He couldn't allow Ole to pay for everything, but all the cashpoints they tried were out of order, so he convinced himself it was safe to pay by card, as by the time the banking system had alerted Interpol they'd be gone. The following morning, before Ole woke up, Robbi went out to fetch breakfast and when he came back with bread rolls and fried fish, Ole was lying dead in the bed with a syringe in his arm.

Robbi had never been aware that Ole was into heroin. Sure, he was fond of his cocktails, and they'd smoked the odd joint together, but nothing more. Nothing to suggest that Ole was a junkie. So when Robbie stood contemplating Ole in the hotel room, stretched out in that unnatural position, eyes half open, a faraway expression on his face, he was convinced they had done this. They had traced his card transaction and sent someone to kill him, only the assassin had murdered Ole by mistake.

Robbi's mind had gone into overdrive, and instead of standing there bathed in sweat crying his eyes out, he'd regained his composure, gathered up his belongings, took Ole's passport and credit cards out of his suitcase and left his own on the bedside table, then he turned the air conditioning on full and vanished into the throng outside. Only when he was on a coach headed for Laos, did he give way to the shock. He trembled uncontrollably, allowing the tears to flow, yet behind all those emotions his mind remained cold as ice, and he told himself Ole's death could buy him peace. If the Bangkok police didn't look too closely at the photograph on the passport he'd left on the bedside table, they'd declare him dead and he'd be free as a bird.

51

The commissioner sat quietly for a moment, staring at Daníel. He knew she was thinking so he didn't say a word. He and Helena had spent most of the day interviewing the couple, alternately ramping up the pressure and being friendly. Daníel had ordered a takeaway lunch for himself, Lárus and the accompanying officers, which they'd eaten in the nicer canteen upstairs, while Helena took Elísabet to the food hall at Hlemmur. But regardless of the approach they took, everything the couple said coincided, and they never put a foot wrong. There were two possible explanations when different people's accounts matched so completely: either they'd got their stories straight beforehand or they were simply telling the truth.

'And you and Helena were completely in synch with this?' asked the commissioner, the same fixed expression on her face.

'Yes,' replied Daníel. 'We swapped information on the app in real time, checked everything straightaway, and it all tallied.'

'Hm.' The commissioner gazed out of the window as if somewhere in the blueness, the mountain, the sea, the sky, some idea about how to confront this unusual case might be found. Then she turned back to Daníel and said: 'We're all frustrated about the lack of new direction regarding the disappearance of Ísafold Jónsdóttir, but we must be careful not to clutch at straws. Instinct tells me this is a lot of nonsense, yet it's hard to dismiss out of hand.'

'My thoughts exactly,' said Daníel. 'However, both parents have asked us to talk to the child. There's a slot available at the Children's House this afternoon. If you give us the green light I'll get Helena to set it up right away.'

'Normally I'd need a very strong reason to authorise an interview at the Children's House—' the commissioner began, but Daníel quickly cut in.

'In this case, though, it's the parents who've requested it. And if my hunch is correct and they're telling the truth, then someone else is filling their daughter's head with these stories about Ísafold. And we need to find out who that is, because they clearly know more than they should.'

The commissioner stared at Daníel for a moment then slapped her palm on the table in the manner of a judge. 'Okay,' she said. 'But I'm calling Oddsteinn to keep the prosecutor's office in the loop, in case your interview turns up a suspect.

'Thank you,' said Daníel, and he placed his hand on his chest in a sign of gratitude.

The commissioner gave a faint smile. 'You know you're much too close to this,' she said.

'Yes,' replied Daníel. 'But we're sure to get some answers today, and if anything new comes up then you hand the case to someone else.'

'Yes,' said the commissioner. 'I'd like this matter dealt with before we assign any more resources to the case. I don't like the feeling we're being led by the nose.'

Daníel stood up. 'You make it sound like the police have nose rings.'

The commissioner gave a little snort and reached for the phone as Daníel closed the office door behind him.

Out in the corridor he pulled out his phone to call Helena to ask her to arrange the interview at the Children's House, but there was a message alert on the screen. He could see it was from Áróra responding to his earlier text. Their secret code was working. In his text he had said he missed her terribly, which signified no developments on the Ísafold case. She had now replied telling him she was on her way to the Canary Islands to relax, lie in the sun and think things over. Anyone intercepting their messages might have observed an innocent exchange between quarrelling lovers. But Daníel understood the message and felt deeply relieved. Haraldur once told him his mother lived in the Canary Islands. And Áróra seemed to have traced him there. He smiled to himself. Of course Lady was sunning herself in the Canary Islands. No doubt with a brightly coloured cocktail to hand.

52

The Icelandic national register didn't keep precise addresses for people residing abroad, so Fríða Róbertsdóttir was registered simply as living 'in Spain'. However, Áróra hadn't needed to search far on Facebook to discover that Fríða lived in Las Palmas. When she landed at the airport, she opened Facebook again and messaged a woman Fríða referred to in several of her posts as her cousin. After introducing herself and engaging in a bit of chit-chat, Áróra asked if they could make a voice call through the app.

When the cousin picked up the phone, Áróra explained the reason she was in touch. 'I need Fríða's address because, as I said before, she's an old friend of my mother's, and I really want to send her some photos I found of the two of them when they were young.'

'I see,' said the woman. 'Wait a minute. My address book is here somewhere.' The woman went away from the phone and Áróra anticipated receiving a barrage of questions about her connection to cousin Fríða before the woman was prepared to give out the address, but this didn't happen. 'Here it is,' the woman said and read out Fríða's address with the postcode and everything.

'Thank you so much,' said Áróra. 'I'm sure she'll be delighted when she gets the photos.'

'I expect so,' replied the woman.

Áróra said goodbye, still marvelling at how open and trusting most Icelanders were.

Fríða lived in a suburb south of Las Palmas, and Áróra took a taxi straight there from the airport. The house was typical of the kind of places lived in by droves of pensioners who flocked there: a small bungalow in a row of identical dwellings, with a tiny south-facing patio and a raised deck with an awning that made it possible for the occupant to sit outside in the shade and enjoy a cup of coffee, or even install a small dining table.

There was no one outside even though the evening sun hung low in the sky, mild and caressing, so Áróra knocked on the pink painted door. She instantly heard footsteps from inside, loud like clattering clogs, and indeed the woman who opened the door wore a pair of classic white nurse's clogs and a floral summer dress.

'*Hola*,' she said in Spanish, peering suspiciously at Áróra. Her expression softened when Áróra addressed her in Icelandic.

'Are you Fríða Róbertsdóttir?' she asked.

'Yes, that's right,' the woman said tentatively, with which Áróra took a step closer, extending her hand.

'How do you do. I'm Áróra Jónsdóttir. I'm the girlfriend of Daníel Hansson from Hafnafjörður. Does his name ring any bells with you?'

The woman looked at Áróra with an expression that suggested she was searching hard in her memory, but then she shook her head slowly. 'No, I don't know him.'

Áróra was about to put her next question when she noticed a photograph on the wall in the hallway beyond. It showed a skinny youth in a high-school graduation cap, smiling a dazzling smile and seeming to stare out at a bright future. There was no doubt this was a younger version of Lady Gúgúlú.

Áróra pointed at the photograph. 'Is that your son?' she asked.

Fríða turned and glanced at the photograph then contemplated Áróra once more, but now with an air of suspicion. 'That's right,' she said. 'That's my son, Róbert.'

'Róbert?' said Áróra puzzled and then recalled the name the mysterious men had mentioned to Daníel. 'Róbert Þór Gíslason?'

'Yes,' said Fríða. 'But, I'm sorry, who did you say you were, and what can I do for you?'

Áróra threw up her hands. 'Yes, forgive me, this is a rather strange situation. You see, I'm actually here on behalf of my boyfriend, Daníel, who I mentioned before. He's looking for your son Róbert. Róbert rented an apartment from him, but two days ago he disappeared and Daníel needs to speak to him urgently. He's worried about him.'

Fríða considered Áróra for a long time then replied rather curtly. 'That is strange,' she said. 'Because my son died four years ago.'

53

Fríða handed Áróra a cup of coffee and apologized for only having instant.

'I always go to my local bar for coffee in the mornings,' she said. Then apologised again, this time for having no milk. 'I can't offer you anything with the coffee either. I decided to eat healthy food when I moved here, no gluten or dairy. It's easy because they have such a big choice of fresh vegetables and fish.'

Áróra nodded, smiling as she contemplated the woman. She certainly looked good on it. She appeared lively and active, and her skin was golden brown, so she didn't take the sun too much, unlike some Icelanders who went to live in warmer climes and ended looking like shrivelled-up leather.

Fríða's claim that her son had died four years earlier tallied with Róbert Þór Gíslason's date of death in the national register; however, having seen the image of the young high-school graduate on Fríða's wall, this made no sense to Áróra. She'd seen Lady Gúgúlú only recently over at Daníel's.

'I believe I dined with your son three or four weeks ago,' Áróra said, realising at once how callous this declaration sounded. She felt herself transformed, suddenly, into another Elísabet, announcing that a dead person was alive, so she quickly added: 'Or at least with a man who's the spitting image of your son, only older.' But Fríða merely smiled as if somehow this amused her. She didn't seem in the slightest bit upset.

Áróra pulled out her phone and found a picture she'd taken at Daníel's dinner party. There was Lady Gúgúlú perched on a high stool, half made up in preparation for her drag show later that evening, wearing the headband she used to keep her hair in place under her wig, but otherwise dressed casually, in jeans and a green T-shirt. Lady Gúgúlú had sat chatting with them while Daníel did the cooking, and when the meal was over she'd gone back to the garage to finish getting ready. It had been a fun evening. Helena and a few of Daníel's other friends on the force, Áróra and Lady.

Fríða looked at the photograph with an impassive expression. The hand in which she held the phone quaked slightly, but this could be normal. She was an older woman.

'And did the man in the photograph, your boyfriend's tenant who you dined with a few weeks ago, say he was Róbert Þór?' she asked then.

'No,' replied Áróra. 'He called himself Haraldur Gunnarsson, as well as Lady Gúgúlú, the stage name he uses for his drag shows at a nightclub in Reykjavík.'

Fríða smiled and looked as if she was stifling a laugh. 'Well, well,' she said and breathed a sigh. 'My son was certainly gay but he was no drag queen. He was a physicist.'

'Lady Gúgúlú also studied physics,' ventured Áróra, but Fríða instantly shook her head.

'This isn't the same man,' she said firmly. 'My son is dead. He drowned in the sea here on the western side of the island. I ident-ified his body.'

It was no use trying to persuade Fríða her son was alive and best known today as Lady Gúgúlú. Nor was it appropriate. No one knew this better than Áróra. She wasn't going to try to con-vince Fríða her son was alive, for the simple reason that she had no firm evidence to back it up. Without that it was wrong to raise people's hopes. She understood better now where Daníel was coming from, and his anger towards Elísabet.

'Had your son been here with you long in the Canary Islands when he died?'

'No, not long. He arrived from Thailand in the autumn and spent one winter here. And he didn't live with me. Naturally, he

wanted to be on Playa del Inglés, because it's livelier there and
he could meet more men like him, if I can say that. He rented a
room from a guy who had a holiday apartment there. But he
visited me here often, and sometimes we met halfway.'

Áróra rose and thanked Fríða for the coffee, then Fríða
walked her to the door. Áróra slung her bag over her shoulder
and turned back to Fríða.

'Has anyone else been here in the past few days asking about
your son?'

A look of panic now clouded Fríða's face. 'No. Who could
that be? Why would anyone come here? He died years ago.'
Áróra observed her closely. Clearly this had touched a nerve.
'Who could that be?' the woman insisted, her voice a little
shriller now.

Áróra smiled apologetically. 'I'm sure it's nothing to worry
about,' she said. In any event, it was good the mysterious men had
so far seen no reason to bother Fríða. She wondered whether she
should let the matter drop, or warn her. She went for the second
option. 'Some rather unsavoury individuals were looking for Lady
Gúgúlú back home in Iceland and they seemed quite convinced
that his real name is Róbert Þór Gíslason. The same as your son.'

Fríða's eyes darted from side to side as if she were searching
for a reply, then at last she murmured: 'Well, well.'

Áróra was making to open the front door when she noticed
a second photograph hanging next to it that she hadn't seen on
her way in. Another graduation picture, only this one was obviously taken at a foreign university. There was the young student
again, this time in a tasselled mortarboard and a red-and-blue
gown. Standing on one side of him was an older man, similarly
dressed, and on the other a man in a suit. Both wore proud expressions on their faces.

'Is that his father?' Áróra asked, pointing at the man in the
suit.

'No, this was taken when Róbert Þór was awarded his PhD at Oxford. The youngest doctor of physics ever to graduate from the university,' Fríða announced proudly. 'There he is with the man who tutored him on his final thesis, and the director of the company that hired him straight after he graduated.' Áróra narrowed her eyes and studied the director closely.

'What company was that?' she asked, and for the first time Fríða hesitated.

'...It's called BH Dynamic Systems,' Fríða said in hushed tones, as though reluctant to say the name of the company out loud. But then it was as if the floodgates had burst. 'They have headquarters in England, in the West Midlands. Róbert agreed to work for them because they promised he could continue the research he started at university. I never really understood what that was. Whether it was some sort of antimatter or radiology. I gave up trying to understand what it was he did long before he went to university—'

'And what sort of company is it?' Áróra cut in, realising that Fríða was babbling in order to try to dissimulate, to direct Áróra's attention elsewhere.

The reason for this became clear when she replied:

'Some sort of ... Yes. Arms manufacturer.'

54

The meeting room at the Children's House was spacious, and a large screen on the wall allowed people to follow the interviews with the children. These took place in a separate area, which most resembled someone's living room at home, with a sofa, a thick carpet and toys. Right now, though, the screen was switched off and the people who'd come to observe the interview with Ester Lóa were busy installing themselves at the table. A microphone had been set up where Daníel was sitting to enable him to communicate questions to the psychologist conducting the interview with the little girl. Next to him sat a young woman called Gunna, a recent recruit at the prosecutor's office, who Oddsteinn had no doubt sent along to observe. Next to her were two members of staff at the Children's House and at the far end, Marteinn, who represented Reykjavík Child Protection Services. They all sat facing the screen, and for a while an awkward silence prevailed in the room.

'Of course, you're aware that this isn't a formal investigation,' Daníel said at last, as if for the sake of saying something. 'Not for the moment, at any rate.'

'Judging from what Helena has told me, this is a most peculiar case,' said Marteinn, the child-protection officer, sliding his glasses down his nose then peering over them at those present.

'Yes, you could say that,' said Daníel. 'Ester Lóa – the three-year-old – is actually here at the request of her parents, who are at their wits' end, and claim to have no idea where their daughter got these stories from about her "past life".' He paused. 'And death.'

'The aim of this interview, then, is to look for signs of abuse?' asked Marteinn, holding his pen above his notepad, as though poised to jot down all the most important points. He seemed like the type who crossed all his t's and dotted all his i's.

'Not exactly,' said Daníel. 'We don't suspect abuse, at least not physical abuse, what we need to do is ascertain whether someone is feeding the child these things she's saying.'

Helena stood behind Daníel, shifting from foot to foot, debating whether to stay put or go and grab a chair from the kitchen. She decided it was preferable to have one on hand, in case the interview was drawn out and she got tired of standing. Better than having to slip out for one mid-interview. She had no intention of missing anything this curious, much-talked-about child had to say.

She left the meeting room and went into the kitchen. She was just picking up one of the chairs when out of the window she saw a car pull up and out of it stepped Elísabet. She put the chair down and walked over to the window. Lárus climbed out of the driver's side and opened the rear passenger door. He unstrapped the girl, who looked like a little pink bundle, and lifted her out of the child's seat. Then he took her round to the other side of the car, pausing on the pavement to slip her hand into her mother's. His eyes strayed up towards the building where they met those of Helena, who waved to him. He nodded tersely then turned on his heel and got back into the car, driving off just as mother and daughter toddled towards the entrance. In her puffy pink anorak, Ester Lóa looked no different from other little girls her age. Her skinny legs sticking out from beneath her anorak were also encased in pink, and as she skipped along by her mother's side, Helena was suddenly gripped by a peculiar sensation that reality was out of kilter, distorted. What could this happy little shrimp know about murder?

55

Áróra had to wait outside the house for a while for the taxi to arrive, and Fríða stood on the deck to keep her company. It had grown dark but there was a warm breeze, and Áróra enjoyed feeling it play on her skin. Fríða seemed most interested in chatting about Icelandic cuisine and customs, and in the end Áróra asked her if she'd ever move back home.

'No,' said the woman. 'I don't feel I can. Not since my son died here.'

Áróra knew the feeling. She couldn't imagine leaving Iceland before her sister's body was found. She'd already probed Fríða about her son's death. Some of the details didn't add up, and a theory was beginning to take shape in Áróra's head. Four years ago, Fríða had gone to the authorities after hearing that a body had been found in the sea off the west coast of Gran Canaria. The body was in bad shape yet she had identified it as her son, Róbert Þór Gíslason, who'd gone missing a week earlier. He was a keen sea swimmer, she said. She recognised his swimsuit. And his necklace. And the tattoo on his foot, protected by flippers from the small, flesh-eating sea creatures found in warm waters.

'Did they check his dental records?' Áróra asked tentatively, but Fríða seemed to have a ready answer.

'I'm not sure it was common practice over here then, but in any case they accepted my identification, bearing in mind what he was wearing, where he was found, and the likelihood of it being him. And in Róbert's case the tattoo was decisive. There's no doubt in my mind. I recognised the tattoo on his foot.'

Fríða adopted such a melancholy expression that Áróra couldn't bring herself to ask whether they'd taken any DNA samples for future use. She decided to let it drop, but when the taxi came trundling along the street she turned once more to Fríða.

'The reason I found you is because you're the legal heir to a summer house and some land close to Selfoss,' said Áróra, instantly noticing Fríða's surprise.

'Really? Well, well,' she said, her eyes darting from side to side, as if she were casting about desperately for something to say.

'Did you not know about it?' asked Áróra, and Fríða shook her head.

'No,' she replied. But then she said nothing. She didn't ask who was leaving her the property, or whether it might be some misunderstanding.

'You're the heir of a semi-homeless man by the name of Haraldur Gunnarsson, an ailing, amnesiac alcoholic who nevertheless owns this property. Do you have any idea why he chose to leave you his estate?'

Áróra expected the woman at any moment to refuse to answer any more of her questions, seeing as how she had no real right to interrogate her. But instead Fríða nodded slowly as though recollecting something.

'Ah yes, of course, Haraldur. Yes, that could make sense,' she said. 'He's an old friend of mine. Maybe he has nobody else.'

Áróra waved to Fríða from the back of the taxi. The woman's puzzled reaction when Áróra asked about the legacy, followed by her peculiar acknowledgment when she pretended to recall her 'old friend' Haraldur, was enough to tell Áróra she was lying. She was lying about everything. Including the death of her son. What Áróra needed to do was to find out why.

56

The photograph of his mother was old now, and he regretted not having the foresight to print out a more recent one from Facebook. He would occasionally sneak a look at her profile, using the various fake accounts he created in various internet cafés. He could see that she'd aged well and was enjoying life in the Canary Islands. But deep down inside he also knew that she felt a void in her life without him, just as he did without her. Still, she'd done a great job of helping him to disappear, and for this he would be eternally grateful to her, just as he was for everything else.

His mother had always been his rock. And the last four years were no exception, even though helping him had meant keeping her distance. Not that she had any choice – she had no idea where in the world he was. But he trusted she wouldn't go looking for him or ask about him, because she knew what was at stake. He felt an occasional pang of guilt when he imagined what she'd say if she knew that he'd been living at home for over four years now. In Iceland. In the same place, moreover. Hiding in plain sight.

He took the photograph down off the cupboard and kissed the glass, then wiped away his lip marks and a tear that had rolled down his cheek when he raised it to his mouth. He wished he could hold her close for real and kiss her warm cheek. The scent of her Nivea cream, her soft permed hair and the absolute certainty that she would always love him. No matter what he did.

She had demonstrated this more times than he cared to remember. The biggest confirmation of all, though, came when Róbert's father, having reached the end of his tether, threatened to send their son away to boarding school and she told him to leave. This happened after Róbert accidentally set the house on fire during one of his numerous experiments involving nail-varnish remover and vitamin tablets.

'It's not enough that he's turned our home into a laboratory for his experiments and that he dresses like a clown – the boy has become a downright menace!' his father had bellowed in the living room.

Robbi had wept as he lay with his ear pressed to the wall of his parents' bedroom, where he had to sleep on a mattress because his room was so badly damaged by fire. But what affected him most was not his father's anger but his mother's response. She replied that it wasn't easy to bring up a gifted child.

Two months after his father left, Robbi was invited to the United States to attend a month-long course for young scientists. When he came back his father picked him up at the airport and told him he and Robbi's mother were getting a divorce. He recalled rejoicing inwardly at the thought of having his mother all to himself, and he didn't realise until long afterwards the true extent of her sacrifice.

His mother had moved to England with him when he went up to Oxford. She looked after him, washed his clothes, prepared his meals and listened to his endless musings about physics, which he knew perfectly well she didn't understand, but which he was keen to share with her anyway. They had scraped by on his grant, his father's alimony payments, and the extra money his mother earned from child-minding and gardening for some of the dons. She'd taken care of her son all his life and then buried him with equal pride. Although of course it hadn't been a real funeral. But the drowned body nobody claimed had been a timely stroke of luck. And had bought him four years of tranquillity.

57

They all sat gaping at the child in astonishment. She seemed content to skip about the interview room at the Children's House and chat to the psychologist who sat on the floor and played with her. The little girl had a slender frame yet her head was disproportionately large, and Daníel tried to recall whether his children had such big heads when they were three years old. Or was it the curls that wreathed the child's face that gave her the same proportions as some of the dolls his daughter had when she was little. Great big heads and great big eyes. She was articulate, talkative and responded clearly to the psychologist's questions.

'Sometimes mummies or daddies or other people tell children that something is a secret. That they mustn't tell anyone about it. Do you have a secret like that?'

'No,' replied the girl. 'My mummy says you can tell mummies everything.'

'This is true,' said the psychiatrist. 'But do you have any secrets with your mummy? Something your mummy has told you, maybe about Ísafold, which you mustn't tell anyone else?'

'No.'

'Ask her again what her name is,' Daníel said into the microphone, and on the screen he saw the psychologist raise a finger to her ear to indicate that she'd heard him.

'My name is Birna,' began the psychologist. 'But I have a middle name, too. It's Lind. So my full name is Birna Lind Hjálmarsdóttir. That's because my daddy's name is Hjálmar and I'm his daughter. What about you?' She prodded the little girl's tummy with her finger and smiled. 'Do you have a middle name?'

'Lóa,' said the little girl. 'Ester Lóa Ísafold Jónsdóttir. She raised her hand in the air as if in triumph, like a player who's scored a goal.

'But isn't your daddy's name Lárus?'

'Yes,' replied the little one.

'Then why are you Jónsdóttir?'

This took the girl by surprise and she gazed at the psychologist through narrowed eyes. This time she replied more deliberately. 'Ester Lóa Ísafold Jónsdóttir and also Lárusdóttir,' she said, cocking her head as though reflecting about this herself. 'My old daddy is called Jón but my other daddy is called Lárus.'

Daníel heaved a sigh. He had exhausted his list of questions about Ísafold's past, and the girl had responded to them all, on the button. Even questions to which he was sure no answers could be found online, and which he'd got straight from Áróra. Names of Ísafold's ex-boyfriends. Details about their camping trips to Þingvellir as teenagers. And when Ester Lóa talked about their pet rabbit dying when they were little, she'd burst into tears and the psychologist had to comfort her.

Daníel leaned in to the microphone again. 'Could we have a word please, Birna?' He watched on screen as the psychologist clambered to her feet.

'I'm going to fetch a drink of juice for us,' she said to the child and walked out of the room. One of the staff members at Children's House, Daníel couldn't recall his name, hurried to the kitchen and dashed back carrying two cartons of fruit juice, which he handed to Daníel.

Outside the door to the interview room, Daníel gave them to the psychologist while they spoke in low voices.

'I don't know what else to tell you,' the psychologist said. 'I find her very plausible.'

'You mean she's been well coached?' asked Daníel.

'No, I mean I see no reason to disbelieve her. It's extremely difficult to coach a child this young this well. Ester Lóa may have the language skills of a five or six year old, but it doesn't follow that her memory and her other intellectual faculties are equally well developed. I find it very hard to believe that someone has been able to coach this child to say all the things she's saying and at the same time forbid her from saying who coached her.'

'Don't tell me you believe she really is Ísafold Jónsdóttir re-incarnated?' Daníel couldn't help giving a little snort.

'Why not? Belief in reincarnation isn't widespread in our culture, naturally, but it's a well-documented phenomenon, you know. This case is by no means unusual; plenty of children claim they can recall past lives. I did my homework before I came here.'

Daníel shrugged. 'Okay,' he said simply, at a loss for words. This whole thing was getting stranger and stranger. 'If you think she's ready, could you get her to talk about how she...' he paused '...died. That's to say, ask her about Ísafold Jónsdóttir's death.'

Birna nodded and went back into the interview room, closing the door behind her. Daníel returned to the meeting room, where the two staff members, Gunna, Helena and the child-protection officer sat staring at the screen. Daníel's thoughts whirled. Somehow the psychologist's words had stirred up new possibilities. Up until now his focus had been on pinning down the parents. Finding some discrepancy in the child's story that proved they had coached their own daughter and that they possessed information they shouldn't have. Information that suggested some involvement in Ísafold's disappearance.

Daníel's reverie was interrupted by the child's soft voice emanating from the screen.

'Could you say that a little louder so I can hear you better?' said the psychologist gently. The two of them sat facing each other on the floor, almost in a yoga pose, Birna clasping the hand of the little girl, whose expression now betrayed a look of dread.

'I woke up and then I was inside the suitcase and everything shook and it hurt so much. I saw a hole and I stuck my finger through and pulled the zip and I saw the ice-bear was dragging me across the lava in the suitcase. Black lava, and I heard some scraping, and strange noises and the ice-bear was crying. And then I fell. Inside the suitcase. I tried to call and call to the ice-bear, but I heard him drive away in the car.' The girl fell silent and the psychiatrist looked at her for a few moments without saying anything, still clasping her hand.

'And then I became Ester Lóa,' the little girl said, suddenly joyful, and she leapt to her feet and seized a doll from the toy box. 'Ester Lóa Ísafold.'

THURSDAY

58

Áróra would have been delighted to spend a day or two basking in the sun and heat in Tenerife. Instead she'd taken a selfie outside the hotel, with palm trees in the background, and posted it on social media above the caption 'Canary baby!' Then she jumped in a taxi and watched the orange-yellow sunrise as she sped back to the airport.

It could be said her trip to the Canary Islands was a bit of a failure. She'd been so convinced that Lady Gúgúlú, whose name she now knew was Róbert Þór, was at his mother's that she hadn't given too much thought to whether the trip was really worthwhile. However, she had brought back new evidence, and that was good. Arguably she could have obtained this over the phone, although she wasn't sure whether Friða would have told her about her son having worked for a big arms manufacturer. Áróra had to drag that information out of her.

After spending the previous evening browsing the BH Dynamic Systems website, Áróra discovered that the company produced various types of missile, missile launchers, mortars and drones, as well as surveillance equipment. But mostly they seemed to lead the field in the development of new types of weapons and surveillance equipment for the military. Their website was adorned with Leonardo da Vinci's drawings and diagrams of war machines, and the yellow-beige parchment made an incongruously attractive background for their missiles and bombs. Áróra couldn't wait to see what kind of reception BH Dynamic Systems gave her when she went there to ask about Róbert Þór Gíslason. She felt sure she would quickly be able to determine whether the company was behind his disappearance, or whether they had something bigger to hide.

Now, as the plane began its descent towards Birmingham Airport, Áróra pressed her forehead up to the porthole and contemplated the landscape below. It was strikingly different to Iceland. A patchwork of green fields broken only by grey roads and a smattering of brown brick villages, which would multiply as they drew closer to the city and finally merge with it. She looked forward to stepping off the plane and breathing in the air. The English spring was glorious. Green, lush and warm. As if joy arrived with the spring birds that came to nest and settle there. In Iceland the spring months were mostly about waiting. People closely followed the weather forecasts and discussed them at length, speculated about when it might be safe to buy flowering plants for their balconies without them withering in an overnight frost. And the first sighting of migrating birds made headline news.

All of a sudden a strange thought occurred to Áróra. What would she do if they found Ísafold? If they found her body, and she and her mother were able to lay her to rest beside their father. When Áróra's mission in Iceland was at last over, would she want to go on living there? Gazing down at the greenness of spring on the ground below, she wasn't sure.

59

It had been a morning from hell for Daníel, in which he'd been assailed with questions from all sides. After the interview at the Children's House, Child Protection Services had decided to remove Ester Lóa from the family home on the grounds she was possibly being exposed to harmful content there, as well as suspected physical abuse. While Daníel had to admit he felt extremely uncomfortable sitting and listening to the child's flute-like voice describe serious physical injuries, the decision by Child Protection Services placed the police in an awkward position. It stepped up pressure on the investigation, moving it beyond the level of an informal enquiry. What's more, he knew it was only a matter of time before the commissioner took the case away from him.

Checking his call register he saw he'd clocked up nearly thirty conversations that morning. A few were him attempting to persuade Child Protection Services to work with the police and take a more measured approach, others were from the media, who'd got wind of the story, several were with the commissioner, and still more were with the girl's parents, who were understandably unhappy. The last time they spoke, Elísabet had shouted at him that they'd trusted the police and had asked the authorities to help them find explanations, only to be let down. This wasn't entirely true, of course; they hadn't gone first to the authorities but to Áróra. Daníel tried his best to calm her down, to explain how this might look from the outside. When a young, innocent child spoke about a murder in such precise detail, it was natural to assume she'd either witnessed something dreadful, or someone had told her these things. And in both instances they had good reason to suspect the parents' involvement. Then again, Daníel wasn't in the best position to explain this knee-jerk response from Child Protection Services, as he himself had wanted to rule out the most obvious possibilities first. Did these ideas come from something she'd seen on TV? Or had her parents, with their knowledge of Icelandic true crimes, and therefore Ísafold's case, simply made the wrong assumptions and then things had spiralled out of control?

It had just gone twelve and Daníel was already collapsing with fatigue. He longed to go home to bed and put a pillow over his head so he couldn't hear the phone. But that wasn't an option. He sat at his desk, turned on the computer and searched the police database, LÖKE, for the report on Ísafold's disappearance. Not because he didn't know it off by heart. But there was no harm in reading through it once more in the light of what little Ester Lóa had said yesterday. And he would take a close look at the forensics on Björn's car.

60

Helena's whole body was telling her she shouldn't have drunk two energy drinks on top of her morning coffee. Her nerves were strung out on caffeine, her feet jogging up and down rapidly under the table of their own accord, as if to burn off some of her excess energy. What she most wanted was to go for a run, but unfortunately her current task required no physical movement whatsoever. She'd been assigned to draw up a list of Ester Lóa's contacts and cross-check them with those of Ísafold Jónsdóttir. She'd finished going through all the child's relatives and found no obvious connections, besides those that were common enough in Iceland – people on both lists who'd been to the same school, belonged to the same sports club at different times, possibly lived in the same neighbourhood – but nothing to indicate a direct link.

She had also been through the staff roster at Ester Lóa's nursery and was waiting for an email giving her the names of all the children in her year, as well as those of their parents. The nursery had refused to give her this list, as Helena didn't have a warrant, so she'd called the city's education department and spoken to someone who allowed her to have a copy after she'd pointed out how bad it might look for the nursery if the police were obliged to get a court order, and how this might be misinterpreted in a number of ways – or words to that effect. Since the advent of social media and its ability to magnify anything that suggested the slightest whiff of a scandal, public-sector institutions had become terrified of gossip.

Helena's computer gave a soft ping to tell her she had new mail. She clicked on the message. The list was more exhaustive than she'd expected and included every child enrolled at the nursery, rather than only those in Ester Lóa's year. Also, since it was in a PDF file, she was obliged to copy and paste the document into Excel to be able to organize it by date of birth. Elísabet had already told them the classes at the nursery were divided by age group, so she would look at the children Ester Lóa's age and their parents to check whether any of the names appeared in Ísafold's contacts or on the police database.

A familiar name jumped out at her as soon as she clicked on the document. Grímur. That rang a bell. She opened the Ísafold file in LÖKE, and there he was. Ísafold had a neighbour called Grímur. She looked back at the list of nursery children. The boy's full name was Grímur Þorláksson and he was three and a half. Might he be the neighbour's grandson? Did Ester Lóa have any contact with little Grímur's family outside school? Did they have weekend play dates? And had Grandpa Grímur maybe been visiting and filled the little friend's head with tales of something he'd experienced? If Helena remembered correctly, Ísafold's neighbour Grímur suffered from mental-health problems.

The caffeine was driving Helena's thoughts faster than she could process them, and her heart pounded in her chest as if she were running flat out. Her hand shook as she clicked again on the school list to check the little boy's parents' surnames. A burst of disappointment shot thought her like a flame, and she felt like letting out a stream of obscenities. Little Grímur's father's patronymic wasn't Grímsson but Guðmundsson. And his mother's was Kristjánsdóttir. No sign of any grandfather named Grímur there.

Damn. She'd hoped she might discover some connection. Something she could take to Daníel and announce triumphantly that she'd found the thread. But maybe it wasn't only that she hoped to make Daníel and the commissioner happy, and get an appreciative pat on the back. Maybe, like most of the other people involved in this case, she was hoping to find a rational explanation for Ester Lóa's stories of her supposed past life.

61

Róbert vividly recalled the sensation that had gripped him when his laboratory was being built. It was anxiety, pure and simple. He'd sat with his back against a warehouse north of the site, watching the carpenters struggle to assemble the rafters with wooden dowels, to a man no doubt cursing him under their breath. Experts in medieval craftsmanship had been called in to instruct them, and seeing as how Róbert wasn't permitted to, nor could he in any simple way, explain what they were going to make inside this building, he murmured something about how the laboratory mustn't contain any metal because he was working with magnets. The outside consisted of a double layer of brick, then three metres of sand for insulation, half a metre of concrete, reinforced with fibre glass not steel, and finally, on the inside, wood panelling assembled with dowels.

As he sat there on the ground, watching this enormous undertaking, his heart had quivered with anxiety. He had estimated the approximate half-life and was fairly sure his calculations were correct, but without any data it was impossible for him to know exactly how much insulation was needed. And then there was the question of whether the project would bear any fruit. He'd been brimming with confidence when he first signed the contract; he'd even wondered whether the research grants he'd received, together with his projected salary, weren't a bit excessive. However, in the context of this vast enterprise, which itself must have cost a small fortune, he realised it hadn't been too high at all.

He'd been convinced of his success. All his experiments and calculations stood up to scrutiny, so in theory everything worked. But as he sat on the dusty ground, the carpenters darting glances at him, their expressions a mixture of contempt and bewilderment, he felt painfully aware of being a twenty-four-year-old brat who probably had no idea what he was doing.

He was roused from his reverie by a golf buggy skidding to a halt beside him. Out stepped the cute secretary from reception. Actually he was the director's son and he looked like a supermodel.

'How do you like your house?' the cute guy asked, contemplating the building.

'It's fine,' replied Róbert forcing a smile. 'I'm just having a few doubts about whether my calculations are right and the walls will hold up. Whether there's enough insulation.'

'Oh, don't worry,' said the secretary. 'Our contractors can build a shelter that will withstand an atomic blast.' Obviously this was untrue, but Róbert appreciated his attempt to boost his spirits. 'You've been summoned to His Highness's office,' the secretary said then, at which Róbert sprang to his feet, brushing the sand off his trousers.

After he'd installed himself in the buggy, the secretary extended a hand. 'Colin,' he said.

Róbert returned the gesture, politely introducing himself. 'Robert Thor,' he said, using the English pronunciation of his name, and Colin smiled.

'I know who you are. Everyone knows who you are. You're our star, our brightest promise. Dad's, I mean His Highness's, favourite boy. I'm not supposed to call him Dad at work, you see.' Róbert laughed and Colin finally released his hand.

Colin drove the buggy off with a screech then proceeded to career between buildings like a madman, his foot flat on the accelerator. Of course, they couldn't go very fast, but enough to churn up clouds of dust, as only the compound's main road was tarmacked – all the others were dirt tracks. Róbert laughed even as he hung on for dear life, and his anxiety dissipated fleetingly and he felt a spark of joy in his heart.

Colin stopped the buggy next to the smaller of the two administrative buildings and pointed to where a brand-new golf buggy stood on charge.

'There you are,' he said. 'That's your car. The latest model with a top speed of around thirty kilometres an hour. HQ doesn't want you wandering round the compound. I think they're afraid they might lose you. Dad also said I should do everything I can to make life easier for you so you can build your superbomb in peace.' He went quiet. 'I don't think Dad quite realises how I might interpret the word "*everything*".' Colin fluttered his eyelids at Róbert, who choked on his saliva and spluttered awkwardly. Was the director's son flirting with him? Colin tossed him the key to the new buggy before vanishing inside the building.

Róbert climbed aboard his new buggy, switched on the ignition and reversed out of the parking lot. He trundled over to the main headquarters, a much flashier building than reception, where Colin's job was to register visitors to the compound. Could this amazingly beautiful man actually fancy him? Skinny, quirky Róbert, who everyone said looked like a nerd? Surely Colin was misquoting his father when he said he'd told him to do everything he could for Róbert. It was obvious he played fast and loose with the truth, since Róbert knew full well his father hadn't told him he was building a superbomb. He certainly wasn't building any bomb in the new laboratory.

62

It was quite a walk from the visitors' car park up to the perimeter fence, and Áróra became warm in the sun. Needless to say, this was the sort of temperature Icelanders could only hope for on the hottest day of summer. If weather like this hit Reykjavík, everyone rushed out to the shops to buy barbecue meat, having already invited their friends for a garden party and invested in sun lotion. Here in the Midlands it was just an ordinary April day, the sun was in the sky, the temperature seventeen or eighteen degrees, and the shrubs along the perimeter fence at BH Dynamic Systems flowering red and yellow.

The main gate into the compound was huge, wide enough for two trucks to pass, but there was no pedestrian gate to be seen. Glancing about, Áróra realised the entrance was through the low office building facing the car park. Next to the door a small notice said *Sign in here*. Clearly they didn't expect too many visitors to the factory. As she approached, the doors slid open automatically and a low buzz came from within, no doubt to alert the receptionist sitting at the front desk opposite the doors.

The man glanced up and smiled winningly at Áróra, who thought to herself he must have got the job because of his good looks. He had dark hair, an oval face, a strong jawline with a five o'clock shadow, despite being clean shaven, and a bright, cheerful smile.

'How can I help you?' he asked.

Áróra walked up to the desk, leaned forward slightly to read the man's badge and smiling amicably as she addressed him by his name. 'Well, Colin,' she said. 'It would be great if you could. I need to speak to the personnel manager, or somebody in human resources.'

'Aha,' said Colin, typing something into his computer. 'In that case you want either Mary or Alfred,' he added, as if talking to himself rather than her. 'Alfred's here in the building. I'll send him a message.' He smiled then suddenly looked worried. 'Unless this is a wage issue, in which case you need to speak to someone in accounts.'

Áróra shook her head. 'No, no. I'm a private investigator. I came here to ask about one of your former employees, Róbert Þór Gíslason. Perhaps you could look him up for me on your computer?'

A look of unease came over the receptionist's face and he grew a little agitated. He leaned in and was about to say something to Áróra when a stout, middle-aged man with a beer belly appeared in the doorway.

'Did you call me?' asked the man, and all of a sudden Colin seemed to recoil. Áróra made to introduce herself when the man's phone rang in his pocket and he pulled it out.

'Hello?' he said into the phone, smiling apologetically at Áróra, who nodded her head. She took a seat on a bench next to the front desk, eyeing the receptionist while she waited. She was curious to know what he'd been going to say. He was now looking down, fumbling with something on his desk. She'd have a word with him on her way out.

The stout man's call didn't take long, and after he'd finished he turned once more towards Áróra. 'Kindly accompany me to my office,' he said amicably, and Áróra rose to follow him.

But Colin suddenly leapt from behind his desk and stood in her way. 'Allow me to take your jacket,' he said, thrusting his hands forward. Áróra hadn't intended to take off her jacket. It was only a lightweight blazer and the building was quite chilly. But something about the secretary's expression made her decide to do as he said, and she slipped off the jacket and passed it to him. He took it, and as he draped the jacket over his arm his hand emerged from among the folds and pressed a crumpled piece of paper into Áróra's palm. She clasped it tight then followed the stout man out into a corridor.

He turned around and smiled apologetically. 'This place is full of corridors,' he said, still smiling, and Áróra smiled back. She continued to follow the man, a few steps behind him, and managed to steal a glance at the note while he wasn't looking.

Don't ask about R! the message said. *Dangerous! Meet me at the Angry Ox at 6.*

63

Colin tried his best not to get agitated as he watched the woman disappear down the corridor with Alfred, the personnel manager. The name Róbert always sent his thoughts into free-fall, and a feeling of dread invaded him. Hopefully the woman would read his note before she went into Alfred's office, and once inside refrain from mentioning Róbert. There was a red flag next to his name on every staff list, meaning security were supposed to question anyone who came asking about him. And this woman seemed oblivious to the trouble she was about to get herself into. In the note he'd made an attempt to meet her in private to warn her not to go asking questions but it might be too late. And maybe she had some information. Maybe she knew something that might confirm his own suspicions: namely that Róbert was alive somewhere.

Because Colin didn't really believe Róbert was dead. Not anymore. After his death had been announced, twice – on the second occasion he'd attended Róbert's funeral in the Canary Islands and mourned him for real – the indications he'd received, the gifts that kept arriving, had convinced him that Róbert was in some remote backwater somewhere and thought about Colin every so often and what they once had together.

The first announcement came as a shock. Colin's father had called him to his office and put on a face intended to convey sorrow, but which failed to conceal from Colin his sense of relief.

'It pains me to tell you this, but it seems that Robert Thor, or Thor as we always called him here, has passed away,' his father said. 'They found him two days ago in a hotel in Bangkok with a needle in his arm. Apparently he died of an overdose.' It had taken Colin a while to digest the news. Firstly, the idea that

Róbert might be dead was so unreal, and secondly it made no sense at all.

'That's impossible,' he said to his father, sinking into one of the easy chairs in his office. 'Róbert isn't a drug addict.'

His father gave a sympathetic sigh. 'A lot can happen in three years,' he said. 'People change, they adopt different life-styles. Meet new people.'

Colin felt a flash of anger at this last remark. His father had always tried to insinuate that Róbert left him for somebody else. He seemed to think if he could change Colin's mind about Róbert, Colin would be sure to tell him if Róbert ever got in touch. When Róbert first disappeared comments such as 'Robert Thor stole from us' or 'Robert Thor has moved on to new hunting grounds' had wounded Colin deeply, but with time they lost their sting and merely made him resent his father more.

'I don't believe Róbert became a junkie in the space of three years,' he declared emphatically. His father sighed once more, exaggerating the phony look of compassion on his face, which made Colin leap to his feet and yell at him.

'If Róbert died of an overdose it's because of you!'

His father rose from his seat. 'Stop this nonsense, Colin. It's no use getting hysterical. I understand that you're upset, but this is unworthy of you.' His father walked over to Colin and placed a hand on his shoulder, and as always when his father showed him affection Colin's eyes filled with tears.

'I know he took his invention with him when he disappeared,' sniffed Colin. 'But I also know that you—'

His father cut him off before he could finish his sentence. 'We,' he said. 'Don't talk about this company as if it were no concern of yours. The shares I own make you a shareholder in BHDS, and you're also an employee. So while you continue to receive a salary from the company that you so evidently despise, I'd be obliged if you used the word "we".'

'Very well,' Colin said, brushing his father's hand off his shoulder. '*We* have been hounding Róbert for the last three years, and if he died of an overdose it's because *we* injected the drug into him.'

'You should listen to yourself, Colin. You need to calm down. You're not thinking straight,' said his father. 'Naturally we want to find Robert Thor. He ran off with an investment worth tens of millions of pounds, which for all we know he intended to sell on the black market. This makes it a matter of national security as well as affecting our credibility as a business. But of course we don't go around killing people. What utter nonsense!'

Colin, who had started for the door, now swung round. 'I think you should listen to yourself, Dad,' he retorted. '*Our* business is precisely about killing people.'

He had slammed the door behind him, but when he got home that evening and had finished crying his eyes out, he called his father to apologise. He'd already lost Róbert; he couldn't bear the thought of losing his father too.

64

Daníel had painstakingly examined all the results of the forensic tests on Björn's car. The Luminol had showed up positive in the boot, where they'd found what at first sight appeared to be a large bloodstain that someone had scrubbed clean. However, subsequent analysis of the samples taken from the scene revealed it to be urine. Containing traces of blood – but urine all the same. And this was actually a stronger piece of evidence, because with blood, Björn might have argued that he was transporting meat. They'd had a previous case where a suspect accused of assault and imprisoning his victim in the boot of his car, claimed the blood traces in his boot came from some frozen lamb he'd brought in from the countryside, which had thawed and leaked through the box. But that wouldn't explain the presence of urine. Urine indicated that a person had been shut inside the boot.

Daníel's concentration was broken yet again by the desk phone ringing. He gave a sigh and got ready to hear the commissioner's voice, but it was reception downstairs.

'There's a man here who wants to talk to you,' said the caller. 'You need to come down.' Daníel heard an angry voice in the background, haranguing those present about the incompetence of the police and Child Protection Services. Daníel scrambled to his feet and raced downstairs.

Lárus was in the foyer, pacing this way and that like a caged animal. Daníel had the impression from his gestures that at any moment he was liable to pounce and strike him, but instead Lárus seemed to freeze when he saw Daníel and simply stood staring at him, his body quivering like a ticking time bomb.

'Come outside with me, Lárus,' said Daníel opening the door. 'We'll take a stroll, go for a coffee and have a quiet chat together.'

Lárus followed him outside and down the steps, Daníel setting straight off along Hverfisgata while Lárus quickened his pace to catch up with him. Moving would calm Lárus.

They'd covered a fair distance when Daníel turned towards him. 'The best thing you and your wife can do is to stay calm. Don't lose your temper and don't talk to the media. Just try to get through this without making things worse.'

Clearly this advice was ill-timed because Lárus stopped dead in his tracks, like a horse pulling up, and now his simmering rage boiled over. 'Stay calm?' he yelled at the top of his lungs. 'Stay calm? After you've taken our daughter away from us? As if we were some sort of criminals?' Daníel was grateful for the traffic noise on Hverfisgata, which partially drowned out Lárus's shouts so they didn't unduly alarm the tourists on the other side of the road.

'I understand that you're shocked and angry...' Daníel broke off mid-sentence as Lárus lunged forward, raising his arm as if to grab Daníel's shoulder.

He shouted, 'You understand nothing—'

And now Daníel cut him off. The movement was automatic, imprinted in his body memory after years on the beat, nearly every weekend subduing drunk men who got aggressive with bouncers, fellow club-goers or terrified spouses in their living rooms at home. Daníel grabbed Lárus by the wrist, placed his free hand on Lárus's shoulder and leaned forward with a rapid movement. It was a less painful hold than twisting someone's arm behind their back, required less force and looked better in the eyes of possible onlookers. Unbalancing a person in this way forced them down onto their knees and made it impossible for them to fight back. Ari Benz had taught him the technique years ago, maintaining it was the best way to avoid getting your uniform vomited on.

'Stop shouting,' Daníel said, calmly but firmly. 'I'm going to hold you like this until you've taken three deep breaths and stopped struggling, okay? It won't help your situation if I have to arrest you for disturbing the peace.'

The tourists across the road had come to a halt and were staring at them open-mouthed, and drivers who had stopped at the lights were staring too. Daníel saw some of them pull out their phones. One took a picture and at least one made a call. No doubt to the police to report a violent incident on Hverfisgata. Daníel turned his face away. He didn't have a free hand to show his police badge, which was hanging on a lanyard round his neck, and, besides, an officer of the law subduing a pedestrian in broad daylight would probably look even worse on social media. Instead he focused his attention on telling Lárus to breathe in and out slowly and hold the in-breath for a count of four. After he'd done this three times, Daníel felt Lárus's body relax and he released his hold on him. He pulled Lárus to his feet and gave him a friendly clap on the back.

'Now let's go and have a coffee and a snack at the Grey Cat.'

65

On his note the receptionist had written *The Angry Ox* and Áróra realised instantly this was a pub. As soon as she reached the car park outside the arms factory and climbed into the hire car, she opened the map on her phone and quickly found the place. In fact it was quite close by. He probably stopped off there after work, as the pub was right next to a train station. It was close on six o'clock and seemed a bit silly not to wait and offer the guy a lift. That was the Icelandic way. Always offering people lifts. Then again, he obviously didn't want to be seen talking to her, and if what he said in his note was true about it being dangerous to ask about Róbert Þór at the company, then she'd better err on the safe side.

She'd given the personnel manager a big spiel about how she was writing an article for the local newspaper focusing on job prospects for young people in Birmingham. He had extolled the virtues of the company before rising to his feet and accompanying her back to the foyer, where he told the receptionist to give her some brochures.

It took her four minutes to drive to The Angry Ox, which was located in a modern, rather box-like building, that had been made to look traditional in a rather lavish way. Green-painted timber cladding covered the corner where the pub was, and flower baskets hung next to the windows. Áróra found a parking space further down the street and sauntered back to the pub. The pavement tables and the stillness of the air made her want to sit outside, but first she entered the pub and joined the queue at the bar. In front of her was a crowd of people thirsty for beer, no doubt employees from the surrounding factories, and she had to wait a while before being served. At last she had a beer in her hand and was sampling it when a voice rang out behind her.

'There are too many people in here. Meet me instead at *The Distillery* by the canal.'

Áróra wheeled round and met the furtive-looking gaze of the receptionist just as he turned on his heel, weaved his way through the crowd and out of the pub. She followed suit, but when she emerged onto the pavement he had gone. She took two sips of her ice-cold beer before mournfully abandoning the glass on one of the outside tables. Still, it was preferable not to have drunk even a small glass of beer, considering she now had to drive into the centre of Birmingham and negotiate the city's aptly named Spaghetti Junction.

It took her half an hour to get there, find a place to park and walk along the canal to the restaurant, which was a converted brewery. After entering, Áróra spotted the receptionist seated at a booth table at the far end of the room, where he couldn't be seen from the outside or from the doorway. She took a seat opposite him and contemplated the food on the table.

'I decided to order some small plates for us,' he said. 'Since we'll probably be here for some time. I think we have a lot to talk about.'

66

Róbert had been terrified when he gave his first presentation, although soon after he started he realised he had no reason to be.
He had opened proceedings with the party trick he'd used at the
university when he originally presented his work to BHDS. On
the table stood an enormous crate of bananas. After the clients
had entered the laboratory, clad in the blue overalls with Velcro
fastenings and felt shoes they'd been supplied with before climbing aboard the golf buggies, he walked around handing each of
them a banana. Seeing the director of BH cheerfully accept his,
the visitors felt obliged to do likewise. Róbert had no idea who
these people were, as he wasn't privy to that information, but he
thought they looked Chinese. After they'd more or less finished
their bananas, he began the presentation.

'Each of you has just eaten a radioactive banana,' he said,
watching the men as they became uneasy, some of them ex-
changing glances while one or two grinned knowingly. 'Don't
worry,' Róbert went on. 'They're perfectly normal bananas, but
something we rarely think about is that all bananas are slightly
radioactive because they contain high levels of potassium, which
is a radioactive substance. However, they would need to contain
much higher levels of potassium for this radioactivity to affect
the human body.' The men smiled courteously and Róbert continued.

'We're surrounded by radiation in our everyday lives: our
food can be radioactive, the materials we use to build our houses,
the stone work surfaces in our kitchens. The sun itself, which
gives life to us all, is radioactive, and will scorch us to death if
we bathe in its rays for too long. Also, the devices taken from
you at the entrance, your mobile phones, emit substantial

amounts of radiation. Under normal circumstances, none of these things are harmful to us. The same is true of our creation. Pax.'

He opened the box on the table, and the men instinctively moved closer to peer inside. They murmured their acknowledgement, although Róbert was perfectly aware the small blob inside the glass sphere wasn't an eye-catching showpiece. He turned to one of his assistants and told him to bring in the steel rod.

'Imagine if it were possible to manipulate isotopes in such a way that the effects of radiation were reversed. Enabling them to pass with relative ease through stone or water, but without affecting living tissue. That the density of potassium in a banana, and consequently in the human body, wasn't high enough for the radiation to harm us, but that once the density in steel reached a certain mass its effects became evident. As is the case with this steel rod.'

The assistant returned with the steel rod and handed it to the director, who smiled before passing it to the nearest visitor.

'Keep it moving along,' said the director amicably, as the five-kilo steel rod passed from hand to hand. The first client to receive it gave an awkward smile, lifting it up and down as if he thought they were supposed to be impressed by its weight. The fifth, however, looked suitably surprised and cried out in alarm as the steel rod began to bend in his hands. The next also let out a cry as the rod oozed slowly between his fingers like playdough.

'Radiation as we've known it hitherto tempers steel and makes it more brittle. Pax, in contrast, softens steel,' Róbert declared proudly.

The men gathered around the piece of steel, and when the director stepped forward and squeezed it firmly, leaving behind the imprint of his hand as if it were clay, the visitors lost their fear of touching the softened steel and burst into cries of joy and laughter.

'For this reason, your colleague who has an artificial hip, and the other one with amalgam fillings had to wait in the office instead of witnessing Pax with their own eyes.' The director now pointed inside the box and the visitors gathered round once more to contemplate the small red-black blob, this time with the respect it warranted. 'May I present to you our latest weapon. A weapon that saves human lives. A weapon that will turn potentially bloody conflicts between nations into trivial squabbles. The world's first victimless weapon. Named after the Roman goddess of peace: Pax.'

67

'Is he alive?' was the first thing Colin the receptionist asked Áróra after she'd sat down.

'Do you have any reason to think that he isn't?' she responded.

'Yes,' said Colin. 'And no. Róbert was declared dead four years ago, but since then I've received proof he's alive.'

'What sort of proof?' asked Áróra, and Colin smiled mysteriously.

'Things I've been sent from online stores here and there, paid for by cards in different names. And always things that had, you know, a symbolic meaning. For us. For me and him. First it was a pair of golfing gloves, because, believe it or not, we met in a golf buggy. Then a book about Frida Kahlo, because sometimes we'd dress up as Frida and go into town. And so it went on, with some package or other arriving at least once a year. Last time it was a wonderful espresso machine. We're both terrible coffee snobs.' Áróra nodded, reached for the basket of chips and emptied some onto her plate. Colin looked at her pensively. 'You're not surprised, are you?' he said. 'You know he's alive?'

'Yes,' said Áróra. 'At least, he was a few weeks ago when I dined with him round at my boyfriend's.' She pulled out her phone and found the photo of Lady Gúgúlú at the aforementioned dinner. Perched on a kitchen stool in a T-shirt but wearing spectacular make-up. 'That's to say if this is the man we're talking about.'

Colin took the phone from her and stared at the screen. Then he placed two fingers on it, zoomed in on Lady Gúgúlú's face and continued to stare. All at once his eyes filled with tears, and they rolled down his cheeks. Then he set the phone down brusquely on the table, got to his feet and stalked off towards the toilets. Evidently seeing the photograph had had a powerful effect on him.

While Colin was collecting himself, Áróra took the opportunity to order half a pint of house ale, which contained the precise amount of alcohol Daníel had told her she could safely drink with a meal and not be over the limit. Then she tucked into her food. It was the typical English pub fare – sausage and mash, steak and kidney pie, scampi and chips – only served on tapas plates, and it made Áróra think of her mother, whom she realised she genuinely missed. She didn't feel guilt over not going to visit her even though she was in England; she really truly missed her. When she and her sister were small, the family would sometimes go out to the local pub for lunch on weekends, and her mother probably still did. Áróra could imagine her tucking into steak and kidney pie, mashed potato, carrots and peas. The peas shiny and green, not grey and shrivelled in their skins like in Iceland. And the potato unsweetened. This was a source of disagreement between their parents. Their dad liked his mash with sugar, Icelandic style, but their mum found it revolting. Áróra sided with their mum over this, while Ísafold backed their dad.

Colin seemed more composed when he came back and sat down opposite her at the table.

'I grieved his loss four years ago,' he said. 'When he was declared dead. That was five years after he disappeared. So it's been nine years since I last saw him. He simply vanished one day, left a note saying he'd gone to see his mother.' Exactly the same as with Daníel, thought Áróra. A note on the kitchen table instead of a proper goodbye. 'Then came the first announcement – of two – that he was dead. Allegedly of a heroin overdose in Thailand. But that turned out to be a mistake. Two years later a body was found in the Canary Islands and Róbert's mother identified it as that of her son. I went to the funeral and cried my heart out for everything we had together that was lost forever.'

Áróra thought Colin might burst into tears again, but instead he took a long swig of beer and sighed.

'And then the gifts began to arrive from various corners of the world, and I imagined him like a nomad with a backpack or maybe a smallholding somewhere in Thailand. He once said if he ever resigned from BH Dynamic Systems, he'd buy a plot of land somewhere and grow vegetables. He was forever talking about Thailand.'

'Did he resign from BH before he disappeared?' asked Áróra, and Colin grew visibly uneasy.

'You're a private investigator, aren't you?' he asked. 'I can't discuss anything that goes on in the company. I'm bound by a confidentiality agreement.'

68

Róbert didn't recall exactly when the reality of it dawned on him. For a long time Pax had been no more than an idea. A scientific theory. And then it grew into a blob the size of a fingernail, a tiny globe that was fun to play with. A sort of party trick that left his guests in awe, marvelling over their host's magic skills and wanting to know how he did it. Which of course he wasn't at liberty to say, since BHDS owned the exclusive rights to Pax and its formula.

But it was probably sometime between his last and second to last presentations that he began to wonder about the identity of the buyers. He had expected to meet people in the metallurgy industry, whom the director had assured him would be among their biggest customers. Manufacturers of all kinds were bound to be interested in something that removed the need to use energy to melt steel, which could henceforth be moulded like clay simply by running it through a Pax chamber. Róbert had looked forward to seeing their reactions. But gradually it dawned on him that the ones most interested in Pax were BHDS's habitual clients: arms dealers and the military. Colin had whispered to him that the Russians were interested in using Pax to create some sort of protective belt around their border, but because of the embargo any purchase would have to go through BHDS's sister plant in India. He had accidentally overheard his father say this when he took some documents to him in a meeting. During his presentation that morning Róbert soon discovered the buyers in the room were Israelis, the day before that, they'd been Americans, and, to judge from their flowing kanduras, the white-clad men now coming down the road were probably Saudis.

Suddenly Róbert saw before him vast quantities of Pax in the hands of all these buyers, and he felt his throat tighten, his mouth go dry. The project was advancing rapidly. They were building another much bigger production site, this time underground, and the design for the containers to transport the material was also well under way – a sort of plastic box using sand as insulation. BHDS would never have invested all this money unless the board was convinced they'd make a profit. Which meant they were already selling Pax. Possibly to multiple customers. Pax would soon cease to be a scientific theory or a party trick and become a terrible reality.

Róbert stood outside the lab and watched the next group of buyers approach. Their white robes threw up fountains of dust from the pathway, and he had the impression the men had slowed right down, as if the world itself were turning more slowly to give him time to order his thoughts. Then it finally dawned on him that within no time at all he would be seeing the effects of Pax on television, and a series of images ran through his head like a newsreel. What would actually happen if two or three kilos of golf-ball-sized blobs of Pax were distributed hither and thither throughout a big city? High-rise blocks and other buildings would soften and become unstable, although here, of course, Pax was better than bombs because the destruction occurred gradually, giving people time to flee. But what then? Everyday tools and forms of transport would be rendered useless; the only way to transport goods would be by horse and cart, or oxen. Health services would cease to function as even syringes would be unusable. Manual work would take over from machines, and how would information get delivered? By courier? Pigeon post? The thought would be hilarious if it weren't so terrifying.

As the prospective buyers drew nearer, Róbert realised he needed to get safely through this presentation, because it would be his last. He was responsible for a looming disaster. His childish indulgence of his own ideas, together with his insatiable curiosity, was about to put an end to seven thousand years of human progress.

69

Colin contemplated this tall, fair-haired woman before him. She seemed pleasant enough in her own way. She smiled a lot, but only ever faintly, then a look of sorrow would cloud her brown eyes and her smile would fade, as if she'd remembered she had no reason to rejoice. There had to be a reason for it, and Colin wondered whether she'd suffered some tragedy in her life, or was sad because she was acting against her own conscience. Employed by BHDS, or maybe the British intelligence services, to find Róbert.

'Who do you really work for?' he asked, and Áróra returned his gaze, as if she were considering how she might convince him.

'I'm actually looking for Róbert as a favour for my boyfriend,' she replied. 'Róbert was his tenant for four years and they became friends. Then last weekend, right out of the blue, he disappeared. He left a note in the kitchen saying he'd gone abroad on family business.'

'Sounds familiar...' blurted Colin, aware of the bitterness in his voice.

'What made it even stranger is that some mysterious guys came looking for him after he disappeared. They beat up my boyfriend, Daníel, and pushed around a colleague of his in the Icelandic police to get the phone off her that Lady Gúgú ... Róbert left behind.'

Colin gave a start. 'What did you say? What did you call Róbert?'

Áróra hesitated. '...Lady Gúgúlú. It's his drag name. He uses it quite a lot in his daily life too.'

Colin couldn't hold back the tears that flowed from his eyes once more, and he picked up a napkin to dab his cheeks and blow his nose. 'That's what I used to call him,' he said. 'I came up with the name as a joke. *Lady* because he was such a big queen, and *Gúgúlú* because he was a mad scientist. Isn't *gúgúlú* the Icelandic word for people with mental problems?'

Áróra pulled a face. 'Yeah,' she drawled. 'In the old days, maybe.'

'Well, anyway, at least now I believe you did meet Róbert. That this drag-queen you knew in Iceland really is him. Nobody else would call themselves Lady Gúgúlú.'

Áróra nodded. She leaned in and lowered her voice. 'I think Róbert is in danger. I don't know why but I think it has something to do with this company you work for.'

Colin considered her carefully. She seemed to believe what she was saying. 'This might have been true a few years ago, but they'd hardly be after him now,' Colin said falteringly, realising it sounded like a question. In fact he was asking her whether she thought it could be true. Whether his worst suspicions weren't simply him being hysterical, as his father had put it.

'I think they are,' she replied. 'These men who came looking for him in Iceland either work for some private security firm or they're British intelligence agents.'

Colin didn't want this to be true. He didn't want to know that his father was still pursuing Róbert after nine years, sending people to hunt him down without letting on to Colin. Without telling his own son that Róbert might be alive.

'I think they recently discovered Róbert is alive and have resumed their search for him after a four-year interval,' said Áróra. 'Have you noticed anything unusual at work? Any unscheduled meetings or visits from the intelligence services?'

'That happens fairly frequently,' said Colin. 'The intelligence services have regular dealings with arms manufacturers because of who their clients are.' He paused. 'I seem to recall a bit of a commotion about six months ago when a whole team of people came storming in and started rifling through everything, but then it was just the tax authorities. Some sort of inspection.'

'Tell me what happened when Róbert left BHDS. You don't need to leak any confidential information about work. Just tell me everything you possibly can about Róbert and his past life that might enable me to find him and help him.'

'With all due respect,' said Colin to this overconfident woman, 'if BHDS and the intelligence services are after him I think I can honestly say nobody can help him.'

70

'It was all very strange.' Colin spoke in a confidential tone. He seemed to have decided to trust Áróra. As if the drag queen's name, Lady Gúgúlú, had been some sort of password to his confidence and he could open the floodgates and unburden himself after all this time.

'Róbert found it difficult at the beginning,' he said. 'When he first arrived and they began building his laboratory, and everyone had such high expectations of him because he was a genius and all that. I think he suffered from performance anxiety. Sometimes he said he regretted accepting a grant to work on his final thesis, because now his sponsor, in this instance my father, or BHDS, had pre-emptive rights over him. He said he felt he'd sold his mind. Of course he was a big drama queen!' Colin burst out laughing but the smile quickly vanished from his face. 'You mustn't think I was in cahoots with my dad to spy on Róbert or anything, but when he found out we were close, Dad asked me to let him know if I thought Róbert was having a hard time.'

'And was he?'

'No, no. Only at the beginning, when he was worried things might not work out. But when everything went smoothly and the board members at BHDS were satisfied with their investment then he was happy too. Actually it was hilarious the way he revelled in his celebrity, still more so the way all those stiff suits fawned over him at cocktail parties, pretending not to notice his pink glitter jacket.' Colin grinned. 'For my part, I was amused at how proud my father was of his semi-son-in-law. Maybe he felt justified, given what a disappointment I was to him.'

'Because you're gay?'

'Yes. That and because I was no good at school.' Áróra considered this well-spoken, handsome young man, and wondered what the story was behind that. But Colin responded before she could ask. 'I was just bad at remembering things, and maths was a closed book to me. I was constantly getting beaten up, and the other boys hated me. So I was miserable at school and dreaded going every day.'

Áróra had heard similar stories before. Bullying didn't exactly have a positive effect on academic achievement.

'Do you know what Róbert was actually working on?' she asked, but Colin shook his head.

'No. I assumed it was some sort of explosive device, a magnetic bomb or something. They built him a lab with walls of sand several metres thick and another even bigger one was under way, a sort of underground bunker where they'd produce whatever it was he was making. They paid him an enormous salary, and he had twenty assistants working for him. People practically genuflected when he went past.'

Colin let out a few short bursts of laughter.

'Then one day it was panic stations, because Róbert had disappeared. And I haven't seen him since. All he left was a note saying he'd gone to see his mother. I called and called, but he never picked up. For a while I hoped he'd just popped over there for a short visit and would be coming back, but I soon realised this wasn't the case, because of all the hoo-hah at BHDS. It was rumoured he'd stolen something belonging to the company. Something of great importance. Security was questioning everyone, and for weeks the place was crawling with intelligence agents.'

'And did they discover anything?'

'No. They hounded me the most, and Dad interrogated me, too. I simply told them everything I knew, which was nothing at all. In the first place I never understood what Róbert was working on, and, secondly, nobody was more surprised than I was when he vanished without trace. We were going to get married. He'd proposed to me.' Colin's Adam's apple rose above his shirt collar as he swallowed. Then he cleared his throat. 'Afterwards, they sealed off Róbert's lab and gave his assistants other posts. A few took early retirement. I was asked to print out the paperwork, so I know some of them received generous severance deals and had to sign strict non-disclosure agreements. That's fairly normal in the armaments industry, as they're all terrified of leaks and industrial espionage. But even so, those were some of the biggest bonuses and the strictest NDAs I've ever seen.'

71

Everything Daníel had intended to get done that day was still hanging over him, so he decided to work late to try to reduce the backlog. The phone had been ringing off the hook, and the commissioner was breathing down his neck, calling or texting to see how things were going. The media hadn't cut him any slack either – not since an astute passer-by recognised the man he had restrained on his knees on Hverfisgata as Lárus, and made the connection between this incident and an earlier tabloid article about Child Protection Services abducting the 'psychic toddler', as people were now calling Ester Lóa.

However, Daníel did manage to calm Lárus down. Once they were seated in a booth at the Grey Cat, surrounded by books and with steaming coffee and delicious-smelling waffles on the table in front of them, Lárus had broken down and wept. He gave a few sniffs and dried the tears running down his cheeks with the back of his hand. And then, his anger having abated, he stammered out that it pained his heart not to know where his little girl was. So Daníel stepped out onto the pavement and called Child Protection Services to find out where they'd sent Ester Lóa.

The cream had melted into the waffles when he came back inside to give Lárus the news that his daughter had been placed temporarily with a couple who had a little girl the same age, and the two were playing happily together. They had explained to Ester Lóa that she was having a sleepover because her mummy and daddy were busy working. Lárus breathed several sighs as he sent a text from his phone, which Daníel assumed was to let Elísabet know how their daughter was doing. Then he dabbed his eyes with his napkin and tucked into a waffle. Daníel did likewise, and could easily have eaten another straightaway, but it didn't feel appropriate. He needed to focus all his attention on Lárus, to try to make him understand the police's position.

He gave the same spiel to Lárus that Elísabet had heard from him that morning, explaining how this looked to the police. New information regarding an unsolved missing-person case coming from a little girl whose parents happened to host a true-crime podcast. Then he asked Lárus bluntly whether he and his wife had coached their daughter to say these things. To say she was Ísafold. Lárus groaned and shook his head.

'Actually, our podcast is on the wane right now because we haven't spent time on it,' he said. 'We had a lot of listeners at first, but instead of growing, our numbers went down. Nowadays everybody hosts some kind of podcast, and we never sold much advertising to speak of. And when Ester Lóa started talking about this past life, we decided straightaway not to run any episodes about Ísafold's disappearance. Out of respect for her. Because although to you this might be nonsense, it's our daughter's reality. She is Ísafold.'

Sitting at his desk now, in the semi-deserted police station, Daníel went over and over in his head what Lárus had said to him. It was getting dark so he switched on the desk lamp. It shone a bright cone of light onto his desk, making the office around him dimmer and hazier. Evidently Lárus believed Ester Lóa possessed memories of a past life as Ísafold.

And there in the darkness and silence it occurred to Daníel that maybe there was some dimension in the universe that was like the gloom surrounding his lighted desk. Something the brightness of our own lives blinded us to. He leaned back in his chair and heaved a sigh. He was on the verge of admitting defeat. It was a feeling he detested. He had never been able to tolerate being baffled by something. He gave another sigh, sat up straight in his chair and reached for his phone. He'd better schedule a second interview at the Children's House. Seeing as how Helena had failed that day to find anyone with a connection to the family, once again it seemed as if the only person capable of providing any answers was Ester Lóa herself.

FRIDAY

72

There was something about this area that brought a lump to Áróra's throat when she came anywhere near it. She had allowed herself to shed a few tears as the plane came into land, seated in her usual spot by the window, face pressed up to the porthole, gazing down at the grey-black lava and the trails and pathways that sliced through it like arteries. This land was a living thing, and now, cruising along Suðurstrandsvegur in the direction of Þorlákshöfn, she had the impression she could almost feel it breathe. She drove past the parking lot on the left, hastily set up to accommodate the vehicles of people trekking up to the crater in the Geldingadalur valleys to see for themselves the fire-hae-morrhaging fissure reaching into the earth's entrails. She herself had little interest in the volcano, despite having been there prac-tically every day while the eruption was ongoing. Instead she had closely inspected a map of the area, located all the trails and pathways likely to be engulfed by lava and walked along the edge of the flow, terrified the molten rock might seal her sister's tomb for all eternity. It still made her queasy when she thought of that vast swathe of land now covered in a thick layer of solidifying lava.

She'd resolved to take the Suðurstrandarvegur route rather than go via Reykjavík. It was a slightly longer way to get to Selfoss, where she suspected Róbert Þór might be hiding out, but with fewer hold-ups. The thought had flashed into her mind while talking with Colin, when she asked him to recall as best as he could what Róbert had said to him before he disappeared nine years ago. And Colin had repeated that Róbert had a dream of buying a plot of land somewhere and growing vegetables. Colin had assumed he meant somewhere warm, but Áróra put two and two together. Seeing as how the homeless man whose national identity number Róbert had adopted owned a plot of summer-house land in Tjarnarbyggð, this made perfect sense. Róbert had been hiding in plain sight in Iceland for the past few years and didn't exist in the system.

Áróra had erred on the safe side and kept her phone switched off after the flight. Hopefully she'd be able to to call Daníel soon with some good news about Róbert/Haraldur/Lady Gúgúlú. She was equally optimistic that Daníel had something to tell her. About the little girl and her parents and how they came by the information concerning Ísafold's fate.

73

Daníel had spent the entire morning preparing for the interview with Ester Lóa at the Children's House, including a lengthy conversation with the prosecutor's office, and a grilling by the commissioner, who demanded an explanation for the image adorning the most-read online news articles that day – that of Daníel restraining Lárus on his knees on Hverfisgata. When she was satisfied she knew everything there was to know, she told Daníel to keep working the Ísafold case and said she would deal with the media. Daníel proceeded to block all incoming calls except those from the station, Helena and a few other colleagues, and of course Áróra. He was expecting a text from her any moment saying the Canary Islands was doing her good and she was ready to carry on their relationship. According to the simple code they'd agreed outside the pharmacy the previous Tuesday this would mean she'd found Lady Gúgúlú: no message meant nothing was happening and a positive one that she had new information.

He parked outside the Children's House, where he was to lead another interview with Ester Lóa in the hope of being able to dig deeper. Instead of looking for clues as to who might be feeding the child information, this time he would take a different tack. Suspend his misgivings for the time being and pretend he believed her. Extract from her descriptions of every possible location – every detail, no matter how trivial, just as if she were a real witness.

He and the child psychologist, Birna Lind, ran into each other at the entrance.

'Good morning,' she said in a cheery voice.

'Good morning.' He held open the door for her and they

walked in together. 'Have you had any new thoughts about Ester Lóa?' he asked, but she just smiled.

'This is a very strange case,' she said. 'Although not the strangest I've come across.'

Daníel raised an eyebrow, and when she didn't volunteer any further information he moved the conversation on. 'I think it would be good if we sat down together briefly to run through a short list of questions you might bear in mind during the interview. Today I've decided to approach Ester Lóa as if she were a real witness, focus on her testimony itself rather than where she might be getting it from. Try to extract as much detail from her as possible.'

'That sounds good,' said Birna Lind. Then, turning to Daníel, she added: 'But if I may correct your choice of words, Ester Lóa *is* a real witness. Irrespective of the unusual circumstances, her testimony matches your findings. Both in the car and the apartment, so I think you should seriously consider the possibility that she might simply be telling the truth.'

'You mean that she is Ísafold reincarnated?'

Birna Lind smiled patiently again, as if she were dealing with a difficult child. 'Yes,' she said. 'Have you never considered the possibility that perhaps we aren't evolved enough to understand everything that goes on in the universe?'

Daníel looked hard at the psychologist. He couldn't figure out whether she believed everything she was saying or was simply trying to persuade him to think outside the box.

'Are you saying you believe her?' he asked. 'You believe that Ester Lóa is Ísafold in a new body?'

'Yes,' said Birna Lind. 'I've read everything I can find on the subject and it's one of those phenomena that hasn't been proven or disproven. There is nothing that says reincarnation is impossible.'

74

Róbert envisaged most of his afternoons like this. At least until autumn arrived. He started with the horse, replenished its water, gave it fresh hay, even managed to lure it over to him with a hunk of bread, which the animal hesitantly accepted from his hand before chewing on it contentedly. Róbert glimpsed a hint of tenderness in the horse's eye, so maybe in the end it would forgive him for the trek across Þrengslin moor.

Then he headed to the coop. The hens always seemed famished and eager for their food. They clucked contentedly and vied with one another to peck at the mix of maize kernels and millet seed he'd prepared for them to increase the levels of polyunsaturated fatty acids in their eggs. He was relieved to see the timid hen venture closer to the rest of the flock. As it pecked away around the edges, he discreetly tossed a few grains its way without the other hens admonishing it. Róbert felt a little wave of optimism as he watched the flock feeding together happily, for the moment at least, and it occurred to him that maybe everything was going to be all right. Maybe he, in his new life as a self-sufficient farmer, was going to be all right.

This sensation deepened when he entered the greenhouse and dipped his fingers in the black plastic barrel he'd filled with water, which was tepid even though it hadn't been exactly sunny that day. The water in the barrel warmed up from simple exposure to daylight and the heat it radiated overnight helped regulate the temperature. The coming days would be relatively warm, but at night the temperature plunged close to freezing.

He inspected the soil in the seedling pots, although he didn't expect to see any sprouts for a few days yet, checked the humidity levels, which were fine, and set the thermometer gauge so he could see in the morning how cold it got in the greenhouse over-night. He kept a record of the temperatures in a little notebook and planned to monitor the effectiveness of one, two or three black water barrels in regulating the temperature, before decid-ing about additional sources of heat. Then he closed the door to the greenhouse and strolled back to the main house.

Now he could jump in the hot pot. It was one of the first things he'd built here, with the concrete left over from the foundations. He had used it frequently those weekends when he was working on the house, to soothe his aching muscles after the building work, to which he was completely unaccustomed but which had left his body stronger and more toned. It felt good to soak in the hot water and gaze at the endless plain stretching away to the sea. Maybe there was no harm in letting himself unwind a little.

Entering the kitchen, he opened the fridge, where he'd put a six pack from the pantry. He needed to be strict about how much beer he drank, because a visit to a state-owned off-licence, Ríkið, was out of the question: those places bristled with CCTV cameras. He had hoarded twenty cases of beer, which would last him forty weeks if he limited himself to two six packs a week. If he was even more sparing he could make it last up to a year. By then he would either have learned how to brew it himself, given up this beer-guzzling habit, or found a way to have it delivered to the house in Haraldur's name. Maybe after forty weeks he wouldn't need to be as careful. With any luck, by then most of the danger would have passed, although nine years' experience told him they'd never give up trying to find him.

Róbert was on his way out to the hot pot with a can of beer in his hand when the alarm went off. Its bleeps sounded frantic, like a newly trapped bird. His heart began to hammer in his chest and a feeling of dread seized him. He dashed back into the kitchen to look at the CCTV monitor. There was no doubt about it. Someone was at the gate.

75

Helena stood in the same place as last time, at the back of the meeting room at the Children's House, jotting down details of the interview with Ester Lóa on her notepad. The interview was being recorded, and she would later transcribe it word for word, but having notes might speed up the process of filing a report on the police database, LÖKE. So far nothing significant had emerged. The psychologist, Birna Lind, had spent quite a long time at the beginning playing with Ester Lóa to build up her trust, before gently turning the conversation to the main subject. Ísafold.

'Could you tell me again about the suitcase?' Birna now asked cautiously. The little girl's eyes opened wide, and even through the camera system the sorrow they betrayed was palpable.

'I was asleep inside the suitcase, and then I woke up and I started crying. And the ice-bear was crying too and he was pulling the suitcase.'

'I can see it makes you sad to talk about this, Ester Lóa, but it's very important you tell me everything that happened. Everything you can remember.' Birna Lind took the child's hand in hers and held it for a while.

'I don't remember anything else,' the little girl murmured dolefully.

Helena saw Daníel lean forward to say something into the microphone then stopped short when Birna Lind resumed talking.

'You told me the ice-bear was crying.'

'Yes. I was crying too, but the ice-bear couldn't hear me. The ice-bear always comforts me when I cry a lot. But the suitcase was closed and he couldn't hear me.'

'And then the suitcase fell with you inside it?' The little girl nodded, her eyes downcast. Helena saw Birna Lind pull out a tissue. 'May I dry your eyes?' she asked gently, but the little girl took the tissue from her and wiped her face herself.

'I want to go home to my mummy,' she said, screwing up her little face.

Birna Lund smiled tenderly. 'You'll be going home to Mummy soon. Mummy and Daddy are busy working and you're staying with the little girl you told me about, what's her name again?'

The conversation continued in this vein, and Helena zoned out for a moment, her thoughts inevitably turning to Sirra. How much she longed to hold her in her arms. How much she looked forward to Sirra's parole, even though she dreaded having to keep up this pretence. To carry on behaving as if Sirra and Bisi were married and Helena was just a friend. She felt her chest tighten at the thought, but was happily able to bring her mind back to the here and now. To the room at the Children's House where Daníel and the other public servants were sitting in front of her, watching the little girl and the psychologist on the screen.

'You also heard the car when the ice-bear drove away?'

'Yes. His car went. And then the man came.'

Helena felt the hairs on the back of her neck stand up and saw Daníel stiffen before her. Birna Lind clearly understood the significance of this piece of information.

'The man? What man was that?' she asked.

The silence in the meeting room was palpable as everyone waited with bated breath to hear what the child would say next.

'The man who was my friend. He took my hand out of the suitcase and he kissed it. I was dead then. But I was still stuck in the suitcase. I didn't become Ester Lóa straightaway.'

'Was this man the ice-bear?'

'No, not the ice-bear. The ice-bear went.'

'Did the man say anything?'

'I love you.'

'He said he loved you?'

'Not me, Ester Lóa. He said: I love you, Ísafold.'

'And did he say anything else?'

'No. He went. Can I have my juice now?'

Birna Lind smiled. 'You can have your juice, but there's one more thing I want to ask you before we go out to have our juice and biscuits. Okay?'

'Okay.'

'I want to ask you: did you hear anything else? Any other sounds?' The little girl thrust out her lower lip and cocked her head to one side. 'Try closing your eyes and thinking very hard,' said Birna Lind, but Ester Lóa shook her head vigorously.

'I want my juice now. I didn't hear anything. Only the airplays.'

'The air ... what?'

'The airplays that fly up in the sky.'

'Aeroplanes?'

'Yes, lots and lots of airplays.'

Daníel sprang to his feet and turned quickly to Helena. 'Black lava and aeroplanes,' he said. 'We need to organise a search of the area around Keflavík airport.'

76

Áróra had no choice but to abandon her car as the heavy wooden gate blocking the road was nailed shut. It also had a conspicuous sign on it prohibiting entry to all vehicles and unauthorised persons. She slipped through the narrow side gate and wondered whether anyone was at home. Viewed from here, the house could well have been empty, yet there was a vehicle by the gate, a grey Jeep with rust on its bumpers, which made it likely the owner, whether Lady Gúgúlú or someone else, was at home. The gravel crunched beneath her feet as she advanced along the path, and all of a sudden she was struck by the stillness. Only in Iceland did you get this stillness. She could almost hear her own heartbeat, the silence punctured only by an occasional fly buzzing past or the squawk of a nesting whimbrel somewhere in the marshes vociferously announcing the approach of spring.

It was one of those grey days, as bleak as they come in Iceland. Low cloud had obscured the mountains she knew were there somewhere inland, and the endless plain stretching south made it difficult to determine where the land met the sea and the sea met the sky amid this unremitting greyness. On days such as this Iceland could seem so uninviting, but then it only took a break in the clouds for the sun to pierce through and bring everything to life, and the landscape transformed into one of the most richly colourful she knew. The white-capped peaks with their myriad shades of blue and violet, the lowlands with their hundred hues of green and black, the red-and-brown scrubland and the tiny flowers, like brilliant specks of blue, yellow and white, that seemed to put all their efforts into colour rather than size, as they knew the Icelandic summer was too short for them to grow bigger. This was one of the things it was so difficult to explain to people in words: Iceland wasn't one country it was many different worlds.

Seeing no sign of anyone as she approached the house, Áróra walked up to the front door, but just as her hand was poised to knock she felt the cold barrel of a gun on the back of her neck.

'Show me your hands!' a man's voice said behind her, and Áróra raised them, pivoting slowly until her eyes met those of Lady Gúgúlú – Róbert.

'Áróra!' he breathed, when he recognised her, his face turning pale with fright, his eyes filled with confusion.

'Róbert,' she said, and the name sounded strange to her as she'd never called him that before. And the fact she knew his real name didn't please him either. He lowered the gun and they hugged one another briefly.

'Seeing as how you've found me it means they'll find me too,' he said, his voice trembling. 'Christ Almighty.'

77

The commissioner appeared unfazed by Daníel's request and considered it out loud, as if talking helped her to think. She leaned back in her chair, rocking gently, and gazed every so often out of the window, as if it sharpened her mind still more to contemplate Mount Esja. The mountain had on its typical spring garb, naked below with a white top. It wouldn't be long before hordes of people began running and climbing up its slopes, breaking their legs on their way down, with the inevitable search-and-rescue call-outs and additional paperwork for the police.

'Of course there's no actual proof, as such,' said the commissioner, turning away from Esja and back to Daníel.

'No, nothing concrete.'

'Apart from the little girl's testimony. And we can consider her a witness, although her young age makes her less reliable.'

'Exactly. Although we can't really treat her memories of a past life as fact.'

'No,' said the commissioner. 'In addition, children hide things in stories. They wrap them up in ways that make them more palatable, depending on how mature they are. Maybe she heard someone describe the assault and she's appropriated it for herself. Maybe she believes it happened to her and she experiences it as memories.'

'I need to tell you, our attempts to discover where she might possibly have got this information have come to nothing,' said Daníel. 'We can't find any connection between the little girl or her parents and anyone linked to the Ísafold case, outside or inside the force.'

'Hm.' The commissioner looked at him pensively, and Daníel hurriedly offered another argument to support his request.

'This search will be the last thing we do based on Ester Lóa's
... testimony. The information is simply too precise for us to
ignore.'

'Very well,' said the commissioner. 'We'll call on the rescue
volunteers to conduct the search. You contact the airport to tell
them to expect increased activity and traffic near the runways.
They'll instruct you on how to operate in the area so as not to
interfere with air traffic.'

Daníel nodded his head briskly. He'd half expected her to call
a halt to this there and then. In reality she'd been extremely in-
dulgent about this investigation, and he felt particularly grateful
to her, knowing how many other cases she had pending.

He rose from his chair and placed his hand on his chest.
'Thank you,' he said.

'You're welcome,' she said. 'Missing-persons cases always get
to me. I think you and I have that in common.' Daníel had
started towards the door when the commissioner called after
him. 'Daníel!' He wheeled round. 'I think Gutti should take the
lead on this now. You'll be his second in command.'

Daníel felt a flash of disappointment but at the same time
relief. She could easily have taken him off the case completely,
so to have Gutti in charge wasn't bad at all. Daníel would remain
in the inner circle, could keep track of everything that happened
and do his bit. After all, he knew the case better than anyone.
He nodded, raising a hand to say goodbye, but the commissioner
was once more contemplating Mount Esja.

78

Áróra rushed round the house after Róbert as he flung some essentials into a backpack and shouted at her a mixture of instructions and requests, most of which she didn't catch.

'The hens have enough food and water for a week before you need to replenish the feeder and the trough, and if not I'm sure Sigurður at Stokkseyri will take them back.' He ran into the bedroom and grabbed a pair of trousers and two T-shirts, which he rolled up and stuffed into the backpack. 'I can't believe I didn't already have a bag ready!' he hissed, more to himself than to Áróra. 'How did you trace me?' he asked then.

'I followed the money,' said Áróra. 'I found the real Haraldur. And his heir.'

Róbert was taken aback. 'Did you meet her?' he said, almost in a whisper. 'Did you meet my mum?'

'Yes,' replied Áróra. 'She told me you were dead, but I didn't believe her.'

Róbert looked close to tears but then seemed to shake them off with a toss of his head. 'My darling mum,' he whispered to himself once more, then shot into the bathroom and flung a few toiletries into the backpack.

'Are you on the run from BHDS?' Áróra asked, scurrying after him.

Róbert stopped in his tracks and looked straight at her. His expression betraying a mixture of fear and relief. 'Did Mum tell you that?'

Áróra nodded. 'Yes. I also met Colin. He told me a few things about the company and that you'd left. But not why.'

Róbert sighed. 'Colin,' he murmured to himself, and his face melted briefly.

'I know that you've sacrificed a lot,' said Áróra. 'And that for nine years you've been on the run and hiding out. But isn't this something you can take to the authorities? The police. The justice minister?'

Róbert gave a hollow sarcastic laugh. 'No,' he said. 'Because it falls under the umbrella of national, even international, security, and the people who are after me have tentacles everywhere. They answer to no one. The only possible solution would be to sell myself to some foreign power in exchange for protection. The United States, Israel, Saudi Arabia. But I don't want that. I don't want anybody to use Pax. And that's number two on BHDS's wish list. If they can't get Pax or the formula or the process from me, they want to make damn sure nobody else does. And the British intelligence service are backing them on this. I literally have James fucking Bond on my heels.' Róbert was talking excitedly as he continued to stuff things into his backpack, then he put on his walking boots and his parka.

'But I'm leaving Pax behind now,' he said. 'I haven't made the necessary preparations to take it with me. But that's okay. They can analyse the prototype all they like; they'll never be able to reproduce it because I kept a part of the process secret.' He hastened towards the front door and Áróra followed.

'What is this Pax precisely? Is it a weapon? What exactly have you created?' Róbert took off towards the stable, Áróra half running after him so she could hear what he had to say.

'I invented and then stole from the company a new discovery, a new material. To put it simply, a kind of radioactive substance that softens metal and renders it unusable. It wrecks machinery, immobilises batteries and so forth. However, it doesn't affect metal if the density is low enough, as is the case in living organisms. In other words Pax isn't toxic, like normal radiation. Metal has to have a certain density, maybe a quarter of a gram or so, for Pax to have any effect on it at all. In large enough quantities it will impact a given radius, so that if, say, a ball-sized piece of it were hidden in a city, it would paralyse everything: there'd be no electricity, no transport, no communications. Do you understand what I'm saying? Cities wouldn't go back to the dark ages, we'd be plunged back into the stone age. Pax is a powerful weapon that BHDS marketed as "the victimless weapon."'

At the stable, Róbert took a hosepipe, placed the nozzle in a barrel that stood next to the outhouse, then ran back inside and opened the tap just enough to ensure the barrel had a continuous flow of water.

'So what happened at the company? You stole the prototype of your inventions and disappeared?'

'I was still in my early twenties back then. I didn't think much beyond my own experiments. I was too preoccupied with breaking through mental barriers. With turning the laws of physics upside down. I've always been interested in quantum mechanics, quarks, wave-particle behaviour and other such perversions.' Róbert gave a little smile, and through the anxiety and the fear Áróra caught a glimpse of Lady Gúgúlú's mischievous humour. 'But it dawned on me what I'd done when the buyers appeared and I imagined how they might use Pax. The superpowers and arms manufacturers would be able to wash their hands of any blood, but if you think it through, the destruction and suffering when all of society's services and networks grind to a halt: floods of refugees, rescue teams carrying emergency supplies on their backs or in a horse and cart.' Róbert heaved a sigh. 'Pax isn't a victimless weapon. It's a weapon capable of enslaving most of humanity. And it's up to me to make sure it never gets used.' He wedged the stable door open and contemplated the horse chomping grass out in the paddock.

'Will you check on the horse for me?' he said. 'You can sell it, but you won't get much, as it can't do the flying pace.' Áróra was about to say something to the effect that of course she'd look after the horse, but shouldn't he slow down a bit, maybe together they could try to think of a solution so he wouldn't need to keep disappearing, but she hadn't even opened her mouth when a helicopter came hurtling across the sky high above their heads. Róbert grabbed Áróra by the arm and dragged her back inside the stable.

'They're here!' he gasped, his legs seeming to buckle under him as he swayed and leant against the wall.

'Are you sure it's them?' Áróra muttered.

Could it really be? How had they managed to do it? Had they traced the ownership records of the summer houses, just as she had? The thought gnawed at her, each possibility more unsettling than the last. Did they speak to his mother, extracting from her the same information she had? Or had they found Colin and pried more from him than he had been willing to share with her? As the questions swirled, guilt grew like a heavy weight in her chest. Had her own actions, her enquiries – or even her phone – unwittingly led them to Róbert? In her quest to find him, had she condemned him instead?

Róbert certainly seemed condemned. His voice trembled as her muttered to himself again and again:

'They're here to take me away.'

79

Róbert watched the helicopter through the window and when it swung north he all but shoved Áróra back outside.

'Now!' he shouted, and they made a dash for the house, Róbert praying the helicopter was too far away and too high up to have spotted them. They wouldn't dare fly very low because of Pax, or land anywhere near the house, but it wouldn't be long before the men on the ground came to arrest him. What about Áróra? He must try to protect her.

'Hide in the hen coop,' he said. 'There's a space under the roof. They won't look there in a hurry. And turn off your phone. They'll be tracking it.'

'It's already turned off,' said Áróra. 'And I'm not crawling into any hen coop. They'll know I'm here – my car is by the gate.'

'I'll take your car,' Róbert said, grabbing the shotgun that stood next to the front door. 'It'll buy you some time to get away.' Áróra seemed to vacillate, like a rabbit caught in the headlights, and when she made to follow him outside he stopped in his tracks. 'The coop is a good place to hide. Wait there until it gets dark then sneak across the moor and head southwest on foot. You'll find a path that leads down to the road.'

This was the only advice he could think of to give her that might work. They'd want to be in and out of there fast. To avoid having to justify a prolonged stay on foreign soil, which meant they might not search too thoroughly. Because once they had him and Pax they'd have accomplished their mission.

'What about you?' asked Áróra. 'And what's with the shotgun? Are you planning to commit suicide by cop, or some-thing?'

He turned to face her, looked into her eyes and spoke calmly.

'I've run out of possibilities,' he said. 'I'm exhausted. I can't take anymore. I haven't the money or the energy to plan another escape. It's over. Will you tell my mum and Colin I thought about them all the time.'

'No, Róbert!' screamed Áróra holding on to his arm for dear life.

He considered wrenching himself free, but Áróra was unusually strong and he'd have a struggle, which he neither wanted nor had time for.

'Áróra, they'll torture me if they take me alive. I don't know if I can stand up under torture. If they torture me I'll give them the formula, and then all my years on the run will have been for nothing. All I can do is make sure they don't take me alive. Hide in the coop and tell Daníel and his brats I said hi.' He gave Áróra a gentle shove, and she released her grip, a look of surrender on her face. But this surrender was short-lived, for he had scarcely taken off down the path when he heard her call after him.

'Don't give up! I'll get you freed. Daníel and I will find you and bring you home.'

He almost burst into laughter, even as the tears rolled down his cheeks and he felt a lump in his throat. He wanted to live. That wasn't the problem. He'd have given anything in the world to be able to grow his cucumbers, see his hens become friends. Even give the poor wretched horse a name. Anything in the world. Except Pax.

He skirted round the hole as he headed towards the gate, but before he reached Áróra's car, he saw them coming down the road. So he tossed his backpack aside and walked out into the middle of the path, crouched and took aim with the shotgun. He wasn't going to give up without a fight. They'd have to shoot him.

80

Which man could this be who Ester Lóa said had come and kissed Ísafold's hand while she lay inside the suitcase, after Björn, or the ice-bear, as she called him, went away? As he drove along Reykjanesbraut, Daníel allowed his thoughts to wander, imagining how the scene might have played out had it been true. The most likely explanation, of course, was that this was a tall story the child was spinning, and the cast of characters would no doubt grow with each retelling.

He had just gone past Vogar when his phone rang, breaking his reverie. It was Ari Benz from the Police Commissioner's Office, so he answered the call using his headset and slowed down.

'What's up, my man Benz?' he asked in a playful voice, but Ari was clearly in no mood for jokes.

'Did you speak to the media?' he replied with irritation. 'About what we discussed the other day?'

'Huh?' Daníel was taken aback; he had no idea what Ari was talking about.

'Right now there's a video on the internet, and in most of the other media, that shows a British helicopter unit arresting a man on the plains between Selfoss and Eyrabakki. And as I understand it the man being arrested is your drag queen.'

Daníel slowed down even more then pulled into the side of the road and stopped the car.

'I assure you I had nothing to do with it. I'm on my way to Suðurnes to meet with rescue volunteers who are beginning a search tomorrow morning relating to a missing-person case.'

'Okay, man,' said Ari. 'I'm not accusing you of anything. It's just I'm in the hot seat right now.'

After saying goodbye to Ari, Daníel hurriedly went onto the RUV website, where he saw reports of a British military operation in Suðurland. Opening one online news channel after another, he read the different interpretations of the incident, all of which showed the exact same video footage. In it a man could be seen from behind, crouching on a gravel path that appeared to lead from a house on the right and continue some distance onto the plain. The man, who was armed with a shotgun, fired at a group of men in black wearing body armour, who were running towards him. Then there was a loud bang and smoke emerged from a big gun wielded by one of the men in black. The crouching figure fell backward as if he'd been hit, and Daníel realised the big gun had fired a rubber bullet. Before he could scramble to his feet, the men in black pounced on the guy on the ground, clapped a pair of handcuffs on him and frogmarched him down the road to where a helicopter was at that very moment landing in a field. It could have been a scene from a movie, except for the crude cinematography and a noise that broke into the recording every now and then, and sounded a lot like clucking hens. On all the news it was duly reported that the man abducted in this dramatic fashion was an Icelandic citizen.

Daníel drove off again, stepping on the accelerator until he reached Grindavíkurvegur, where instead of going straight ahead to Keflavík, he turned left towards the Blue Lagoon. He intended to take Suðurstrandsvegur, the road that ran along the south coast in the direction of Selfoss. Because although he himself knew nothing about the video, as he said to Ari Benz, he had a pretty shrewd idea who had recorded it and posted it online.

He dialled Áróra's number, and after a few rings she picked up. She was breathing hard, as if she'd been exerting herself.

'It's good you called,' she said. 'Do you mind coming to fetch me from Ölfusár Bridge? I've been running over hummocks for two hours and I'm just about done in.'

'Áróra, what's going on?'

'I lay for ages in the hideaway in Róbert's hen coop – Lady Gúgúlú's hen coop that is – and managed to film him being abducted by helicopter. Then those same agents came with a van and a truck and proceeded to bury his weapon, or whatever it is, in what looked like a container filled with sand. I don't think they saw me get away, and right now I'm heading towards the Ölfusár river, southwest of Tjarnarbyggð. Would you mind hurrying up?'

There were ten thousand questions Daníel wanted to fire at her, but she was clearly in no state to answer even one of them. He gathered from her panting breath that she was still running.

'Keep your phone switched on,' he said. 'I'm on my way.'

Daníel stepped hard on the accelerator and sped south along Grindavíkurvegur. He was glad he'd taken a patrol car, because now he had every reason to use both the sirens and the flashing lights.

81

The rescue workers sat with serious faces and listened to Helena. She admired their concentration, despite the fact it was getting close to dinner time and most, if not all, of these people were volunteers who'd just completed a full day's work. At six the following morning they'd all be here again in their red overalls, ready and willing to take on a hugely laborious task with no guarantee of a good outcome, as was often the case when people got lost in the Icelandic wilderness. Helena had made it clear to them that on this occasion they were searching for a dead body.

This was the last group to whom she was giving the same spiel, and she wondered how on earth Daníel had persuaded the commissioner to let him call out a one-hundred-strong team. He'd said something along the lines that he and the commissioner agreed it would be a one-day search and good practice for the volunteers.

'Since what we're actually looking for is human remains we're also on the look-out for any past signs of suspicious activity. You'll all be given plastic refuse bags, so pick up anything you see, because the idea is also to clean up the lava around the airport. However, if you come across anything significant, such as clothing that looks as if it's been lying there for a long time, take a picture with your phone then call the team leader, who will have paper bags like this, which come in two sizes.' Helena held up the evidence bags to show them. 'Place the items in the bag. Needless to say, wearing gloves.'

'I thought you always used plastic evidence bags,' one of the male volunteers put in. Helena smiled. It wasn't the first time she'd heard this.

'Generally speaking paper is better, because fingerprints can get damaged when they come into contact with plastic, and damp evidence can go mouldy inside a plastic bag. We use plastic bag for things like drugs. But mostly we use paper ones.' The same question had arisen in six of the ten groups yet somehow Helena managed to act as if she were hearing it for the first time. 'TV cops, on the other hand, always put everything in plastic bags,' she added. 'It looks better on film.' The group laughed and she laughed too, despite having made the same quip six times in two hours. It was always good to lighten the mood. 'To recap: take a picture, call the team leader, use gloves to place the item in a bag and then mark it with the coordinates.' The team leader now rose to his feet, and Helena gave the group a final reminder. 'If you see anything out in the lava you think might be suspect, call your team leader, who has instructions about when to get the police to go and have a look.'

The group dispersed, and the majority left the rescue squad's HQ, but a handful remained behind to check some of the equipment for the following day. Helena went into the canteen and saw that Gutti had arrived at the scene.

'Where's Daníel?' he asked, and Helena shrugged. She'd assumed he'd be here by now.

'The last I knew he was on his way.'

'Do you want to grab a burger?' asked Gutti. 'I need you to bring me up to speed on the case, tell me exactly what we're looking for. I don't want to lose face tomorrow when the volunteers start pelting us with questions.' Helena nodded, grabbed her jacket and Gutti followed her towards the door.

She glanced back over her shoulder. 'I think we're going to need fries and mayo ketchup with that, this is probably the strangest story you've ever heard.'

82

Áróra took the bathrobe Daníel handed her after he'd taken her clothes down to reception to have them cleaned.

'You smell nicer now,' he said, kissing her ear, and she heard him breathe in the aroma of her freshly washed hair.

'Thanks,' she said, and laughed. 'That's a helluva romantic compliment.' She wrapped the bathrobe round her, sat down on the bed and switched the television on with the remote.

'The news isn't on for another five minutes,' Daníel said, sitting down next to her and stroking her back. Then he whispered: 'You realise this search here at the airport is to follow up on the information from Ester Lóa and her parents. We don't expect to find anything.'

'I know,' said Áróra. She didn't expect anything to come of it either. After all, she'd searched the area thoroughly herself. Still, she was grateful to Daníel for making it happen. For standing by her. 'But it's always fun to get to stay at a hotel in Keflavík,' she said with a grin, and Daníel chuckled.

'I don't think it's so bad,' he said. 'Although I know you're used to more luxury.' He gently stroked her back once more. 'Are you sure you're okay?'

Áróra shrugged. 'I think so. Apart from cramp after running across that moor, and the stench of hens in my nostrils. Actually, they were excellent hosts. They didn't bother me at all.' It seemed Róbert had made the roof space in the coop for this very purpose. A trap door prevented the hens from getting in, so it was relatively clean, and he'd designed it like a shooting hide so you could stretch out comfortably. At the gable end, beneath the eaves, he'd installed a small triangular window that overlooked the path running between the house and the outhouse, and it was through this aperture that Áróra had been able to watch events unfold. Stored in the roof space were two bottles of water and a shotgun, which she didn't touch but which in a strange sort of way reassured her, though she had little experience of guns and had always avoided them. As a close-combat woman, Áróra regarded the distance a gun created between you and the person you were injuring a form of cheating.

And there she lay for over two hours, aiming not a gun but her phone through the aperture. She had filmed Róbert being abducted by helicopter. She'd also got pictures of the truck lowering some sort of gigantic plastic container to the ground, and the efforts of the men scurrying back and forth, followed by another truck emptying a big load of sand into the container. She assumed the motive for all this was Róbert's weapon, and they were preparing to transport it. From what Colin and Róbert had told her, the gadget required prodigious amounts of insulation.

'Well,' said Daníel, raising the volume on the television. The news theme played, followed by reports of a significant earthquake swarm on Suðurnes, which might or might not herald an eruption, a political analyst speculating on whether the government coalition was on the brink of collapse, and finally the news they'd been waiting for. The video of Róbert Þór's abduction was broadcast alongside an interview with the justice minister, who claimed not to know of any foreign law-enforcement agencies or military groups operating on Icelandic territory, but admitted the video looked suspicious and he would make sure the matter was looked into.

Áróra gave a sigh and let herself flop backward onto the bed. Daníel lay down beside her, placed his arm over her and held her tight, and before she knew it she'd fallen asleep.

SATURDAY

83

Áróra wasn't merely angry over the morning news. She was foaming-at-the-mouth-furious. Daníel had left for the search area just before six, and when the hotel restaurant opened shortly afterwards, she'd gone down for breakfast. Then she'd gone back upstairs to her room in time to catch the justice minister telling a barefaced lie to anyone wanting to hear namely that the video of Róbert's abduction with the helicopter, gunshots and helmeted men in black, was actually the work of foreign film school students, and the individual abducted wasn't an Icelandic citizen at all but a foreign student. He went on to say that all this speculation about the man in the video being Róbert Þór Gislason was pure nonsense, since the aforementioned Róbert Þór had been dead for four years, as could be seen in the national register. Evidently they intended to cover this up.

Áróra knelt on the bed, repeatedly punching the mattress to release the violent rage that gripped her so intensely it was all she could do to stop herself from trashing the room. It was strange how aware she was of losing control, as if she were watching from outside as she pummelled the bed to vent her rage so she wouldn't do something foolish. She went on pummelling until her arms ached then she slowed down. Daníel wouldn't have to foot an embarrassing bill for damages. She let herself fall onto her back on the bed, breathless and spent, and she had an overwhelming desire to cry.

As so often in the past her father's voice came into her head. If she'd done badly at a contest he used to say: 'When your adrenals pump loser-hormone into your blood, that's when you need to fight it with all your might. Then you need to focus your brain. That's where your true strength lies.'

Áróra took three deep breaths, all the way down to her belly, then she stood up, grabbed her parka and marched out of the hotel and down the road to the petrol station. When she got there she gave the sales assistant some cock-and-bull story about how her car had broken down close by and could she make a call as her battery was dead. The man eyed her suspiciously as she pulled out her phone, looked for Colin's number and dialled it on the landline.

'BHDS have got Róbert. Go out to a store right now and buy a burner phone,' she said the instant Colin picked up. 'I'll be in touch via an app called Signal. I need your help.'

84

At first Róbert wasn't entirely sure what kind of transport he was on, as they'd taken him on board with a bag over his head. But now, the rolling motion as well as that distinctive smell that seemed like a mixture of iron, engine oil and sea salt, told him he was on a ship. They wanted to get him out of the country as fast as possible, via air or sea, and not long after the helicopter they'd initially bundled him into landed he felt everything sway beneath him.

He was locked in a windowless cabin below deck, probably close to the engine room, judging by the rumbling sound he could hear. No one had spoken to him or offered him anything to eat or drink, but he'd prepared himself. He knew what he was going to say to anyone willing to listen. He was going to plead amnesia. Avail himself once more of Haraldur's identity. He would tell them about the numerous electro-shock therapy treatments that had all-but destroyed his mental faculties. Haraldur had certainly done him a great service, but since Róbert made sure he received a kind of regular user's fee that topped up his disability benefits, he had few qualms about continuing to use Haraldur's identity. Or about how he'd stumbled across his personal data in the first place.

Róbert had got hold of Haraldur's details indirectly, through a psychiatrist he'd been dating named Kristján. On one of the five mornings they'd spent together, Kristján had got up early, saying he had a session with 'a fascinating case', as he put it. A man who'd suffered total memory loss after receiving electro-shock therapy for depression, which wasn't unusual, except that he never got his memory back. When Róbert asked if the man was elderly, Kristján had replied: 'No, roughly your age.'

And it was those words, 'roughly your age', that gave him the idea for a possible solution. While Kristján was having his shower that morning, Róbert rifled through his briefcase, found Haraldur's medical file, copied down his name and national identity number and then went to find him. Haraldur had been most friendly when Róbert fell into conversation with him downtown. He'd bought Haraldur a beer and they chatted about this and that. Then Róbert returned the following day and after a brief exchange discovered that Kristján was right: Haraldur's memory was completely gone. Save for his early childhood, he recalled nothing of his past, and seemed incapable of forming new memories; he remembered nothing from the day before and behaved as if he were meeting Róbert for the first time.

Now he would try to use Haraldur's name and story yet again. Claiming it was he, as Haraldur, who'd lost his memory and that they only need look up his medical records. He would swear he'd forgotten the formula for Pax, that he remembered nothing from that time and had only been on the run because he was convinced he was being followed. He didn't suppose they'd fall for it, but he'd give it a try. Leaning against the wall, he felt the engine vibrate in his back. A peculiar calm washed over him as he closed his eyes. So it had come to this. The running was over. After nine years they'd caught him. He only wished the gun had fired a real bullet instead of a rubber one.

85

Daníel had never known the air this still on Suðurnes. Yet as he and Gutti stood next to the rescue squad's control vehicle, gazing out over the lava towards the airport, not a hair on their heads stirred, as if the world itself were waiting with bated breath for what the day might bring.

'Do you believe in any of this stuff?' Gutti asked, biting into his sandwich, which was tightly wrapped in tin foil and looked homemade. Daníel felt a flash of envy. He wouldn't mind being the kind of guy who brings a snack to work, instead of standing in the middle of a lava field in the early hours, hungry and without any coffee inside him.

'I don't really know what to say,' replied Daníel. 'I veer between thinking it's complete nonsense and that the child must be close to someone who knows something.'

'What about the other thing?' asked Gutti. 'You know, the reincarnation stuff? Do you believe in that?'

Daníel shook his head and smiled. He didn't want to say too much, especially after the dressing-down the psychologist had given him at the Children's House, although truth be told he didn't really believe in reincarnation, even if meeting Ester Lóa had sown a seed of doubt in his mind. That said, he couldn't completely rule out the possibility that reality had another dimension to it. Lady Gúgúlú had taught him that much with his scholarly lectures on quantum mechanics.

The noise of jet engines punctured the morning stillness, and barely had the first aircraft begun its descent towards the airport than the landing lights of the next one became visible in the distance. Gutti glanced at his watch.

'Flights arriving from the US,' he said. 'We have this din to look forward to all fucking day.' The drone of the engine intensified as the plane drew closer, and when it glided above the runway Daníel had the impression the landing gear was skimming the heads of the volunteers dressed in red.

'I wonder what the pilots will think when they see all these red midgets milling about at the end of their runway?' Gutti said, and chuckled.

The aircraft braked on the tarmac with a piercing screech then the noise died away.

'All incoming aircraft have been warned about the search so they won't be fazed,' said Daníel. 'But we can only work during daylight, as we're not allowed to use search lights at the end of the runway.'

'So the search is just today?' asked Gutti.

'Yes,' said Daníel. 'We have one day.'

'Good,' said Gutti, taking another bite of his sandwich. Evidently Gutti didn't regard this as a dream assignment, but at least he wasn't bitching about having to babysit Daníel. He seemed to be getting less cranky with age.

'There's coffee inside,' said Gutti, and Daníel followed him gladly into the control vehicle, where one of the volunteers gave them a chequered thermos flask.

They helped themselves to coffee. Daníel had left the hotel before breakfast, so the aroma from the flask smelled better than it normally would. Gutti raised his cup, Daníel did likewise and they clinked. Then Gutti fell to talking with the volunteer about house prices on Suðurnes, and Daníel checked his phone to see whether he had a message from Áróra, which he didn't. He sent her a heart emoji and said good morning. Then he continued to sip his coffee and listen, half-heartedly, to Gutti discuss building-lot prices, prices per square metre, inflation and interest rates.

He had almost drained his cup when a call came through to the volunteer's radiophone.

'We have something here,' a nasal-sounding voice said through the speaker system.

'What is it you have?' the volunteer said into the radiophone.

'Ask them to take a picture and send it to us,' said Gutti. 'We can't go rushing out onto the lava to check every piece of rubbish they pick up.'

But when the response came over the radiophone Gutti and Daníel looked at one another and rose as one.

'It's a suitcase down inside the fissure,' said the voice.

86

'Are you at an internet café?' asked Áróra, and Colin confirmed he was.

'And I've created a fake user profile, bought a burner phone that looks like it's single-use only so I hope it doesn't conk out, and as you can see I'm talking to you on the Signal app. Everything just like you told me.'

'Good,' said Áróra. 'Were you able to buy the flash drives?'

'Yes,' said Colin. 'I bought four.' These were mini-flash drives that resembled small, flat plugs when inserted into a USB drive. 'What do we do now?' Colin said then, and Áróra sat down at the little desk in her hotel room and took a deep breath. She needed to concentrate on guiding Colin through what he needed to do while at the same time staying calm.

'Remember when you told me about the people from the tax office who came to conduct a search at BHDS?'

'Yes,' said Colin.

'It gave me an idea. Tax authorities don't generally carry out this kind of raid unless they suspect some irregularity.'

'Okay.'

'Well, if I can find dig up something, preferably on your father – sorry to say – I may be able to help Róbert. Strike some sort of deal whereby Róbert gets immunity in exchange for me not revealing information about your father's, or BHDS's, taxes. It's a bit of a long shot, but then again maybe not.'

'It's not such a long shot,' said Colin. 'That day the tax people came, my dad asked me to run up to his office, grab his laptop and take it home with me.' Áróra breathed a sigh. This was promising.

'I'm sending you a link right now. Type it into the browser exactly as it is, with the HTTPS, two forward slashes, etc,' she said. 'Then press enter and a menu option will appear on the screen. You need to choose "Go Dark".'

'Okay, wait a sec.' She heard Colin tap the keyboard and she guessed from his breathing that he was holding the phone between his ear and his shoulder. 'I'm clicking on "Go Dark" now,' he said, and let out a little gasp. 'Wait, what happened? The screen's gone black. Did I do something wrong?'

'No,' said Áróra. 'Wait a minute.' She counted the seconds in her head before texting the code to Colin on Signal. 'You should see a seven-digit box open up. Type in the code I just sent you.' She heard more tapping.

'Yes!' said Colin gleefully. 'It's worked. I can see a message from you.'

'Excellent,' said Áróra. 'Now, click on the link in my message, download the app and copy it onto the first flash drive.' She waited, her phone pressed to her ear, until Colin confirmed he'd done what she said. 'Now do the same with the other drives.' After he'd finished doing that, she gave him instructions on how to erase his digital footprint from the internet café computer.

'Shall I stick these in my dad's computers now?' he asked, and Áróra could tell he was outside from the traffic noise in the background.

'Yes,' she said. 'We need to access all your father's computers.'

'He only has two. One is his home computer,' said Colin. 'But I don't know the passwords.'

'It doesn't matter,' said Áróra. 'The instant he logs on, Trojan keylogger activates the malware program, then I'll be in and can see everything on his computer. All you need to do is insert the flash drives. In the most inconspicuous place possible.'

'Okay,' said Colin. 'His home computer is a desktop so I can put it in a portal at the back. The one he uses at work will be trickier, as it's a laptop. He has a board meeting at eleven. I'll sneak into his office then and insert the flash drive.'

'Message me on Signal when you've done it,' said Áróra.

She hung up, closed her eyes and clenched her fists, the way she did when she was a child and tried to make her wishes come true by willing it with all her might. If Colin pulled this off, Róbert might stand a chance. All she could do now was hope he didn't get caught red-handed and that his father, the director of BHDS, didn't notice the flash drives in his computers.

She opened her eyes and glanced about. Seeing as how she didn't have her laptop with her, she really needed to drive to Reykjavík to fetch it, but she was without a car and didn't want to bother Daníel at work. Today was the day when she wanted him to be one hundred percent focused on what was going on with the search. And she wanted to stay close by. In case they found something. Even though she knew it was unlikely. She wanted to stay put in Keflavík today.

She eyed Daníel's laptop on the bedside table. She could quickly download her software onto it, disguise the IP address and then erase everything after she'd finished. Daníel need never know she'd used his computer to carry out a completely illegal online hack. And besides, she was doing it for Lady Gúgúlú. For Róbert. Daníel's best friend. In the internal debate Áróra had with herself, this argument worked. She grabbed Daníel's laptop and opened it. She knew the password. It was: *Áróra*.

87

Daniel was grateful to Gutti for not being bossy or overbearing, despite being the lead officer on the investigation. On the contrary, he seemed to regard the case the same way the commissioner had presented it to Daniel, as more of a collaboration. Gutti handed him a pair of disposable rubber gloves, and after one of the volunteers had given them some work gloves to put on over them, they began slowly to descend into the fissure. They were wearing harnesses – the suitcase wasn't very far down but there was no way of knowing how deep these lava fissures were, and the volunteers insisted they wear them for safety's sake. Things could end badly if one of them lost their footing, or a piece of lava gave way under their weight, the man who'd strapped them into the harnesses had explained. Daniel saw Gutti grin and was half expecting him to make some quip about being happy to test out their kit for them, but it never crossed Daniel's mind to quibble. He assumed these volunteers had pulled enough people out of every type of fissure and crevice to know what they were talking about.

They took their time going down, staggering their descent so they could approach the suitcase from different sides. The fissure quickly narrowed so they were able to place one foot on either side of the rockface, inching their way down, legs akimbo, until they were within touching distance of the suitcase.

The suitcase was large and had probably once been red but had faded to pale pink. It was covered in a thin film of black dust, aircraft soot or volcanic ash. Slipping off the safety gloves, they took pictures of it on their phones as best they could, given they were both in rather awkward positions. The zip opening was on Daniel's side and he glanced at Gutti, who nodded. He pulled the tab, but the zip wouldn't budge. Despite being made of plastic it seemed to have rusted or melted shut.

'Do you have pliers?' he called up from the fissure, and soon after a pair was lowered on a cord. He gripped the tab with the pliers and yanked. The zip moved but needed a few extra tugs to get it round the corner so he could open the suitcase wide enough to see inside.

'It's obviously heavy,' said Daníel. 'It hasn't shifted with all this pulling.' Through the gap he was able to make out the sole of a shoe. He pushed it gently but the shoe didn't budge, as if it were cemented inside the suitcase. Daníel then yanked the lid open wider, thrust his phone inside and snapped the camera several times. The flash flared out through the gap and he pulled out his phone and examined the photos. The first two were out of focus and showed a grey blur, but the third clearly revealed the lower half of what had once been a face but was now a set of naked teeth fixed in an eerie grin.

Daníel waited for the sensation that often seized him when he encountered death, a kind of flickering light in his head, but it didn't come. Instead a sudden shudder ran through him and his back turned cold, as if an icy blast had risen from the fissure. Looking up, he met Gutti's eyes and nodded, then he called up to the volunteers who stood peering down at them from the edge of the fissure.

'Yes. We have the remains of a body here.'

88

It never ceased to surprise Áróra how predictable tax evaders were. Most of them used offshore shell companies, happy in the knowledge that cooperation between different countries' tax authorities was feeble at best. Many hired tax lawyers in Hong Kong or Switzerland who specialised in hiding money, and that's when the schemes became a bit more complicated. Finally there were those who took kickbacks from clients for promoting their interests in the companies they worked for, and who stashed the money in offshore tax havens like Tortola, the Cayman Islands or Panama. The director of BHDS, Colin's father, fell into this last category.

At around eleven o'clock, Áróra had received a message from Colin on Signal telling her he'd placed the flash drive in his father's work computer. Then she'd sat in front of Daníel's laptop in the hotel room in Keflavík, ready to go straight to work the moment Keylogger copied the director's password after he logged in to his computer. That happened at twelve-fifteen, and since then she'd been rummaging through his files and found exactly what she'd expected to find. Although she imagined a man of his stature would have covered his tracks better. That was the other thing that never ceased to surprise her about people who believed they had a right to cheat their employers and the society in which they lived: their arrogance. No doubt they considered themselves too smart or too lucky, or their relationship with God too special for them ever to be found out. She'd been ready to call on the Copenhagen-based hackers she used occasionally, but it hadn't come to that. She'd been able to access all the director's files herself, using her scant knowledge and the excellent software for which she paid an exorbitant fee on the black market every year but which was worth its weight in gold. She downloaded copies of the director's bank statements from his bloated offshore account in Panama and took a screenshot of the first page.

The deposits were scandalous enough to provide Áróra with the leverage she needed to negotiate Róbert's release. The tax authorities generally posed the biggest threat to people with off-shore accounts; however that threat was manageable, as the ones who got caught pleaded ignorance, insisting they had no idea that money was taxable. Or they claimed they had every inten-tion of paying, and had simply let it slide. Such cases usually ended with a fine being slapped onto the original tax bill. However, the tax authorities aside, the people who would be most interested in the deposits into the BHDS director's account, and where they came from, were his fellow board members, or indeed the British authorities.

Áróra created a fake Gmail account and sent a message to the director's private email address, which Colin had given her, and which he used exclusively to communicate with family and friends.

Her mail contained only a screenshot from his offshore account and a brief message: *How much is it worth to you to keep this secret?*

89

Helena had the impression she was in some chaotic dual sounds-cape as she stood at the edge of the fissure, instructing the volunteers on how to handle the suitcase while they tried to place a strap under it in order to hoist it to the surface. On her left Daníel stood talking to Jean-Christophe about processing the scene, and on her right Gutti was speaking with the commissioner about getting a pathologist out there.

Helena ordered the men inside the fissure to hold off for a moment, they weren't going to hoist the suitcase just yet. Maybe she was being over-anxious and wanted to control everything down to the last millimetre. Then again Gutti had sounded deadly serious when he gestured towards the fissure and said: 'Don't let them wreck anything.' This was why she wanted to ensure everything went smoothly. She would only give the order to hoist when Daníel and Gutti had both finished their calls.

Despite the stillness in the air, Helena had started to shiver as she stood shuffling her feet next to the fissure. She jumped on the spot to warm herself up and shook her arms to get the blood circulating. She dreaded seeing what was inside the suitcase. What grisly state must a body be in for someone to be able to cram it into a suitcase? Even if it was extra large, what in Iceland they called 'American size'. She turned her mind to something else so as not to think about broken bones or sawn-off limbs until it was absolutely necessary. Better to think about Sirra. About how everything would be after she came out of prison. Sirra was obliged to stay at a halfway house for a week, where she would eat dinner and sleep. But Helena had already resolved to change her work schedule so she could spend as much time as possible with her the first few days after she got out. She and

Sirra could have lunch together and while away the afternoons in bed.

Helena was roused from her reverie when the volunteer she had sent to fetch plastic sheeting approached the fissure carrying a large roll of it over his shoulder. They set to work spreading out the plastic over a relatively flat area so the suitcase could be set down and examined. Seeing the rescue vehicle trundle back down the track, she hoped they'd brought some kind of tent to erect over the suitcase. She had sent for one after gleaning from Daníel's conversation with Jean-Christophe that the forensics team would be delayed, and with it the work tents they used, because she knew Gutti and Daníel wouldn't want to wait to look at the contents of the suitcase.

She heard Gutti say goodbye to the commissioner on one side of her, and soon after Daníel bade farewell to Jean-Christophe, who'd obviously given him instructions. Helena called out that they were ready to the volunteers with the rope and pulley next to the fissure, the man operating the winch on the rescue vehicle and those hanging between the rockfaces below. Then the three colleagues stood by and watched the pink suitcase being lifted out. The volunteers took it slowly, following her instructions, and once the suitcase was clear of the fissure the man operating the winch moved it above the plastic sheeting before lowering it gently to the ground.

Helena, Daníel and Gutti walked over to where the suitcase lay on the plastic sheeting and contemplated it with something akin to awe. It always felt odd finding a body, only this time it was particularly strange because all of them knew, or were pretty certain, that the suitcase contained the body of Ísafold, Áróra's sister.

Daníel crouched next to the plastic sheeting and pulled on a pair of disposable gloves, then leapt to his feet again when a voice reached them from inside the fissure.

'Hey! Bring back the straps. There's another suitcase down here!'

90

The director's reply came within an hour of Áróra sending her email. This must mean he hadn't consulted a lawyer or advisor and was probably going to deal with the matter on his own, which was good news. Áróra wasn't the slightest bit concerned he might go to the police, and there were five million reasons why. In pounds. His reply was guarded yet open. Evidently he was feeling his way into this, because the bank statements made it impossible for him to pretend the money wasn't his. So he simply asked:

What do you propose and what assurances do I have that you'll keep your side of the bargain if I pay up?

That was all he said in his message. And was exactly what Áróra would have wanted. He didn't seem flustered, nor did he ask futile questions about who she was, or try to claim the account had nothing to do with him. Áróra sat down to compose an email setting out her demands. She decided to use plural pronouns to make it seem like some group was behind this.

This isn't blackmail. We don't want your money. We demand that Róbert Þór Gíslason is freed tomorrow. We also want a redundancy agreement from BHDS taking into account nine years' earnings equivalent to the salary of a professor at a top university, which is what Róbert Þór would have been receiving if he hadn't fallen into your clutches. In exchange Róbert Þór will sign a non-disclosure agreement and you can keep the Pax prototype. (Yes, we know about Pax.) We'll be in touch tomorrow via video link and Róbert Þór had better be by your side and in good health. Once we've explained the agreement to him he will sign it, because all he wants is to be free to live in peace. In addition, you will see to it that Róbert's name is deleted from all the lists of all the intelligence services, and that all the private security firms and law-enforcement agencies that have been persecuting him cease to do so with immediate effect.

Áróra grinned to herself as she pictured the director's face when he read this and wondered who this 'we' might be. She carried on writing.

If you fail to comply with these demands, no doubt the BHDS management board will be interested in examining the documents we have in our possession, and will want to question you about what you did in exchange for the consultancy fees you received from various clients, among them governments and even countries sanctioned by the West. Oopsy! The British authorities might be equally interested to see these documents. And we don't just mean the tax authorities. Then there's the press, who'd doubtless have a field day with them.

None of this will happen if you free Róbert Þór tomorrow at 16h00, with his redundancy agreement in his hand. A balance of terror will then exist between us: Róbert Þór's life and liberty against your riches and reputation.

Áróra pressed send and felt as if a hundred butterflies were fluttering in her stomach. She sat staring at the screen for a long while. No doubt the director was sitting at his end, anxiously awaiting her demand letter. He would read it straightaway, but then would he make an immediate decision or take time to reflect? That was the question.

The computer pinged telling her she had mail and Áróra opened the message with a trembling hand.

I agree to all your demands.

She leapt to her feet, skipping round the room a few times. Then she opened Signal and called Colin. Without waiting for him to greet her, she shouted down the phone:

'I think our plan worked!'

She heard Colin laugh and saw him before her jumping for joy, just as she was, but she didn't hear what he said because just then the door opened and Daníel walked in. His face was pale, his eyes clouded with sorrow as he looked straight at her.

She lowered the phone and stared at Daníel. He nodded and she knew. He didn't need to say it. They'd found her. They'd found Ísafold.

91

Even though Áróra had prepared herself mentally for this moment for so long, she felt nothing like she thought she would when it arrived. She'd expected her grief would somehow burst forth. That she'd be beside herself with sorrow, unable to stop crying. But clearly that was someone else's way of grieving, because her sorrow was silent. Nothing boiled or raged inside her, instead it felt more like a painful burning sensation had invaded her whole body. She allowed Daníel to lead her by the hand all the way from the car to the fissure, and signs of the intense activity that day could be seen everywhere. The gravel track had become a mud bath in places, and alongside it lay clumps of moss torn from the lava by car tyres and people walking.

They came to a halt next to the deep fissure, and Daníel peered down inside it.

'So she's been here all this time,' said Áróra.

Daníel put his arm over her shoulder and pulled her close for a moment. 'Obviously we haven't made a formal identification yet, but from the necklace you identified I think it's safe to say we're ninety-nine percent certain we've found Ísafold's remains.'

'And Ester Lóa told us this?' said Áróra, and she heard Daníel let out a soft sigh.

'Yes. Her parents have been taken into custody and will be interrogated over the coming days.'

Áróra felt annoyed by this, but was too upset to give it any emotional space and protested only feebly. 'But maybe it's just the child, Daníel, and has nothing to do with her parents. Maybe she senses things. I always had the feeling, too, that Ísafold was around here somewhere.'

'Possibly,' said Daníel. 'She's been right about some things and

wrong about others. In any event, we'll get to the bottom of it.'
He drew her to him once more, only this time he held her for a
while. 'You need to call your mother,' he whispered into her hair.

Áróra nestled against his neck, breathed in his scent and
closed her eyes. A sudden weariness came over her. As if she'd
been running a race that lasted years and must now admit defeat.

'I'm half kicking myself for not looking along this path,' she
said. 'I searched all the other trails and pathways round here.
Even the sheep tracks. But this is so close to the airport it's a no-
fly zone for the drone, so I put it on hold, along with all the other
places I planned to cover on foot.'

'You know it wouldn't have changed anything for Ísafold,' he
said. 'Clearly she's been here right from when she disappeared.
Although, of course, it would have spared you and your mother
a lot of suffering. I've seen it in other missing-persons cases; it's
not knowing that wears people down.' They continued to peer
into the fissure, a cool breeze ruffling their hair as if the wind
were doing its best to be gentle at this delicate moment.

'I want to see her,' Áróra said turning towards Daníel.

He took her hand in his and looked at her hard. 'No, Áróra,'
he said. 'You don't want to see her. Believe me.'

'I realise she's probably just a skeleton, but I feel as if—'

He cut her off before she could finish her sentence. 'The body
is saponified,' he said. 'It's not a skeleton. And you'll never be
able to erase that vision from your mind. It's not the image you
want to keep of your sister. Trust me on this, darling Áróra.'

She gazed at him bewildered. 'Sapo ... what?'

'Saponified. The suitcase is plastic and sufficiently sealed for
no oxygen to get in. That means the body didn't decompose in
the normal way, it turned ... Well. Into soap. Actually.'

Áróra looked into his eyes but instead of protesting and demanding to see Ísafold, as they both might have expected, she
simply nodded.

'There's something else I need to tell you, Áróra, and it's a strange development.' Daníel stepped back a few paces from the fissure and Áróra followed him.

'What is it?'

'We found two bodies. Two suitcases here in the fissure,' he said. 'It looks as if Björn was also murdered. All this time we, and not just us but poor little Ester Lóa, mistakenly assumed that Björn murdered Ísafold. Someone else seems to have murdered them both.'

ONE MONTH LATER

92

'I had no future at BHDS in any case,' said Colin as he sat on the edge of the bath, his hand stirring the bubbles that filled the tub. Áróra had lent them her apartment for a few days and had gone to stay with Daníel in Hafnafjörður. They'd been using the time to rediscover one another, share the experiences they'd had during the past few years, fill in all the gaps and unanswered questions. 'Dad never really trusted me after you disappeared, he kept me working in reception, but now, after I was caught on camera putting the flash drive in his computer, he's asked me to resign.'

Colin had sat calmly and contemplated his father when he'd demanded he resign from his job, and he immediately felt a new kind of inner freedom. Colin had always known his father wished he was more like him. He'd often hinted to Colin that they might develop a closer bond through work. And in spite of all the disappointments over his poor results at school, and then the whole uproar when he came out of the closet, Colin had the impression his father clung to the hope that one day they'd find they had a few things in common. At first his father insinuated that Colin's job in reception was just a start and later on he'd be given a promotion that would bring him closer to his father in the workplace. And then, when Róbert appeared on the scene, Colin's father seemed to regard the young scientist as a joint project of theirs. During the years when Róbert worked for BHDS, and he and Colin had lived together, all Colin and his father talked about was Róbert, and they never did anything together without Róbert coming along. At times Colin had the impression Róbert was his father's son and he was the son-in-law. But this didn't bother him. He was just happy to have both Róbert and his father, and that they got along so well.

But when he listened to his father describe how he could never trust Colin again, not after he betrayed him by giving Áróra access to his computers, he felt the bonds of guilt that had tied him to his father all these years fall away. The bonds that had kept him working in his father's company, living in the apartment his father had bought for him, wearing the clothes he approved of that weren't 'too gay'. Colin had risen to his feet, walked over to his father's desk and planted a kiss on the bald patch on the crown of his head.

'I know I've been a disappointment to you in so many ways, Daddy dearest,' he said. 'And I'm sorry for that. You've been a disappointment to me, too. But we're stuck with each other. I'm your only son and you're my only father.' Then he handed him the letter of resignation he was carrying in his pocket and told him he was moving to Iceland. With Róbert.

'He assures me that neither you nor BHDS have anything to fear from him. He also told me that since his invention is back in the company's hands the intelligence services have left him alone.'

'Pax,' said Róbert now, shifting his position in the tub. 'We called it Pax. A name that was at once appropriate and inappropriate.' Róbert's face had taken on a melancholy expression again, so Colin scooped up a handful of bubbles and placed them on his head, making him look like Father Christmas.

'It doesn't matter now,' Colin said. 'You're free and so am I. Free from my dad and everyone who kept you on the run and me stuck where I was when you disappeared.'

'I'm sorry I left you behind with all those problems,' Róbert said dejectedly, taking hold of Colin's hand. Colin squeezed his in return.

Róbert had changed. He was no longer the same shy but optimistic youth he once was. There was a sadness in his eyes, he was ironical and prone to flare up over the slightest thing. Yet the instant they met, what they'd had between them was rekindled. As he clasped Róbert's hand and contemplated him half-submerged in bubbles, he could scarcely believe how well they still clicked with each other. The two of them were so different and at the same time so in harmony. Their zany humour, their sensitivity, their passionate natures. It was all still there, as if the relationship had been sitting in a freezer but had now thawed and come back to life with renewed vigour.

'Now's your chance to make it up to me,' Colin said winking at him, and it was as if a weight had been lifted from Róbert. He clasped Colin's hand tighter and drew him towards him, down into the bubble bath. Colin yelled.

'No! Don't! Not in my clothes!' Colin had only just got up and was on his way out to the corner bakery to buy some of those delicious Danish pastries for breakfast. But Róbert's strong arm gripped him like a vice and since his clothes were now wet, he yielded and returned Róbert's kiss.

93

Áróra looked across the room to where her mother sat with Ester Lóa on her lap, feeding her rolled-up pancakes. The wake was coming to an end and people were beginning to drift away, taking their leave of Áróra with warm embraces and words of condolence. Áróra marvelled at how little she felt she needed them. Only days after Ísafold's body was found she realised she'd already come to terms with this very outcome. Most important of all was her relief at being able to talk about the loss of her sister as her death. Somehow everything had become more natural. Ísafold had been gone a long time, and Áróra had grieved her, yet people hadn't been able to offer their condolences. They couldn't say 'I'm sorry for your loss' because it automatically implied Ísafold was dead. Which nobody knew for sure until a month ago.

She'd seen Björn's funeral announced a few days earlier, and even though it was clear by now that he hadn't murdered Ísafold, since he himself had been murdered, Áróra had no intention of attending. She'd gone to the aid of her battered sister too many times after he'd beaten her black and blue. And apart from his brother, Ebbi, none of Björn's relatives had come to her wake. Áróra was glad to see Ebbi; he had always been good to Ísafold.

Daníel placed his arm around Áróra's waist.

'I've always considered it an act of charity to offer people sandwich loaf after a funeral,' he said.

Áróra smiled. 'The healing powers of mayonnaise,' she said. And it was true. Sharing food with friends and relatives, receiving their embraces and their warmth did something for the soul after the tears had been shed, and after what Áróra found still more difficult, her mother's tears. Now she watched as her mother broke another pancake in two and gave half to Ester Lóa. Joy shone from both their faces.

'It does seem a bit odd to invite them to the funeral when they're still officially suspects,' said Daníel, and Áróra saw his face full of misgivings as he watched Ester Lóa's parents try to prise their daughter from Violet's embrace, presumably because they were ready to leave.

'Maybe,' said Áróra. 'Yet deep down I know they had nothing to do with Ísafold's death. I can sense it in my bones. And I've decided to listen to my intuition more from now on.'

Daníel hummed. 'At any rate, your mother seems happy for them to be here,' he said. And it was true. Violet was delighted. They'd barely filed out of the church behind the coffin when Ester Lóa came bounding over. Áróra made to embrace her but the little girl flew straight past her and flung her arms around Violet. Then she trotted back to her parents and Violet asked Áróra in a shaky voice whether this was *the child*? After that she'd sat with Ester Lóa on her lap throughout almost the entire wake.

'Yes, she does,' Áróra said, slipping her hand beneath Daníel's jacket and feeling the heat of his back through his thin dress shirt. 'I thought to myself that if Ester Lóa is Ísafold, or possesses some part of her soul, or whatever happens during reincarnation, then coming to the funeral would comfort her. Being here to see Ísafold's last farewell.'

'That makes sense,' said Daníel, and now she felt like kissing him. He was so kind. He'd been so patient with her throughout the funeral preparations, accompanied her at every step and been amazingly kind to her mother as well. Maybe he was being too kind. The longer she'd been off the steroids the more ashamed she felt of her behaviour during those weeks when she was still taking them. Her moodiness and how she'd treated Daníel. One day she would confess to him about it.

'Well, my love,' her mother said, linking arms with her. 'Are you going to help me find my coat?'

Áróra went with her out to the foyer of the reception hall, found her mother's coat and her own at the same time. Then they walked arm in arm out into the afternoon, and were greeted by a cold north wind and a cloudless sky.

'Everything here is so blue,' her mother said. 'Blue mountains, blue sky, blue sea, wherever you look.'

'And everyone blue with cold,' quipped Áróra, but the joke appeared lost on her mother. Evidently some things just didn't translate.

'Won't you be coming home to England now?' asked Violet, and Áróra gave a start. She'd been expecting this question but not today. 'Now that we've buried Ísafold next to your father. Isn't it time you came home?'

Áróra turned to her mother. 'I knew you'd ask, and I thought I'd be ready when we found her. But I can't just leave without knowing what happened. We always thought Björn killed her, but now everything is back to where it started. And I feel I need to be here in Iceland while the investigation is still ongoing.' Áróra had expected her mother to raise an objection. Try to persuade her. But instead Violet grinned and started towards the car.

'Might this have something to do with your uncle?' she said with a mischievous backward glance.

Áróra let out a deep sigh and hastened after her mother. 'For the hundredth time, Mum: Daníel is *not* my uncle!'

94

'I still don't understand how Áróra pulled it off,' said Daníel, clapping Róbert on the shoulder. 'But I'm so glad you've come back safe and sound.' He would need to get used to calling him Róbert, having always thought of him as Haraldur, although Lady Gúgúlú was as valid as before. They had come into the kitchen to make coffee while Áróra and Colin chatted at the dining table in the living room. Daníel had cooked roast leg of lamb with all the trimmings, and set the table using his best plates and cutlery to celebrate his friend's return from hell.

'We all have our weak spot,' said Róbert. 'If it isn't money it's reputation. And Áróra found the director of BHDS's weak spot.'

'Do you mean she somehow blackmailed him?'

'Couldn't we say she used her methods, and that you're better off knowing as little as possible about them?'

Daníel hummed. He'd never fully understood how Áróra found the money people hid all around the world, but what Róbert said was probably true – he was better off not knowing because it was probably close to being illegal. For all their resources the police didn't have much success discovering whether people had hidden money in tax havens. Yet Áróra seemed to have no difficulty digging up this type of information.

'But you are safe now, aren't you?' asked Daníel. 'They won't come after you again?'

'I'm safe. And I'm free. For the first time since I started working for BHDS as a young man. Don't get me wrong – the years I spent here in the garden were wonderful, and I was safe because they actually thought I was dead – but I was never truly free. I was constantly expecting someone with links to the company to find out by chance that I was alive, and then I'd have to disappear again. More conclusively than if I'd died, you see. And it turned out to be true.'

'Well, anyway, I'm glad it's over and you have your life back.' Daníel held back from saying that he wished Róbert had felt able to confide in him about his troubles, because he realised his friend and tenant had wanted to shield him from all this mess.

Besides, Róbert seemed much more serious since he came back, as if his brush with the company had taken its toll on him, and Daníel wondered what they'd done to him while he was in captivity. Róbert hadn't wanted to talk about it and put up his usual shield, Lady Gúgúlú, who wriggled out of everything, erecting an impenetrable barrier of philosophy and physics that would have made any attempt to discuss it futile.

'I've just met my mum for the first time in four years. I'm going to stay with her for a while in the Canary Islands, but apart from that I'm going to live in my house in Tjarnarbyggð. And Colin is moving in with me,' Róbert said and smiled. 'We've decided we owe each other some time.'

Daníel felt another pang of regret. All those hours he'd spent out in the garage, moaning about his relationship with Áróra, and Róbert had never once mentioned Colin. He wanted to bring that up too, but decided it could wait. This evening was supposed to be a celebration.

'We'll be coming to town regularly, though, as I plan to do the odd drag show. My first show will be called *Lady Gúgúlú Returns!*, and then *Gúgúlú's Three Resurrections*.' Róbert adopted a stylish pose to give him a taste of the glamour that would surround the performance. 'And if you insist, I can babysit those insufferable brats of yours,' he said, and Daníel laughed.

He'd often been close to feeling jealous of his children's affection for Haraldur/Róbert, whom they called Auntie Gúgúlú and greeted much more warmly than they did their father on their visits to Iceland.

'And I'll continue to look after your hens when you go to visit your mum,' said Daníel. 'It's a luxury always to have fresh eggs.' He opened the little box of confectionery and placed it on the tray next to the coffee pot and cups. But before carrying it out to the living room, he turned to Róbert with a look of curiosity.

'You kept a chunk of this secret weapon of yours buried in the garden all these years?'

Róbert smiled. 'In an insulated box and so deep down it only affected a few square metres, most of which was solid rock. Did you really never wonder why all your garden tools broke or bent when you tried to use them on the "elf patch"?' he said, making quotation marks in the air with his fingers.

Daníel mustered a smile but inside he felt something close to pain.

'You fed me all kinds of myths and nonsense about elves you claimed lived in the rock, when all the time it was some kind of radiation.'

Róbert put on an astonished face that Daníel wasn't quite sure was sincere. 'Oooh,' he drawled. 'So you believed it?'

'No,' Daníel replied tersely. 'I don't believe in elves. Not as such. Maybe I took it as a sign that there might be something ... you know, something else. Some other dimension or power. That this mess we human beings have created isn't the final rung on the ladder of our existence.'

'Oh, darling,' Róbert said, seizing the coffee tray from Daníel and marching into the living room. 'If you believe what your senses consider to be reality *is* in fact reality then you haven't understood a word I've said to you about the inner life of the atom.'

ACKNOWLEDGEMENTS

It is always a great pleasure to present a new book to English-speaking readers, and *Dark as Night* ('Dauðadjúp sprunga' in Icelandic) is no exception. Although I have completed this series in Icelandic, the release of each new translation allows me to feel that 'first-reader' excitement anew. Seeing the new covers and receiving feedback from readers across the world is truly a special experience, and I am deeply grateful for the chance to share my stories with you all.

This opportunity to reach readers worldwide would not be possible without the invaluable work of translators. I would like to extend my heartfelt thanks to Quentin Bates, who translated the first three books in the series. Quentin not only captured the essence of my work but also played a significant role in shaping the series by coming up with the titles that have become so well recognised.

Changing translators midway through a series was an unnerving experience, but I am grateful that it has turned out so well. I would like to express my deep gratitude to my new translator, Lorenza García. Lorenza has done an excellent job on this book, and it has been a genuine pleasure to work with her. Her dedication and skill have ensured that the story remains as compelling in English as it is in the original Icelandic.

I owe a huge debt of thanks to everyone at 'Casa Orenda'. Publisher Karen Sullivan and her fantastic team have been incredible throughout this journey. A special mention must go to my editor, West Camel, who has always made me feel that my work is in the safest of hands. His insight and careful attention have been invaluable in bringing my books to life for the English-speaking audience.

As always, my hope is to entertain and thrill my readers. I hope you enjoy *Dark as Night* and find the story as captivating to read as it was to write. Thank you for your continued support and enthusiasm; it means the world to me.